A Feather in the Rain

For My Extremely Talented Friend,
Tom —
Thanks for the most treasured quote
of all.

2005

A Feather in the Rain

by

Alex Cord

FIVE STAR **PUBLICATIONS**
INCORPORATED
Chandler, AZ USA

Linda F. Radke, President
FIVE STAR PUBLICATIONS, INC.
P.O. BOX 6698
CHANDLER, ARIZONA 85246-6698

All characters and events described herewithin are completely fictitious and any similarities between persons living or dead is purely coincidental.

Library of Congress Cataloging-in-Publication Data

Cord, Alex.
A feather in the rain / by Alex Cord.-- 1st ed.
    p. cm.
I. Title.
PS3603.O7342F43 2005
813'.6--dc22

                                        2005002837

Printed in the United States of America

Editor: Paul M. Howey
Project manager: Sue DeFabis
Cover design: Barbara Kordesh
Cover illustration: Buck Taylor
Interior and cover flap illustrations: Carla Garner
Interior design: Janet Bergin

Dedication

This book is for my
dear son,
Damien Zachary Cord,
who is with me
for all time.

Acknowledgments

My name is Alexander Daniel Viespi. I am the son of Alexander Viespi, Sr., and Marie Palladino Viespi. I am the brother of Robert and Marlene.

I am filled with admiration for my son, Wayne, for whom much has been difficult and yet he makes it all seem easy. I am the grandfather of his beautiful twins Jake and Alexandria.

I am the proud and grateful product of this amazing family. I am honored and humbled by the love, kindness, generosity, and support they have always shown me.

And ultimately, I want to say, "Thank you, Baby," to The Great Dane, Smoky Boy—Susannah Cord, my wife, the treasure of my life, who has shown me what true love really is. I did not know that such a feeling could exist until I met her. Smoky changed my life from straw to gold. When I am separated from her, I feel wrong in the world.

Special Thanks

To the mighty Janette Anderson for her steadfast belief, unyielding perseverance, and faith. To the angels that put her together with the perfect person to publish this book. And to Linda Radke, the perfect person, whose perception, wisdom, and sensitivity are so profoundly appreciated. Special thanks to Sue DeFabis, for your gentle patience and to Paul Howey, for your eagle eyes. Thank you, Carla Garner, for your fine illustrations and Janet Bergin, for the beautiful design. A big thank you to Jennifer Selberg for all her energy behind the scenes.

Thank you to John Shirey, M.D. for your medical advice, Dale Schneider, D.V.M., for your expertise in equine chiropractic and acupuncture and John Thoma, D.V.M.

Thanks to the Kays for their unconditional friendship.

I would like to express my gratitude to the artists who have enriched my life - in person and/or through their work - and to name just a few of the multitude, most of them friends: Bing

Crosby, Ernest Borgnine, Sammy Davis, Ken Atchity, Van Heflin, Coco Marshall, George C. Scott, Slim Pickens, Ben Johnson, Chuck Connors, Eartha Kitt, Jean Simmons, Edmond O'Brien, Robert Fuller, Jennifer Savidge, John Steinbeck, Kirk Douglas, Sam Peckinpaw, Lawrence Olivier, Marlon Brando, Peter O'Toole, T.S. Elliot, e.e. cummings, William Shakespeare, Tennessee Williams, Cormac McCarthy, Annie Proulx, Hank Williams, Wilbur Smith, Andrea Boccelli and countless others.

And lastly, my most profound gratitude to Buck Taylor, a truly gifted artist, a great friend and a kindred spirit, who knows too well the truth contained herein. Thank you for the perfect cover. I could not have dreamed it better.

A Note to Cutters

Please allow the license I have taken with dates of actual events, with geography and with the dollar amounts and number of contestants. I respect your sport and see it as a thing of great beauty.

My hat is off to the founding fathers: Buster Welch, Shorty Freeman, Don Dodge and Matlock Rose, to name just a few who have made cutting what it is today.

Prologue

All things have their time to live and die. Leaves have their time to fall. Buds have their time to bloom. Flowers their time to wither in the wind and cold. The sun has its time to rise and set. The stars their time to shine and fade. But Death abides by no rules of time or season. It seems to delight in thwarting the hopes and dreams of mortals with no regard to good or bad, old or young. Death knocks without discrimination at the doors of hovels and castles alike with only the promise of sleep in the bosom of the earth unless we choose to believe that there is more and observe how the dim eye of the dying brightens with its last light.

1

Cuttin' Horses

No floor, nor earth beneath his feet, he floated in dazzling rays of golden light. A thinning silver strand joined him yet to the body, cold and still on the bed below. He could hear the faint sobs of his mother in the corridor. His father seemed small and bowed in a chair beside the bed.

He was quitting the flesh and blood, the sky-blue eyes and blond hair and the quirky grin known as Damien Zachary Burrell.

Zack, as his dad called him, was only twenty-six. There were bright, even joyous times in his short, troubled life, but somewhere behind the golden glow of Zack lurked a dark unwillingness to want to live.

Though he had vacated the flesh, as Damien Zachary Burrell he still had things to do. Living people and their anguish would remain real to him for a time to come. He'd left behind a wounded, crippled father who worshiped him and struggled under a burden of doubt and self-blame. Tranquility was a distant thing yet to be achieved. Zack was not at peace.

———✦———

A grim evening sky thickened over the Houston Astrodome. The acrid aroma of horses, cattle, and straw hung in the moist air. A mosaic of pickups and horse trailers jammed the vast parking area.

The millions in prize money won annually in the cutting horse world had given birth to syndicates, shareholders of equine stock residing in stalls, and a fierce atmosphere of intense competition.

The now glamorous, high-dollar sport grew out of the dust of everyday ranch work, sorting cattle to be sold or doctored, separating strays out of large herds. Cattle naturally want to bunch together. It takes a horse with the cunning athleticism of a cheetah to cut a cow out and prevent it from darting back to the herd. A rider can't make a decision and communicate it quickly enough to get the job done. The horse must have the desire and ability to react instantly to his own reflexive decisions.

Twelve hundred pounds of hot muscle and bone quivered between Jesse Burrell's legs as the brown mare squatted deeper into her hocks. She pinned her ears and poked her nose at the cow desperate to get around her. Tapping the earth with her front feet like a boxer bobbing, she dared the cow to try. The herd behind the mare was where the cow wanted to be. It drew her like a magnet. She darted to the right. The mare, a flashing, mirror image of the cow, cut her off. She dove to the left. In a sweeping blurred arc, the mare cracked over her hocks, splattered out in front of the cow and stopped her dead. Locked eye to eye, she blew in her face and shuddered her shoulders. Jesse stared at the cow, the breath of the mare hot in her face. Overwhelmed, the cow quit. Jesse picked up light as a feather on the loose reins. Instantly, the tense mare softened, came out of the ground-hugging crouch, and stood alert. The savvy audience whistled and whooped in boisterous appreciation as Jesse

4

turned her back to the herd to cut another cow.

Jesse Burrell had the gift—the feel, the sensitivity and balance, and the willingness to listen and hear what the horse tells him. The mare was stout, very quick. She could jar a lot of people loose. But when Jesse was on a horse, he gave up part of himself to the horse and the horse did the same. They came together as a single entity— a brilliant, graceful poem of flesh and blood in motion.

He had thirty seconds before the buzzer would sound ending his two and a half-minute run. He looked between the mare's ears at the cattle milling in front of her and decided on the brockle-faced heifer. He drove the heifer out in front of him and just as he dropped his rein hand on the mare's withers, the cue to go to work, it happened. His concentration faltered. A blade of grief slammed through him. Why always at the weirdest times would he see his son's face and realize it would never be there in the flesh again? Doubts about his ability had begun to creep into his consciousness. His financial life needed oxygen. If he could just keep these last few seconds together and get a good challenge from the heifer he could win $23,500, a decent dose of air.

The heifer made two quick moves. The mare matched them. The cow dashed for the wall and Jesse just wasn't there. The mare sensed his absence, and in that microsecond of confusion the heifer scooted under the mare's neck and made it back to the herd. The run was over and Jesse had blown it. He looked down and shook his head as the crowd applauded in support.

He rode out of the arena stroking the mare's smooth hide with his fingertips. He leaned low along her neck and spoke a soft apology.

There was a time when the mistake he'd just made would not have occurred. He'd have won the twenty thousand dollars and tossed his $400 hat like a boomerang and not care if it ever came back. That was when Zack was still alive. Before the hollow feeling, the paralysis that would overwhelm him, the red-hot impulses to lash out a cocked fist to the face of someone merely impolite.

He pulled off the bridle and shoved the saddle on a rack in the trailer. Abbie arrived on a gust, a turbulent swirl of woodfire hair, freckles, and a flashing smile. "Bummer. Jesus, you guys were awesome, man, till that brockle-faced kamikaze dove right through you." She'd moved straight to the sweaty mare and had her arms around her neck, kissing her nose. "You were a good girl, what a good girl." She poured liniment and vinegar into a tub of water and plunged a sponge to the bottom. "You disappeared," she said to Jesse. "I turned back for a second and you were gone." She sloshed water on the mare with a practiced hand.

"If I hadn't had a brain fart, it wouldn't have happened." He grabbed a beer from a cooler in the bed of the pickup and popped it as he moved among the horses softly with a hand stroke here and there as his eyes scanned for anything amiss. He heard Abbie saying, "You were such a good girl." Unmindful of her clothes and the sopping hide, she nuzzled the mare and slapped the sponge on her neck splashing her own face.

Jesse stood at the head of a magnificent sorrel, a three-year-old stud colt. He nickered as Jesse's fingers lit on the small white star above his eyes as softly as a butterfly and circled the path of the hair. The colt's head dropped, his eyes began to close. With his other hand he stroked his ear, pulling gently, massaging the base. He ran his hands reverently over the powerful haunches. His registered name was Bueno Bar Tab. Jesse called him Buckshot. This was his Futurity prospect. When he first saw the colt struggle to its feet on wobbly legs glistening wet from the womb, he knew he had a good one.

Getting this colt to The Futurity was probably the best reason Jesse could come up with for going on with the business of living.

The rules for The Futurity prohibit a colt from being "shown" prior to it. So Jesse hauled that colt everywhere to get him used to the excitement, the sights and sounds of the cuttings. He'd ride him in the warm-up pens then tie him up and let him stand to learn patience. Jesse took a hold of the base of Buckshot's tail and let it slide through his hand as he moved to the gelding tied next to the colt and patted him softly. They were strong, agile, powerful athletes, sensitive as raw nerves, delicate as fine porcelain. He could hear Abbie rattling on as she scraped water from the mare.

She had a natural feel for a horse and damn sure loved them, all of them, not just the pretty ones or the talented. When she first came to ask Jesse for a job she stood square in front of him, all five feet of her. "Mr. Burrell, I know you're one of the best. I'm a great admirer. I hear you're a hard guy to work for..." She broke into that wide-eyed grin, only a little embarrassed by her boldness. "But I think I could work for you and you'd be happy." He liked her right off. He'd just fired a girl for taking off a bridle without care, letting the bit clang into the horse's teeth.

"Saddle that bay mare there." She went right to it. Every move smooth, experienced, sensitive. He watched her step aboard and pick up the reins. She had a real light touch, no fear and a lot of feel. The mare was not one to do you any favors either.

That was three years ago. She was twenty years old and working toward a master's degree in psychology at Texas U part time. Jesse figured she spoke about a thousand words to every one of his. Though she'd never express it openly, it was clear she had a crush on him even though he was a couple of years older than her father.

He stepped up into the tack room. Abbie looked out from under the mare's belly. "Not a terrible day, Boss. Your two non-pros were in the money. Old Apple-butt is gonna be all over you now."

"Man, you got a mouth on you. She could be walking up here any minute now. She heard you talk like that she'd pinch your head off."

"I know. I got my eye peeled. Besides, her perfume gives me a two-minute warning." Suddenly, she dropped her voice. "Here she comes." Then in a singing whisper, "She got spurs that jingle jangle jingle..."

Daryl Ann Henley, recently divorced from Brian Henley, head council for Omega Oil did step to the jingle of silver spurs on a pair of thousand dollar custom-made Paul Bond boots with tall green scalloped tops, six rows of multicolored stitching and red and yellow butterflies inlaid. Tight Wranglers painted on the Mackintosh butt and a white silk shirt rippling over ten thousand dollar breasts, she moved with confidence, flaunting sexuality. Auburn hair sleeked back revealed a flawless arrogant beauty beneath the 20x black hat with the trendy cutter crease. "Hi, where's Jesse?"

"In the tack room. Nice job showing your horse, Mrs. Henley."

"Thank you, Abbie. Ah've told you, you can call me Daryl Ann."

"Thank you, ma'am."

"Ma'am is not Daryl Ann. Abigail."

She smiled, "Thank you, Daryl Ann."

She climbed up into the tack room. Jesse was sorting equipment for the trip home. She stood so close he could feel her breath on his face. "Jesse Burrell, had some bad luck. You were lookin' pretty shiny till that brockle-face run through you like a train. Hey, let me buy you supper with some of the money I won."

"Thanks, but I'm just gonna grab a couple of hours sleep and hit the road early."

"Ah'm not takin' no for an answer." She pushed him against the wall. Slowly pressing against him, she walked her fingers up his chest and around his neck. She tilted her face till her tongue could reach out to lick his lips.

He looked her dead in the eye. "Daryl Ann…" By God, there's a sweet smelling heat rising from her. "Any man in his right mind would kill to be in my boots right now. But I am not in my right mind. I wish I were."

<hr/>

He shut the door to his room, peeled off his clothes, stepped into the shower and turned the water hot enough to kill a lobster.

Stretched out on the bed, a cold mass of aloneness crept over him like a flow of clay. He thought about his son, dead. Gone. How is that possible? Dear God. How do I ever get to understand this, live with it in some kind of peace?

Behind shut lids a squall of tears rose, spilled, and tracked his cheeks to the pillow. He blinked and stared at the ceiling. His gaze slowly moved to the far corner, down to the shadowed wall of drapes. He ceased breathing.

Damien Zachary stood there, clear as day. Jesse bolted upright and blinked his eyes. The boy was there with that little half smile. Jesse whispered, "Zack…say something. I know this isn't a dream." Zack's smile widened. Jesse heard himself say, "My God, I miss you so much." He edged forward on the bed.

The young man looked as if he would speak. But language didn't come. The glow around him began to dim, the image soften, until he faded totally and was gone. Jesse left the bed and went to the spot where Zack had stood. He reached out to pull the drape aside. He looked down at the parking lot dimly lit, then up at the starless sky. He went to the bathroom and threw water on his face. Looking in the mirror, he thought, it's been a long time since I've owned a real smile.

2

The Plaza

The venerable entrance to the Plaza Hotel in New York was being used as the backdrop for a glossy magazine fashion shoot. Camera grafted to his face, the photographer, an amalgam of undefined creatures, clicked and crawled and cooed, climbing about the stone and marble like something primordial yet to develop legs. A woman in gray wool and a wine-colored scarf blown by a huge fan, was the focus of his attention.

Holly Marie Bassett's traffic-stopping, head-turning face had glamorized the covers of countless magazines. Her perfect legs had strutted the runways of Paris, Milan, Tokyo, and New York. She'd been wined and mined by royalty, shutterbug trash, and a yogi "guru." Like most beautiful women, she required constant reassurance of the fact that she was.

Eric pulled the camera from his face and stood surprisingly erect. She smelled the cigarettes on his breath. "Baby, what's going on? There's something missing. You're not giving it to me. We're losing the light. C'mon Baby, you gotta turn it on." He whirled to his assistant. "Give me all you can on that reflector. Let's go!"

The hotel room was jammed with equipment, designer clothes on rolling racks, makeup and hair paraphernalia. The people that went with it all were packing up. Holly sat in the bathroom blotting tears. Eric leaned against the door talking to her in the mirror. "I think we got it. But, Jesus, Holly, it was like pulling teeth. What's the matter with you?"

"I don't know…Maybe I need a rest…"

"A rest? Who rests in this business? You rest when you're dead. Go home. Drink a half bottle of Merlot and get some sleep. Your eyes look like two slices of pepperoni." He kissed the top of her head, lit a cigarette, and left.

The rent on her puny one-bedroom apartment on the East Side was about the same as a mortgage payment on a Texas ranch. Not much of a place to call home, but it kept the rain off a gypsy's head. The kitchen was a sink, a two-burner stove, and a half-pint fridge lined against a wall. It was almost never used. Mainly Cokes, bagels, and an occasional dose of brown rice fueled her.

She leaned against the wall as if she'd been clubbed, her face streaked with tears, her legs about to fold. As the last of her strength ebbed, she slid slowly down the wall and dropped her head on her knees.

Tony stood there in his slickness wishing he could be anywhere but where he was.

"What makes me think?" She said it to the floor, then wearily raised her head as if it were a great weight and behind a cascade of tears looked at him with tired eyes and said, "I don't think…I know. I know because she told me. She told me the things you said about me while you were screwing her. 'I'm frigid because I'm really in love with my dead brother.' Am I making that up? It's written all over your face."

"Well, maybe if you'd let go of your brother, I wouldn't be

12

screwing somebody else." Tony brushed a hand lightly over his hair as sleek as a blackbird's breast and glanced at his watch.

"You're such a low-life." She sobbed, "And my brother's got nothing to do with it. I knew it. I've known from the start what you are. I deserved you for being so stupid. My brain must have died with my brother." She struggled to her feet and walked slowly toward him on unsteady legs as she reached deep inside of herself for just enough power to pummel his chest and beg him to leave. Tony covered his head as she raised her arms in an incomplete gesture. "Get out...please...get out. Get out!"

With his slamming of the door, she summoned the energy to get to the bedroom, gather his stay-over clothes in her arms and rush out to the empty hallway. The elevator light indicated its descent. She leaned over the handrail at the stairwell and tossed the clothes and sneakers. She watched them tumble twelve stories to the lobby floor. He appeared from the elevator next to the heap. When he looked up, she was gone.

She spread her forearms on the mantle and put her cheek on her stacked hands and wept. She raised her watered eyes to gaze at the tousled head and lopsided grin of her brother Brad in a silver frame. "I want you back..." she said, releasing a plaintive wail from a tortured heart. "Everything I ever hoped for...it's all gone. Oh, God..."

3

On the Road Again

It was 6:30 a.m., a threatening cloudy dawn. Jesse backed the truck into position under the trailer hitch and got out.

Five horses stood tied outside the trailer. Abbie was wrapping Buckshot's tail. Jesse stepped up, coffee in hand, looking dazed. Abbie, grinning behind Buckshot's butt said, "Good afternoon, Mr. Burrell, sir. Hmm, looking pretty sparky this morning."

"You don't shut up, I'm gonna choke you to death."

"Uh-oh! Is this gonna be a long ride home? Should I take a bus?"

"Let's load 'em up."

"Think it'd be a good idea to hook up the trailer first? Be hell if we stop for gas and find out we left the horses in Houston."

He took a last swallow of coffee, shook out the cup, and threw it at her. "I am gonna kill you."

It was close to four hundred miles from Houston to his place on the outskirts of Bandera. Behind dark glasses, though the day was dark, he drove in silence, watching the left front fender swallow the broken white line. Respecting his clear desire for solitude, Abbie had her headphones on and her eyes shut. His glance fell on her. Instantly her eyes popped open and she smiled at him. He grinned and turned back to the road. A minute later he stole a glance at her again. Her eyes opened. When he turned away they closed. He began to think about the little dynamo curled next to him and what a treasure she was.

4

"That Son of a Bitch"

He slowed the rig to pull in to the truck stop at Brenham. Abbie sat up wide-eyed. "I want some candy bars. I need some strokin'." She undid her legs and pulled her sneakers on.

Jesse eased the rig into the station looking for an unoccupied pump with easy egress. A van was just about to pull out. He started slowly forward to the pump. Out of nowhere, a Japanese sports car whipped in front of him and stopped at the pump. A tall dark-haired man with a black barbered beard got out. A woman remained in the car. Abbie said, "That son of a bitch!" Jesse pulled up close behind the car and rolled down his window. "Excuse me, sir, but I was pulling up to that pump. Maybe you didn't see me."

The man began to take the nozzle from the pump. "Big deal," he said, opening the gas cap.

"I don't think you want to do that, sir. It's not polite. If you'll just pull ahead and let me get my gas, you can get in behind me."

The man ignored Jesse. "Sir? You don't want to do that." The man turned from his task and looked at Jesse with an insolent smirk then turned away and inserted the nozzle.

Jesse eased his truck forward crunching the California license plate and pushing the car ahead until it was out of his way. The woman's head had snapped around, the nozzle pulled free of the tank. The man, roaring like a speared elephant, charged toward Jesse's side of the truck. As he reached for the door handle, Jesse pushed the door open with force enough to slam the man back into a concrete column next to the pump. Jesse leaped from the truck, clamped his hand around the man's neck pinning his head to the column and drove his fist into his guts. He felt the man's gorge rise under his grip. His fist re-cocked to smash the man's face. Through his rage he saw that the man, though bigger and younger, was stunned. Jesse hissed through his teeth, "Do you want to push this, mister, or do you just want to get in that stupid red car and drive the fuck out of here?"

The man stared, his eyes getting wider, his face redder as his air was being choked off.

"Answer me, you smart son of a bitch."

The man managed to gasp, "Okay, okay."

Jesse let him go and the man stumbled toward his car. Abbie stood dumbstruck.

They'd been back on the road an hour before she spoke, which was pretty much a record. "You know, I've never seen anything like that. The more I think about it, it was beautiful. An exquisite manifestation of pure rage. And then..." she tried to find just the right words, "...suddenly...a rational thought. Cool. I swear I thought you were gonna kill him." Then she giggled and said, "And so did he."

His voice was dry. "I don't know what in hell's wrong with me."

Abbie looked at him for a moment. "Your son died. That's what in hell is wrong with you. It's only the worst thing that can happen to a human being. You need to cut yourself some slack, Jesse. Besides that asshole had it coming. He'll think twice before he pulls that shit again." Two minutes later, she added, "You know you could talk to me about it. Hard as it may be for you to believe, I could listen. And I'm pretty damn smart."

He smiled and reached out to ruffle her hair. "Don't I know it."

She remained silent to see if he would offer any more. He didn't.

"Want me to drive?"

He shook his head.

"Want a sandwich?"

"Yeah."

"Good. I'm starved." She dove into a bag of groceries and pulled out bread, turkey, mustard, pickles, and a tomato.

5

Death in
New York City

Holly Marie Bassett moved like a hurricane ravaging a small town. She was packing. After ten years in New York she was preparing to depart. The decision had not come easily. She had loved the city and her lifestyle, at least to the extent that she ever thought about it.

Holly Marie was more complex than a spacecraft. Not even her own superior intellect was keen enough to fathom herself, and it wasn't for lack of effort. Self-knowledge was her avocation.

With purpose formed by her beauty, and a pace driven by her industry, she'd gone where the fast lane took her. Gotta catch the 6:25 to Madrid, gotta get my hair done, gotta get to the gym, need another pair of shoes, gotta stay thin. Layer upon layer of stress and anxiety, and an overwhelming sense of emptiness took their toll, as romantic fantasy became reality without fulfillment.

Two years ago, her kid brother by one year, Brad, her best

friend, her strongest ally, half of herself, was killed in an act of random violence on a sidewalk in New York City while waiting for his fiancée to come out of a market. For Holly, it was a cannon ball in the guts.

Now, she had come to the end of a headlong rush to nowhere. She was tired and in spite of an over-populated voice-mail and a bulging phone book, alone. She wanted to go home and see her "mommy" and her father. She wanted to be a little girl again and curl up in her mother's arms and be healed. She wanted to be a comforting parent to her mother and father and take them in her arms and help them to heal. She'd already booked her flight to Denver.

6

The Lazy JB

The sign at Jesse's place said, "LAZY JB, Sport Horses Trained, Bought and Sold, Jesse Burrell, trainer."

A pair of streaking masses of fur, one big, one small, flew across the yard to meet the Ford as it pulled up to the barn. Blizzard was a Queensland heeler, a forty-pound compact combination of relentless energy and aggressive intelligence seeking a task. Dozer was his pardner and opposite, a thickset, heavyweight golden lab, kind-eyed and handsome. A pipe smoker in a cardigan tolerant of Blizzard's relentless challenges to wrestle.

Dozer had been Zack's dog. Every once in a while, he'd cock his head and flick his ears in a surge of attention to something only he could sense, the way he used to look at Zack. Dozer was homeless, wandering lost and hungry at a construction site when he found Zack. When Zack got down with a dog, he became luminescent and giggling —a child pure as sunlight. Jesse had said, "I never saw him that open with a person…but with dogs? He'd lie down in the grass and use a dog for a pillow and they'd let him and like it."

They turned the horses loose in the arena to kick out the kinks and roll in the sand. Jesse's hired hand, Ricardo Valverde, had brown skin drawn tight over fine bones. Thin as a hoe handle, hard as a hound, he appeared stained by strong tea. He went straight to cleaning out the trailer and unloading the tack.

A black pygmy goat sneaked up and pressed his horns against Jesse's leg. Chauncy lived in his own world, subscribed to no pecking order, and took no shit, nor did he give any. Jesse felt he was kind of like him.

Abbie tucked the horses in, then stood square in front of Jesse and said, "Well, I guess that's it, Boss. I've got three classes tomorrow morning. I should be here about one-thirty, okay?"

"Okay." He put his arm across her shoulder and walked her to her car. "Thanks." He leaned down and kissed the top of her head. She looked up smiling, then got into the dusty old "bug" convertible and drove down the dirt drive. She shared a little place in Austin with another student, Alissa, a dancer studying banking, and Alissa's boyfriend, a computer nerd.

He sat deep in a leather recliner next to a wall of books with a scotch in his hand and John Coltrane easing from the speakers. Dozer was flopped on the floor. He'd built the house of stone and wood, stout posts and beams, weathered board and batten. A massive river-stone fireplace sported a thick plank mantle disarranged with family photos, unpaired spurs, old bits, and fat candles in iron holders. A wall clock was framed with trophy buckles of silver and gold, testimony to glory days. Photos of cutting horses and team roping were scattered everywhere. Splashes of bright Navajo rugs covered parts of the clay tile floors. A film of dust covered everything. He needed to get Ricardo's girlfriend, Nellie, in there to do the place up.

Any evidence of female occupancy was long gone. It'd been more than twenty years since moth holes had appeared in the fabric of his marriage and Jolene moved out. A year later, she was married to the owner of a string of wholesale furniture stores. While she pranced around the tennis courts, her new husband golfed, smoked cigars, and indulged her costly whims.

Dozer followed him across the yard in the cool quiet night to the barn. The horses in stalls shuffled as they entered. The horses were used to the sound and sight of Jesse. He was the man who straddled their hearts. He stopped at each one, speaking softly, and stroking its face.

At the end of the barn aisle, Jesse climbed a flight of stairs to a second story loft with a door, locked. He stepped in and reached for the light switch. He shut the door behind him with a churchly reverence. It was a no-frills bunkroom. A plank bed with blankets and a pillow, a tin stove, an unpainted chest of drawers under a mirror, a corner bar for hangers behind a curtain on rings, a small table, two chairs, and a cramped bathroom. That's all there was to it.

The ranch had been a sanctuary for Damien. The loft was his space. Jesse sat on the bunk, and cupped his chin. His eyes fell on the motorcycle poster, and another of a Sports Illustrated swimsuit queen sporting breasts crafted by a master. Next to the posters, a section of old barn siding had been framed as a background for a collection of feathers fastened with unseen dabs of glue. The plumage of the Red-tailed Hawk, Brewers Blackbird, falcons, doves, owls, ravens, the Green-tailed Towhee, and the Cinnamon Teal formed a polychromatic palette that Damien would add to in his quiet times. Jesse turned to look at the pillow where his son's head had rested. He brought it to his face in search of a lingering scent of the Polo cologne Zack favored because his love, Melinda, whom Jesse thought might save Zack's life, had said it was sexy.

The resident owl hooted from the gnarled cottonwood behind the barn where Damien's boyhood swing still hung. And then silence. He lay down on the bed and stared at the ceiling. "Damien..." The word flowed out of him on one long breath.

With a groan, Dozer eased himself to the floor next to the bed.

7

Holy Rood, Ravens and a Sign from a Spirit

He stepped out, coffee in hand, to a cold moist morning, the iron sky a haven for demons. He went back into the house, grabbed a blanket-lined jacket and went to the barn.

"I'll be back in a couple of hours." He told Ricardo what horses to have ready to ride, then got in the Ford and drove out.

A ribbon of blacktop snaked through a wide expanse of pale, wind-bent grass. Wipers thwacked away the light rain. He turned in between brick columns bearing wide-flung iron gates and entered another world. Edgar Allen Poe might have been standing barely visible behind the swirling mists as host.

He drove slowly along a single lane of gravel, the crunch of tires the only sound, through a verdant grove of solemn oaks arching out the sky. He pulled to the right, stopped, and got out.

Nary a soul in sight. A flock of thirty ravens, crouched in their black feathers, grouped on a gathering of gravestones. He pulled up his collar and snugged his hat walking toward them. They scattered, rising to vanish in the leafy darkness.

A wet weaving of dead grass, fallen leaves, dark feathers and twigs formed a dense duff carpet that silenced the stepping of his feet. He stopped to face a small neat stone with rough chiseled sides and a smooth polished face that said, Damien Zachary Burrell, October 3, 1976 - July 7, 2003.

Unconscious of the rain-drip off his hat brim inches from his eyes, he stood entranced by the dates as he relived his son's life from Jolene birthing him to God taking him.

His eyes were swimming. He looked skyward, the light rain diluting his tears. "I miss you, boy." He shook his head and looked back at the stone. The wrenching agony seared his soul. "I know you're here right now. I can feel you."

He shoved his hands into his coat pockets and looked around. It was a soothing, sacred place where angels assembled to conduct their business. He said, "Come on, take a walk with me."

Ambling aimlessly among aisles of stone, he looked up again through the drizzle at the slate sky and said, "Give me a sign, Zack. A feather, anything." Feathers had been a thing between them since Zack was a little kid. They'd watched a hawk stoop to a pigeon in a cobalt sky. A tail feather from the hawk had fallen out of the collision and landed at Zack's feet. He had stuck it in his hatband and deemed it a symbol of good fortune. It was the start of his collection. But even as Jesse spoke the words, he realized the ground was strewn with the dark feathers of ravens, sparrows, and little brown birds perched on limbs looking like leaves that had forgotten to drop. Finding a feather would have little significance.

The thought was no sooner complete than his gaze was drawn to the sodden ground. There not two feet in front of his right boot toe landed a still fluttering, bone-dry, pure white, down feather.

He bent quickly to pick it up, taking off his hat to shield it from the drizzle.

It was absolutely dry. Impossible. It was white as snow. A four-inch plume of fluff. He held its fragile softness lightly in his hand.

Emotion overran its banks and flooded his throat. He began to laugh aloud. He reached for the knotted neckerchief, pulled it free, and with a mother's care wrapped the feather in its folds.

And he laughed. In joy and amazement, he walked and laughed with tears in his eyes. He told Zack how cool that really was. Then he laughed again. And the ravens heard a sound they'd never heard before.

8

A Living Legend

He listened to the machine and picked up when he heard Larry Littlefield on the other end. Larry had won the coveted title of "World's Champion All-Around Cowboy" an unprecedented six times. He was a living legend. He had parlayed his fame into a mini-empire of several successful businesses and still maintained celebrity status as host of a TV show about horses. He acted in films, appeared at rodeos, horse shows, and cuttings. He was a gentleman, a husband, a father and a damn good friend.

"Got a deal goin' up here at the Colorado Springs Rodeo. Might be kinda fun for you. They're wanting to do a pro-celebrity cuttin' to raise money for the Cystic Fibrosis Foundation. Bunch of big corporations are sponsoring the thing. Hotel is donating rooms. Bring a couple of horses, meet some good folks, maybe catch yourself a movie star. And we'll be doing some good for these kids with CF. Whuddyuh think?" It seemed he'd said it all on one breath.

"I think you ought be selling beach houses in Nevada. When do I need to be there?"

He gave him the dates and said, "Come up a few days early if you can. I got a bunch of horses to ride and we'll get around a little."

9

A Team Roping Jackpot

Floyd Cox's place was a dust bowl churned by trucks and trailers maneuvering for space.

About thirty-five teams were entered. First place jackpot winners could take home a little more than one thousand dollars each. But the toughs were there. The eighteen-year-olds with faster-than-the-eye-can-see hands swinging ropes they keep next to their beds at night. In the mornings, one hand aims the urine, the other fondles the rope. It was gonna be a tough roping. Five steers. You could be fastest on four, miss one and you'd go home empty.

Billy Diggs' brown and white head horse was like the heavy equipment he drove. Hugely muscled and athletic, standing quiet till asked to go to the task. Then he could drag a rhino to Albuquerque at the end of a rope. And he could run some, too.

Jesse's red roan, normally a quiet, soft-eyed, gelding when not at a roping was now a coiled steel spring in a sweat-shine from his ear-tips to his tail. He stepped as if on hot coals as Jesse eased him toward the heeler's box, on the steer's right side. This was their last steer. They'd caught four. They needed this one and they'd have to be quick. They still had a shot.

Billy's placid paint walked into the header's box on the steer's left and mechanically turned front with his eye on the captive steer and waited. Nice horns, thought Billy as he visualized his perfect loop snaring and coming tight. He looked across the steer to the other side at Jesse trying to settle the impatient roan into the corner for a good start. Jesse shook his loop, caught Billy's eye, and nodded. Billy nodded to the chute man who tapped a trigger and the brindle steer shot out of the chute with Billy and Jesse in hot pursuit. Billy swung once and delivered the loop to the horns, jerked the slack and in a blur dallied the rope around his saddle horn and turned left, taking with him the flying steer. Jesse rounded the corner with his loop whirling and his eyes locked on the hopping hind feet of the steer. In perfect time he placed the loop where the feet were headed and roped them out of the air. As the roan stuck his tail in the ground, Jesse jerked his slack and dallied. The arena judge dropped his flag. The bullhorn squawked, "Eight flat. Diggs and Burrell." Not fast enough for first, but they'd get their entry money back and then some. They'd had a good day.

Floyd Cox was a youthful half-century old, with silver-white hair and a white mustache traveling down each side of his mouth terminating at his jaw. The chew behind his lower lip looked like he harbored a golf ball. The brightest blue eyes twinkled above shining red cheeks. When afoot, he traveled on bandy legs under a trophy buckle obscured by his belly as if he were fleeing a fire. No stroller he.

He could tell a story and loved to laugh. Jesse and Billy were just finishing untacking their horses when he rolled up with a Coors in his hand and spat.

"Goddamn, you boys roped good today." Then he launched right into it, rapid-fire. "So this ol' boy decides he wants to git hisself a guard dog. So he goes out and gits a goddamn Rottweiler with a neck on him like a tree trunk and takes him home. That night that son of a bitch terrorizes the entire family. The wife locks herself in the bedroom, and the kids just make it to their rooms with this son of a bitch a-chewing at the doorknob. He catches the family cat, kills it, and eats the damn thing. The ol' boy jumps on the phone to the vet and says, 'Doc, this is one rank son of a bitch. I don't know what the hell to do with him.' Vet says, 'Bring him round here tomorrow and we'll castrate him. See if that quiets him down.' Next morning the ol' boy snaps a stout chain on to the collar and sets out. This Rottweiler is a-pullin' and a-haulin' and a-jerkin' this ol' boy down the street. He finally gets him stopped at a crosswalk. There's a pedestrian walking on the other side of the street. That dog makes a lunge at the chain, breaks the snap, and takes off like a rocket after the pedestrian. This guy is a-runnin' for his life, his knees to his chest. That dog is snappin' at his heels. He makes a leap through the air, tackles the guy to the ground, and jumps on his chest. He is just about to tear the guy's throat out when up comes a-runnin', pantin' out of breath, the owner. He reaches down, grabs the collar, and jerks the dog back just in time. He looks down at the terrified guy on the ground and says, 'Jesus man I'm sorry, I apologize. I was just now taking this son of a bitch to the vet to have him castrated.' The guy looks up and says, 'Castrate him hell. You need to take that son of a bitch to a dentist. I could tell from a block away he wasn't gonna fuck me!'"

Jesse and Billy roared while Floyd giggled with delight as if he hadn't heard it before.

Seemed like Floyd had told the story on one breath, words flying like bullets. When he'd finished he spat brown juice and took a swig of Coors. Seemed he had a compartmentalized oral cavity that allowed him to do both at the same time.

On the drive back home, Billy extended an invite from his wife Kathy Sue. Her cousin Marlene from Oklahoma City was coming to visit for a few days and Kathy Sue would like for Jesse to come to supper. Billy said, "She works for the newspaper. I met her once.

She's about halfway ornamental. She might be too needle-witted for a feller like you though." Jesse said he'd come. He was thinking more about the food and a couple of hours with Billy's boys than meeting a new woman. A small sadness moved in his heart, and he turned away from Billy to look out the window.

10

Marlene

The first thing people noticed about Kathy Sue Diggs was a cascade of blond hair she could sit on. Seeking recognition for something deeper, she had cut it all off and now sported a two-inch pixie shag framing her pretty scrubbed face.

When she opened the door, Jesse damn near fell back. Her hand fussed in her hair. Jesse said, "Wow! That was a bold move." His grin grew wider as he studied her face. "You look great. I mean beautiful." She knew he meant it. He thrust forward a handful of wildflowers and a bottle of red wine.

Mason, a lean fourteen, was the quieter, more cerebral of the boys. He was a talented rider and held Jesse in the highest esteem. He greeted Jesse with a grownup handshake and the news that Billy and Lucas were out back tending the grill.

Billy had thawed a brace of pheasants he'd shot last season and was doing a hell of a job making them look like a magazine cover with the rambunctious Lucas wielding a pepper mill.

Marlene McAdams had a body to stop a Mormon in mid-sermon. An abundant luxury of shining, jet-black hair bespoke a Cherokee ancestry. She was big-city glib, confident, educated, and politically informed. But she didn't hit you over the head with it. Jesse found her to be a very attractive and pleasing woman.

In the kitchen, Kathy Sue carved hunks of apple pie and slid them onto plates as Marlene dropped a generous scoop of vanilla ice cream on each one, saying, "He's amazing. Every time he says something, it's a surprise. He must spend half his time reading. And foreign films. I bet he's the only man in Texas that's ever seen a foreign film." She licked her fingers. "He's a horse trainer?"

"One of the best. Billy says he's half horse," said Kathy Sue.

"Which half?" She snickered. "I didn't say that. He sure is interesting. He seems a million miles away even when he's looking straight in your eyes."

"Yeah...I think he is a million miles away. When his boy died, most all of Jesse went with him. Jesse was a pistol, always laughing, playing jokes on people, always up for a good time. The boy was everything to him. He raised him by himself."

"No woman in his life?" Marlene licked vanilla ice cream off her fingers.

"Not so's anyone would notice. He never seemed to miss having a woman much. Oh, I'm sure he had his quiet little things going on now and then. The women are all crazy about him. But mostly he seemed to keep to himself...his boy, his horses, and his dogs." Kathy Sue had loaded a tray with pie. She picked it up, shook her head at the sadness of it, and making a little lip sound said, "He sure would make somebody a catch."

Jesse stood, patted his belly and asked Marlene if she'd like to walk some of it off. Ambling under the stars she shared some privacies of her past and secret hopes for her future in a frank and open way. Jesse listened.

Hardly a leaf stirred as they sat on the tailgate of the Ford, feet dangling and no sound between them. She followed an impulse and reached out and touched his cheek in a sweet and gentle way. Her voice seemed to come from afar. "You're a good man, Jesse. You've got kind eyes."

Marlene knew that at least for now it wasn't going any further. She inhaled the night and sighed. "Well, I guess I'd better go on in."

He smiled and nodded.

"I enjoyed meeting you Jesse. Maybe we'll see each other again sometime."

"I hope so."

She put her face close to his and swept him up in her huge brown eyes and softly placed her lips on his and said goodnight. She turned and walked away.

He watched her go, enjoying the swinging flare of her hips, knowing she was aware. She waved her arm without turning back.

11

On the Lam

Though thin as a pen, Holly tossed the stuffed duffel into the overhead bin like a farmer bucking hay. She punched it back so the door would close, then climbed into the window seat and crammed another bag under her feet. She wore dark glasses, a ball cap over a ponytail, and a soft white shirt under her brother's blazer, jeans, and handmade buckskin moccasins. By the time the plane took off, she had her notebook in her lap, a pen in hand, and headphones on. A half-hour later, she took a deep conscious breath and blew it out as if to purge herself of New York.

There was no attempt on her part to draw attention to herself. She wore no makeup or visible adornments of any kind and hoped to be undisclosed behind the incognita of black lenses. Yet an aura compelled even the dullest eyes to follow her. Aware of the guy in the tie next to her feeding figures in columns to his laptop, she hoped his occupation would last the length of the flight. At that moment, he stopped typing, pinched his chin, then turned to her and said, "Are you going home…or are you leaving it?"

Holly pulled her headphones to one side. "Sorry?"

"Are you going home or are you leaving it?" He was a Rogaine user, in his early forties, who if fluorescence could give one a tan would be brown as a berry. Instead he was the color of the belly of a whale.

Holly was amused. Then she said, "I'm not sure."

He waited for more. There wasn't any. Then he asked if she wanted to explain.

"I'm going to see my mommy."

"Your mommy?" It had traces of challenge and ridicule.

Holly simply smiled and replied, "Yes…my mommy." She replaced her headphones and turned to glance out the window and then down to her notebook. Rogaine man ceased to exist.

She began to write in a distinctive artistic scroll, unhurried, recording stampeding thoughts and surging emotions as well as words could capture them. She knew one thing for sure. This flight was portentous. Where it would take her was not spelled out on her ticket. She adjusted a pillow under her head and closed her eyes.

12

Colorado Bound

The last thing he stuffed under the seat was a snub-nosed Smith and Wesson three fifty-seven magnum. He turned to Abbie to repeat last minute instructions, to which she replied, "Get in the truck and go!" Then she reached up and pulled him down to her and planted a kiss on his cheek and said, "Be safe."

He stopped in Kerrville to top up the tanks and get a second coffee. Back on the road, the country poured open on each side. His mind wandered in its own corridors as he listened to Patsy Cline lamenting calamities of love. The haunting echoes of her voice converted music into portraits of his soul.

Straight ahead in the shimmering distance of the empty road, he saw Zack as a nine-year-old boy learning to ride a skateboard, coming at him fast, blond hair flying, eyes wide and howling with joy and the pride of achievement. One of the beautiful memories of Zack loving life. Before the darkness came on him.

13

The Sweet Scent of Kiowa

The contrast between New York City and Kiowa, Colorado, where the deer and antelope play and its population of eight hundred and seventy-six people was a numbing shock. Her dad had always wanted to live in the west and be a cowboy. So there they were on ten acres in a small redwood house with a barn and a couple of pastures with three horses, two dogs, five ducks, and a goat named Bingo. She spent the first forty-eight hours in a trance. She slept and walked and slept and walked again.

The setting sun streaked the sky with flame and lavender. A breeze blew the sage-scent across the porch where she sat and ruffled her hair. She hoped that here with her parents, they could confront the grief of her brother's death and somehow heal.

Holly crawled between the chilly sheets of her grandmother's ornate bed. Incense and a candle burned. She closed her eyes to meditate. Coyotes were yapping along the hills to the south and there were calls from the northward rimlands, cries that seemed to have no other source than the night itself.

14
The Tar Ribbon

The country had begun to put on fancier duds. As the sun painted warmth on the rockscape sprouting tufts of green, he began to come out of himself and notice the world around him. At Pueblo, he crossed the Arkansas River with its stony palisades and muddy flats. The road, instead of just lying there reached out and demanded attention as it wound through limitless pasture flecked with sizable cattle herds. A buckaroo in chinks and wildrag was easing along on a plain-looking gray behind a bunch of heifers. One busted out on her own. The cowboy and the gray sprang to life whirling and streaking through the tall grass after the cow and, cutting her excursion short, turned her back to the herd. The action put a smile on Jesse.

The sky was an untroubled lucent pearl. A stream accompanied the road for a while, then coiled off through soft meadows. He took off his hat and stuck his head out the window. The sudden mountain coolness blew through his hair and filled his lungs. He heaved a loud sigh into the wind. "Damn, this is pretty country."

15

Ruby and the Bear

At the rodeo grounds at Colorado Springs, the stable manager told him Larry Littlefield had been there but had to get on over to the hotel. He got his horses set up in a pen, unhitched the trailer and drove to the hotel.

The young woman at the front desk handed Jesse a message and went to the computer to check his reservation. The message read: "Had to get back out to the ranch to prepare for the arrival of guests for a shindig tomorrow. Put your horses up and come on out." As the desk clerk pondered the computer, the shadow of a big man fell across him. He turned toward a bright-eyed flashing smile in a round face under a clean black cowboy hat. He had silver and black hair. A dark mustache made the smile shine even more. He was barrel-chested, tall, a powerful presence with a jovial spirit. He said, "Are you Jesse Burrell?"

"Yes, sir."

"I thought so. I was just with Larry, he told me to look out for you. He had to run back to his ranch. He said for you to get your butt out there." He laughed and extended his hand, "I'm Henry Bassett. Most people call me Bear. It's good to meet you."

Jesse took his hand. "All right, Bear. Good to meet you, too."

"I'm doing publicity for the event. Can I buy you a drink before you go?"

As they walked toward the restaurant, Jesse noticed that Bear's polished boots had spent more time on carpet than they had in stirrups. They sat at a small table near the bar where a diet Pepsi waited. Jesse followed Bear's glance to the woman approaching with a destination-oriented stride. She wore a long skirt, boots, a flowered shirt, fringed jacket, and an old-time Charlie Russell Stetson. Hardly anything over five feet, she was trim and neat with the bone structure women dream about and a smile that made Bear's pale. She took Jesse's hand in both of hers, looked deep in his eyes and said how very pleased she was to meet him. Ruby meant it and he knew it. She sat behind the Pepsi her husband had ordered for her.

There was about them an open willingness to be perceived as who they were with no attempt to disguise or deceive. It didn't take long for Ruby to say that Larry had told them about Jesse's son and how truly sorry they were. Jesse was a little taken aback, but it seemed it was something she needed to say. She took his hand again in her delicate palms, and through the radiant smile said, "We lost our son, Brad. He was twenty-seven." Jesse saw a small disturbance occur in her face. The smile vanished and returned as quickly as it left and she continued her thought. "Almost...three years ago," she leaned forward as if to share a hushed confidence. " And you know, Jesse dear...I wish I could tell you it gets easier. Maybe one day. Anyway, we know what you're living with and our hearts are with you." She smiled big and warm.

Jesse nodded.

As Ruby told of the violent act that took their son, Bear sat silent, sad-eyed, pain-wracked stone, till he caught Jesse's glance and smiled wanly. Ruby went on to express their gratitude for having had their son for the time that they did, and to tell how fortunate they were to have "the most beautiful and talented daughter. And she's just come home from her life in the big wide world to be with us for a while."

16

He turned off the paved road at Florissant into a dirt road maze through the alpine mystery of the Front Range. Round a bend, a lush meadow billowed where a band of horses arched grazing with a pair of mule deer does and a fawn. At the distant end of the valley, Pike's Peak, snow-capped and bronzed by sun-wash, jutted toward the heavens.

Barely discernable among the thicket of conifers and aspens stood the beginnings of a Gallus gate, two peeled upright cypress poles, ungated and wanting a crosspiece at the top. He turned in through a forest corridor bordered by an incomplete cypress fence. About an eighth of a mile through the trees, things opened up. He could see the house and barn. The pond across from the house mirrored a stand of black, spear-pointed spruce, a flock of ducks painted on the still water. A pair of tepees stood white against the green meadow next to the pond.

Larry was at the hitch-rack in front of the barn pulling a saddle off a horse as Jesse walked up. He turned smiling, flung the saddle on a rail, and came to Jesse. He shook his hand, eyes atwinkle, saying, "Goddamn, it's good to see you." He introduced Jesse to young Roxanne. She was tall, strong, kind and gentle and was to Larry pretty much what Abbie was to Jesse. Reaching for a snaffle bridle, he said, "Why don't you get on that buckskin there. I want to ride this colt up in the hills a little bit. This ol' vet I know bought him and he's a little too much for him so he dropped him off here for me to work him for a while. I'd like to trade him out of him. This is a pretty nice colt."

That was non-stop Larry—riding horses, training, trading, running a business, emceeing a charity event, and hosting people he didn't even know, and he did it all with a kind of offhanded ease. His wife, Rosie, and their ten-year-old daughter, Linda, were in the house cooking for the twenty or thirty people who were expected tomorrow.

Larry led the way at a trot across the meadow behind the barn. They rode over a rise through a stand of aspens and sage, then down a slope alongside another alpine tarn dotted with ducks. They kicked up into a lope. The colt flung his heels in the air like a whip-crack. Larry looked back at Jesse and laughed. Hell, he was six times world's champion cowboy; this colt would have to get up pretty damn early to worry him. The trail stretched out in front of them for quite a ways over rolling meadows. Pretty soon they were side by side at a canter, then a gallop, and then the race was on. The buckskin was big, powerful, and could damn sure cover some ground. The colt, light and airy, possessed the competitive aggression of youth, and plumb refused to let the big buckskin nose ahead. Jesse gave himself up totally to the charge until he could no longer tell where he ended and the horse began. They breathed as one. The same pounding heart seemed to serve them both. Jesse was rooted in the buckskin's being. He glanced down at the spinning grass and flashing hooves reaching forward pulling the earth to him as if to accelerate the rotation of the planet. They flew over the trail like warring Comanches whooping and hollering, laughing like loons, wind whipping tears from the corners of their eyes.

They cut off the trail and crossed country where the footing became less commodious. Still blowing from the run, they picked their way over the rocks to a promontory overlooking the ranch. They stepped down and loosened the cinches. The horses took up the slack with swelling sides and lowered their heads to the slim pickings between the rocks. Jesse and Larry hunkered on the gray ledge.

The silence of the woods and the valley below was deep. They sat without words till a wind rustled and a cloud mass blotted the lowering sun casting streaks of bronze and purple through the trees. Jesse spoke, as if his voice had rusted, "Every which way you turn on this place, you're lookin' at a postcard."

"Yeah, I've got a real fondness for this country," answered Larry as he reached into his stained vest pocket and came out with a thin silver flask.

Jesse pointed off at the distant mountains. "Look at that light." A thin silken sash of violet strung between two peaks binding them one to the other. "Makes me wish I could paint."

"You could paint my barn." Larry held out the flask. "My dad brought this up from Arizona. Some old teamster makes the stuff in his barn. Tell you what, I think it's better than Wild Turkey."

Jesse took a mouthful and swallowed. "Damn." He handed it back to Larry who did the same and then gave the flask to Jesse again. And so it went. There seemed to be in the silence between them a license to communicate in thoughts and feelings as roadmaps for words. Larry pulled off his sweat-darkened hat and scratched in his hair that was longer than cowboy culture would dictate. Larry was always his own man. Finally, he spoke. "So how you doin'?" He turned his head and peered with ice-blue eyes, inquisitor-like, straight into Jesse's face. "How are you really doin'?"

A huge feeling had been gathering in the privacy of Jesse's heart. It took a while, but before he knew it he was talking like he'd never done before. "You know what…Meeting those folks Bear and Ruby.

She got me going, telling me about her son…she talked about it so easy. Made me realize what I'm holding inside. Sometimes, I feel like I'm gonna explode…other times, I feel like I'm dead."

Larry handed him the flask. "I left you a drop, hell, you're a guest."

Jesse emptied the flask. "I have to remind myself to breathe. Sometimes I just quit breathing." He filled his lungs with Colorado Rocky Mountain air and slowly let it out. He turned over the flask and absently shook it. "I can't help thinking I could've been smarter. Seems like I should've been able to…prevent it."

"Well, you know that's not true."

"Still it seems like I…like I could've…done more…" He laid back, adjusted his head on the rock, pushed his hat over his face and spoke into the hat. "I used to smile a lot. Now, I have to remind myself to smile. I've lost my fire."

"It's gonna take time…you probably never get over it."

"I swear to God, sometimes I feel…sometimes I feel like I could just fold it all up…real easy."

"How do you mean?"

He handed the flask back to Larry. "I don't know. Just…kinda quit. It's like I lost that fighting edge. And yet let some son of a bitch look at me about halfway cross-eyed and I'm likely to offer to tear his head off. I've never been like that. I'm gettin' to be a cranky bastard. It's a mighty wonder anybody'd want to be around me."

"Well, you know I never did care for you much myself. So I can't say as I see all that big a change. You got a woman in your life?"

Jesse shook his head.

"You got too much venom in you, son. You need to do some horizontal two-steppin'. A man can't live on floggin' yer mutton alone."

"I've been around for more than half a century…and I'll tell you what. I don't believe I've ever been in love. Not really. No, sir. And you know what? I don't believe I'd know it if it bit me in the ass." He uncovered his face, sat up, and squinted off at the changing light. With the flamboyant paintbrush of sunset came a sudden brief downpour to rinse the day.

17

Holly Marie Bassett

Larry was out of the tepee pissing before the sun came up.
"Goddamn, son. You gonna sleep all day?"

Jesse knotted up in his bedroll. "Hell, man, it's dark out there."

Under a marbled sky in a chilled morning mist, they gathered a
mixed herd of Herefords and Brahmas and drove them into the
pole-fenced arena that looked like it'd been there since 1896.
Roxanne rode down from the barn trailing a string of horses to be
worked and some for the guests who wanted to ride

Larry was a warm and generous host, just not long on formality.
He'd ride over to the fence and shake hands, then go back to cuttin'
or turning back cattle for Jesse as they worked several horses.

Bowls of pasta, salads, beans, bread loaves, and rolls covered the
big wooden table in the house. Out on the porch, a home-welded
barbecue spewed plumes of chicken and beef-scented smoke rising
to the rafters. Among the porch group scattered around tables,
benches, and railings were the CEO of an airline sponsoring the

event and his young son, neighbor ranchers, a veterinarian and his cowgirl wife, a TV star and his actress wife, two more actors, a lady country western star, and Bear and his wife Ruby. Digger and Brantley, unshaven Texas Rangers who'd stopped on their way back to Texas from a hunting trip, were tending the meat.

A galvanized tub filled with beer, soda pop, and ice stood against the wall. Larry fished out an armload of Coors and passed them around. Jesse and Larry greeted Bear and Ruby who jumped up and gave them each a hug, shining her smile on them.

Jesse was standing at the barbecue with Digger and Brantley when he heard the screen door behind him open and shut. He made the slightest movement with his head and turned. Then he turned back to the fire. His head snapped back to the door again. She was carrying a plate of food and looking for a place to sit. She wore Wranglers, boots, a good black hat, and a pale blue silk shirt, shy and tentative about the way it contacted her body. With the help of a light breeze it would touch her breasts, cling for a second, then flutter away. She focused on Bear and Ruby and walked toward them. Even in the smallest movement there was something hauntingly familiar about her and yet he knew he'd never seen her before, or anyone remotely like her.

She squeezed in next to Bear who was in an intense discussion with the airline executive, and balanced the plate on her knees. Bear stopped to introduce her with customary paternal pride. She smiled and nodded politely with genuine interest in whatever he was saying. As she turned toward Ruby to answer a question, she caught Jesse staring at her and smiled at him, then spoke to her mother.

He felt immediately clumsy but his eyes would not leave her. He took in every point of her. The face, the figure, the honey-colored hair, the way she was dressed. He could smell her from where he stood. He took it all in and stored it as quick and keen as lightning. Under the black brim of her hat, the smoky blue-gray eyes caught him again and for the briefest part of a second she smiled easily while turning from an inquiry by Rosie about the food to some-

58

thing Bear was saying about the upcoming event.

"Jesse!" It was coming from behind him and finally broke through his trance. He turned to see the unshaven, unbreakable jaw of Digger saying, "You want ribs, a burger, or 'gospel bird'?"

"Gospel bird. Thanks."

"Chicken?! You're a Texan, aincha son? You need to eat beef. We're in the cattle business in Texas. We don't raise no damn chickens."

"Tell you what. I'll eat whatever you put on that plate."

Jesse had turned back to what drew him like the moon draws tides. What was it that haunted him? Yes, he could see her mother's smile and the cheekbones and that she got her tallness from Bear and the fineness from Ruby. But there was something in the way she moved.

He was depositing bones in a trash bag when Bear stood beside him popping a Coors. "Have you met my daughter Holly?"

"No, sir."

They moved to where she stood in a circle. Bear put his arm around her and puffed up. "This is my daughter Holly Marie. Holly, this is Jesse Burrell. Larry says he's a great horseman. Holly has just come in from New York. She's been working back there as a fashion model. Holly wants to learn to ride a cutting horse." It was something Bear had done ever since she was a child, get his children right out there. "Go and shake that hand. Look 'em straight in the eye." Holly was used to it, but what was natural for Bear wasn't always easy for her.

She took his hand in hers and held it warmly. Smiling the brood mare of all smiles, she looked into his eyes. "It's an honor to meet you, Mr. Burrell." She bowed slightly at the waist as a yogi or Buddhist might.

No one had ever said it's an honor to meet you, Mr. Burrell. He felt his face flush and found it almost impossible to look at her directly. "Please, call me Jesse." And in that instant he was seized by a fever of the flesh he had never in all his life experienced. How could such a thing happen? She was probably younger than Zack would be. But this was a feeling over which his mind had no power. She let loose a flight of elaborate bright balloons in his heart.

"Well, we're gonna ride some more. Maybe rope a little bit. C'mon down to the arena, we'll get you on a horse."

It was ever so slight but her face pinked a little and she felt an agitation inside of her as the molecular structure of the space between a man and a woman was altered. She hesitated for a second then said, "Really?"

"Sure. Have you ridden at all?"

"As a girl in the Midwest, I used to ride hunters."

Bear had gone back to discussing the event with a circle of supporters. Jesse and Holly started down the steps to the path that led to the arena. "I think riding the hunt seat is about the best foundation there is. Lot of cowboys are scared to death of a flat saddle. If you can ride that, you can ride anything." He suddenly realized he was talking about three times more than he normally would and was sure he sounded stupid. Yet he couldn't seem to stop his mouth. "I'll tell you one thing. You look the part."

She may not have been on a horse in a while, but it didn't appear that way. She was tall and lean with the unflared hips of a teenage boy. She sat up straight but relaxed, an extravagant natural arch in her back lending an air of elegance. Jesse sat the big buckskin and trotted alongside giving small hints and elaborate praise as they went, his mind a chaotic blizzard of thought.

Holly knew well how to suppress nerves and function under stress while appearing cooler than a glacier. She tried to concentrate on what he was saying but found distraction in the easy rhythm of his flowing with the horse. And there were his hands. Large, long-fingered, as articulate as a guitarist's, the reins draped loosely between them, as he seemed to command the big horse easily by virtue of his will.

As she watched the horse move, an image came to her of the huge heart pumping within the vaulted cathedral of ribs between his knees and blood pulsing to muscles and sinews that articulated the legs and drove the hooves to imprint the earth.

His glances were quick, furtive, like a child hoarding contraband sweets. A pearlescent sheen appeared beneath the down along the pout of her upper lip and caused his tongue to moisten his own. He trotted close beside her feeling the warmer air. For an instant his knee brushed hers. They were both aware.

She had a light touch, a willingness to be soft. She was balanced and poised as they cantered a big circle around the arena. He showed her how to ride for the hard stops that were a big part of a cutting horse's defensive maneuvers. Jesse said, "You wouldn't be putting me on, would you? You look like a ringer to me."

"It's been more than fifteen years since I was on a horse."

He shook his head. "Let's get you in there and cut a cow."

"You think so?"

"You're ready."

"Oh, my God. I can't believe I'm going to do this."

She rode into the herd with a white-knuckled grip on the saddle horn. Jesse said, "Relax, concentrate on the cattle and trust the horse."

She did a helluva job for a first-timer, and delighted in Jesse's praise. She could barely contain herself as she glanced toward the fence to see Bear and Ruby, beaming and Bear giving her a thumbs-up.

In high spirits, she extended her hand. "Thank you so much, Jesse. That's the most fun I've had…" She puffed out her plump pink lips and blew away some tension as he took her hand and held it for what seemed a week. He was the first to let go. "That was just great," she said. "Thank you so much."

"You did a good job."

"Well, thank you." There was something unique about the way she said thank you, an uncommon dimension of sincere connection and appreciation. "Bear's got a couple of horses at our house but he and my mom never seem to have time to ride lately. You got me started now. I'm going to have to go out there and get the old gray mare back to where she used to be." Then she gave him a look he could have poured on his pancakes. It wasn't playful and it wasn't designed. It just was.

He felt that his life had just doubled in value. A bolt of fear shot through him. Then a part of him wished he hadn't met this woman, that she hadn't looked at him like that. Like what? Maybe there was no like that. Maybe he'd added that.

Larry called him. They were ready to rope. When Jesse got his horse backed into the box, Larry grinning across at him said, "You better catch. She's watching." The young longhorn fired out of the box and damn near outran them, but they cowboyed-up, caught the steer, and made a hell of a run out of it.

After a few runs, Bear called across the arena saying they had to get back to town. Larry and Jesse rode over to say goodbye. Bear said, "We've still got to play host to some of the celebrities and press at the hotel. Thanks for a great day. We'll see you guys tomorrow."

Holly reached her hand over the fence toward Jesse. "It was very nice to meet you. And thanks again for the lesson. That was so much fun."

"Will you be at the rodeo tomorrow?"

"Oh, yes. Bear's got me working. We're doing a video on the whole thing. So I'm the official interviewer and camera operator. Maybe you'll let me interview you?"

"I'm not real good at..."He saw a look of disappointment at the thought of him refusing and immediately said, "okay, why not. If I make a fool of myself, you can always cut it out, right?"

"I'm sure you won't make a fool of yourself. Are you staying at the hotel?"

"Tomorrow. Gonna stay out here tonight." He simply could not look at her.

Taking in the surrounding panorama, she said, "This is the most beautiful place."

And all the more so because of you, he thought. "It is that," was all he could say.

"Well, see you tomorrow then. Bye." She smiled and the sun brightened. Then she turned and headed up the hill following Bear and Ruby. As he watched her go the tense bob of her buns pumping her arched back up the hill, the swagger of her arms, he suddenly realized what it was that haunted him. Though totally feminine, and Zack completely masculine, she moved like his son. That's what it was. The thrusting bounce of his heels off the ground and the easy swing in his shoulders. The thought chilled him. He watched her all the way to their car, daring to wonder if she might look back. She did not. He was almost glad.

18

The Event

People milled among the vendor booths and food dispensers while the grandstands began to fill. A TV news van sprouted wires, microphones, cameras, and the personnel to work them. Like a hummingbird, Bear moved among them all, gathering celebrities and organizing interviews. Holly had traded her cowboy hat for a baseball cap to accommodate the bulky camcorder on her shoulder. She wound through the throng with supple ease, a hod carrier's stamina, and the resolve of a combat photographer.

Susan Hampton, a glamorous blond villainess in a James Bond movie, was Jesse's celebrity partner for the cutting. She sat tall, confident in the saddle looking down at what she could see of Jesse under his hat brim as he adjusted her stirrups. As he touched her calf, guiding her foot into the stirrup, he kept trying to look around her to see if he could spot Holly.

Susan, accustomed to men fawning, falling, and fighting over her, could not comprehend this cowboy's lack of interest and wondered what in hell he was looking for. At the practice pen, he saw she could ride better than he'd expected. He coached her while she cut three cows and told her she was ready. "Really good job. If I can hold up my end, we'll do all right. You can stay on him. Just let him walk awhile. He's not used to this altitude." Susan thanked him and turned the horse around to circle the pen.

He knew she was there before he turned his head. Holly Marie had come up behind him. "And how are you today, Mr. Burrell?" There was something wicked in her smile.

Immediately, he felt left-footed, humpbacked, one-eyed, tongue-tied, red-faced, and stupid but somehow managed to reply with equal formality, "Well, thank you. And you, Miss Bassett?"

"I'm fine, thanks. Do you think maybe we could do a little interview?"

He noticed again the light glisten of moisture on her upper lip. He could swear she seemed just a little shy. There was a need in him to find what imperfections he could in this creature so far beyond the reach of such a common mortal as himself. "Sure. That's a lot of stuff you're carrying."

"I'm pretty strong...but it is getting warm."

"Where would you like to do it?"

"Over by that trailer would be fine."

He stood down and leading the horse, followed her. Watching her springing, leggy stride he felt a dry tightening in his throat even as he smiled and shook his head.

She adjusted him to the angle of light she preferred. As she pinned a microphone on his shirt, he breathed in the heated scent that perfumed his brain and sent his heart everywhere at once. As he tumbled into a trance, he heard her distant voice say. "What would you like to talk about?"

Before returning to total consciousness, he said, "I'd like to talk about you marrying me."

It was too late, the words were out, and the bell could not be unrung. It was the dumbest thing he could have done. And all for

66

wanting to be slick, for not wanting to be the toe-in-the-dirt country bumpkin. Surely, she would take offense even if she didn't show it, or at the very least see him for the ultimate rube that he was.

Like newly veined porcelain, a pink shine colored her cheeks and her smile broke wide and shyly. She turned away in slight embarrassment and then as she looked back at him said, "Really? That would be something."

"I can't believe I said that. Excuse me. My mouth just ran ahead of my brain."

She kept smiling and clearing her throat, trying to get past the moment of knowing her face was flushed. And in it all he thought, she's not offended and maybe, am I dreaming, is she mildly amused?

As she stood next to him, though separated by eighteen inches of space, he felt as if something of her was rubbing against him. Her most important pursuit seemed to be making Jesse feel good without a trace of effort. So he told her he was born on a kitchen table, which was true, and that he had no brothers or sisters and grew up lonely and sensitive. Then he laughed and she wasn't sure what to believe.

"And so you drove twenty-two hours hauling horses all the way up from Texas to help raise money for these kids?"

He nodded and bit his lip.

———⋙◆⋘———

Jesse had just cut a couple of cows to tune his horse and was letting him relax before the work. A man and his wife approached with a ten-year-old boy in a wheelchair. The boy's eyes were wide with wonder and excitement. The gentle father handling a program requested an autograph for his son. The boy began to push himself out of the chair and walk with gasping effort toward Jesse. Jesse confessed that he was nobody famous. But Danny wanted his autograph because he was a cowboy.

Jesse looked at the boy's father. "Would Danny like to get up on this horse? He's plumb gentle."

Before the father could respond, Danny broke into a keyboard smile and whispered hoarsely, "Yes!"

The father lifted him up to Jesse's outstretched arms. Jesse slipped him into the saddle in front of him. They walked off. The boy looked as if joy might cause his face to burst. Then Jesse stepped off and walked alongside as Danny rode by himself. When they got back to the parents, Jesse lifted Danny to the ground.

He rested in his chair and held the oxygen mask to his face. Jesse signed the program and ruffled the top of Danny's head. He felt the rush of heat in his throat and smiled. When he turned back to the horse, he saw Holly in the distance with her camera aimed at him. When she saw him look, she took her eye from the viewfinder and looked at him directly.

The hotel was top-of-the-line Rocky Mountain Resort— redwood, vaulted ceilings, glass, and modern sculpture in a spacious lobby.

In a room packed with hundreds of people, a bartender was pouring Jesse a straight scotch when Susan Hampton, the bad Bond girl, glided up, batting lashes like tarantula legs, and pursing lips on the verge of bursting from a collagen overload. She thanked him for his help with the cutting and gushed over what a great horse he'd let her ride.

"Well, you did a fine job. You would have won, if I'd been judging. I think that country western gal paid off the judges."

Her attempt to engage him further was thwarted by the intrusion of one of the sponsors of the event, which gave Jesse a reason to drift away. He spotted Bear and family at a table with several others in animated conversation. The all-seeing Bear called to him as he stood up. "Jesse." He walked over and clasped one hand on his shoulder and shook the other. "Come and meet some friends."

Richard Running Deer was one of four Native Americans seated with the Bassetts. A well-known artist, he had donated a painting to be auctioned for the benefit. The Bassetts were proud of his work and their friendship. Holly smiled politely and shook Jesse's hand. An observer might have called him cool but indeed he was hoping that the conflagration within wasn't blazing on his brow.

The room had filled with heat. Jesse stepped into the lobby to find a door to a patio when Holly was returning from the ladies. "Are you leaving?" she asked.

"No, I…I just wanted to get some air."

"It's pretty warm in there."

"Do you want to get some air?"

She looked at him curiously and nodded, "Yes."

He opened the door and stepped aside as he touched her shoulder to guide her through. She felt cool, thin and smooth. The night was hushed, the moon demure behind a silvery veil in a starless sky. He asked if she had any plans.

"Oh, it's hard to say. I've got to find my mind first, before I can get it to think. There's plenty of work to be done. I'm going to help my dad in his PR business. I like to write. I like taking pictures. We're going to put up a tepee, a big one. Something Bear has always wanted to do. I don't know. I'm just going to see what happens. And you? What are you up to?"

"Well, I…I've got a colt back home I'm gonna take to The Futurity. He's a pretty good one." He smiled, feeling foolish for not being better at conversation and was beginning to hope for a rescue. "Would you like something to drink?"

She didn't answer immediately. Instead, she looked at him almost as if she hadn't heard. He wanted to ask what she was thinking about but the whole idea unnerved him. Then she said, " Okay."

He held the door as she walked in. He caught her scent of musk and amber, the air made sacred by her presence. He watched the swinging slope of slender shoulders and the straight tapered back beneath the swirl of hair. In the landscape of his heart, the earth gaped and sucked him headlong into a pit of loneliness and despair. She stopped to greet some friends. He drifted off.

Susan Hampton made one more attempt to connect with Jesse,

then moved on in pursuit of easier game. Just as Jesse thought he could vanish, Larry intercepted him and said, "So, did you make a deal?"

"What?"

Mischief in his eyes, lopsided grin pulling at his face, "Bear's little girl. She sure is a pretty thing."

"Are you crazy? Little girl is right. I've got boots older than she is."

"I don't know…she might be older than she looks."

"Not enough."

"I don't know. I think you're missing a bet. I see things. She's interested in you, son."

"I can't even look at her. I'll bet I'm older than her father."

"You just look older. You need a young woman. Hell, we all do. It's natural. Older men need younger women. Young men need older women. Works out real good for everybody. I remember when I was about twenty-two I had me a woman was fifty. And, man, I'm here to tell you it doesn't get any better than she was. She had hell trying to get rid of me."

"Why am I talking to you?"

"Cuz I'm a smart feller and I know what I'm talking about. Anyway, if you want to be stupid, go ahead. Listen, why don't you stick around for a few days. Stay up at the ranch and help me work those horses. Oh, and that Susan Hampton asked me why you wouldn't pay her any mind. I told her you was an odd feller and that I thought you was gay."

Jesse chuckled and shook his head. "I'll see you in the morning."

"You're making a big mistake. That gal is gonna be dreaming about you tonight. Two of 'em gonna be dreaming about you. And you going home alone. Damn, you're a sorry son of a bitch."

Jesse waved over his shoulder as he headed across the lobby.

He closed the door to his room behind him and stood rooted to the spot by some unbidden thought that held him paralyzed in its grip. *Maybe I should load up and hit the road right now.* A clawing fear of the lack of purpose and meaning to his empty loveless life filled him with despair.

The Smith and Wesson was a slick little unit with custom sculpted cherry-wood grips to accommodate his oversized hand. Like a polished wooden nude, it was a soothing thing to fondle. It was loaded. He rubbed it over his face slowly noticing the smell of oil and gunpowder and thought about what that final moment would be like to actually consider putting the barrel to his temple or in his mouth (which would be the better choice?) and pulling the trigger. The physical thing couldn't be much. What about the mess? Someone would have to clean up his splattered brains and bits of bone and blood all over everything. And what about the folks he'd leave behind? Not too big a thing. His momma and his father were already gone. Speaking of old Clyde Burrell, he'd kick up the graveyard over this. He'd be waiting for me on the other side, arms folded, tapping his foot, and looking at his spur until I stood before him waiting for the storm.

Abbie would sure feel bad. She'd be angry, disappointed, wounded. She'd think I was a fool. He snapped open the cylinder and tipped the copper and lead-headed bullets into his palm and rolled them together like dice. They were smooth with oil sheen and made a comforting sound. He slid them each into their chambers and clicked the cylinder shut. He kept the gun in his hand.

The thought was damn sure intriguing. He'd get to see Zack on his new turf. Meeting this Holly Marie Bassett...why in hell did that have to happen? Jesus, I've got to get the hell out of here. Out of where? No matter where I go, my mind is coming with me. Unless I lose it. Now there's a thought. Goddamn. I've got to quit this.

———◆———

Abbie, sprawled face down in the pillow, groped for the phone and got it to her mouth. Before she could say hello, the voice on the other end said, "Wake up. No sleeping allowed."

"Damn. You caught me laying down on the job. I'm sure there's something I ought to be doing at one in the morning besides sleeping."

"I can think of lots of things."

"So can I. In fact I was dreaming about one of them when the phone rang, thank you very much."

"How was it?"

"It was great up until that point."

"Let me know how it turns out. How is everything?"

"Aside from the barn burning down everything is fine."

"Say you're kidding."

"And the house too. Sparks carried from the barn." She laughed. "I'm kidding. How're you doin', Boss? You having fun?"

"Yeah. I'll be back in a couple of days. I'll call you from the road. Go back to sleep."

"I wish. I hope. See ya. Hey. Bring me back an Aspen leaf."

19

arry was loading saddles into his trailer. "I'll be there for The Futurity. We're gonna do some filming there. I want to see you win it, son."

Jesse smiled. "Call me when you're on your way. Thanks for inviting me up. I had a good time."

"Thanks for coming." He stepped down out of the trailer stuffing a pinch of Copenhagen into his lip. "Everybody's been bragging on you, saying what a nice guy you are. Specially Bear and Ruby. Course I told them they don't know you like I do. Holly didn't say anything though. I figure that Susan Hampton told her you was a sissy." Larry stood in front of him and said, "You're a good man. Take care of yourself. You want to talk, call me or get your ass back up here." Over their handshake, he said, "Drive safe."

Jesse nodded, "You, too." He turned and walked toward his rig.

The horses were tied to the trailer ready to be loaded. Bear and Ruby came to say goodbye and tell him how much they enjoyed meeting him and to come visit at their little place up north. He thought he'd probably never see them again. It saddened him. "Tell Holly Marie I said goodbye. I enjoyed meeting her."

Bear said, "Oh, she said she wanted to come and say goodbye. She should be here in a minute. Well, we'll see you. You come and visit us. We mean it now." Ruby put her arms around Jesse and said, "We love you…you and Damien will be in our prayers." She felt so small in his arms. He thought he mustn't hug too tight or risk cracking a rib. But when she looked up into his eyes, he saw the power and strength. She smiled at him and walked after Bear who turned to take her hand.

Jesse waved. "Adios." He turned back and started to load the horses. As he stepped out of the trailer to get the second horse, she was standing there.

A spine-thrill of delight went through him and then the thud of a brick hitting him in the chest. She stood hip-cocked in a Zack stance and then shifted her weight just exactly as he would. Then she made a totally girlish move completely her own as he walked up to her. He imagined her pale breasts behind the fresh white shirt below that apricot triangle of neck and tried to still the tremor he was sure she could see. Her lips shone like licked red candy and he wished she would just say goodbye and leave. No, he didn't. He wished she would stay forever. He wished he could grasp her hand and put her in the truck and take her home to Texas. The intoxicating brown fragrance of her mesmerized him. She reached out her hand. He took it. In that formal, extremely polite way that she had, she thanked him for the riding lesson and said how nice it was to have met him. She hadn't seen him poking a pistol barrel into the hollow of his cheek. She didn't know he had visualized his brain like a flung pizza splattered on a wall.

She stood there for a moment in silence, as fair as a lily, those smoky blue-gray eyes scanning his soul. A breeze lifted her hair and caressed her neck. He wished he'd been that breeze.

Her eyes fell to his hands that could uproot a tree, hands that could caress a woman's softness.

Feeling like an oaf in a ballet class, he managed to tell her to "get out there and ride those horses y'all have. You've got a real good feel." Of all the things in the world a person could say, this is what I come up with. Good. Real good. You should've pulled the trigger.

The next thing he knew he was watching her walk away again, only this time he wouldn't be seeing her tomorrow.

20

A Long Ride Home

He drove clean through Colorado and saw nothing. An oppressive melancholy had closed in like a dense fog. He ached with a
crushing desire he had never felt before. The more he realized it was
never to be satisfied, the deeper he despaired.

The more he tried to push her out of his mind, the more insistent she became. He imagined himself picking up the cell phone,
telling her he loved her, turning around to go back and get her and
taking her home to Texas to spend the rest of his life with her.

The polished brightness of twenty-four-hour fuel dispensing
paraphernalia gleamed under the lights as he tended to the needs of
the truck. He bought a bag of pretzels, a chocolate bar, a Coke, a
coffee, and a ready-made sandwich purporting to be turkey.

He stopped at Dalhart to let the horses out and shut his eyes. A
little after three in the morning, he pulled out of the rodeo grounds
and aimed for Lubbock. He reached into the glove box and took out
a small, antique leather box. Embossed in silver, its lid bore a

pastoral scene of lovers on a hillside near a castle. Jesse's mother, Francis, had told him it was her mother's, made in England. Now it was skimming over a Texas highway and carrying in it a pure white wing feather from a Texas angel. Jesse flipped the lid and set the box on the seat, took out the feather and held it up to his cheek. It was the softest, most delicate thing, lighter than a breeze and soft as a flower scent. He moved it slowly over his face to tickle above his eyes and under his nose. Then he drew it across his lips and put it back in the box.

Ragged chains of silent lightning ripped the dark dense night to the east. Dead ahead, a tall truck studded with colored lights like a dreadful giant Christmas tree loomed out of the darkness and rumbled by, shuddering Jesse's rig.

Eventually, day broke upon a smoking reach of rolling grassland with a long red sunrise pouring its syrup over the golden hills at the edge of the world. He thought how easy it would be to call Larry and get the Bassetts' phone number. He even let his hand touch the phone. Then what? Ask her if she misses you? Git a holt of yerself, boy. She ain't even on the same planet you are. Think about the colt, The Futurity. In a few hours, you'll have him under you.

21

Home Again

Blizzard and Dozer escorted the rig to its place near the barn. Abbie's hair was covered with a red pirate's bandanna tied tight under a green ball cap from Cullen's Feed Store. Beaming, she looked down at him from the horse she sat on. "Good afternoon, sir. What can I do for you?"

"Well, ma'am, how about a job?"

"Well, sir, the only job we have available is mucking stalls and hauling manure."

"Fine. Just what I need. Some shit in my life."

"Then you've come to the right place."

"Don't I know it."

The sorrel colt stood gleaming, burnished copper in the dusty sun shafts. He snuffled as Jesse placed his arm along his neck and stroked between his ears. He slipped off the halter, bridled him, and stepped into the saddle. He walked the colt off on a loose rein. The horse stretched his neck long and low then tossed his mane and his spirit set his feet to dancing. Jesse just let him go. He broke into a trot, kicked his hind feet in the air, and shook his head as he moved into a canter. Abbie liked to watch Jesse's every move on a horse. He never seemed at odds with a horse, even a rank, uncooperative son of a bitch. She'd seen him ride plenty of them. He was constantly trying to let them know that he'd go along with them or at least meet them halfway, and that it really wasn't a big deal.

Jesse pushed ten head out of the herd and sat facing them, deciding which one he would cut as he allowed the rest to drift back to the bunch. A black and white Angus cross was face-to-face with Buckshot. The reins dangled loosely as Jesse squeezed his legs as a signal and the colt transformed into a brewing storm in hide and hair. He pinned his ears and all but spit in the cow's face. The cow made a quick move. The colt squatted and dove to counter. The cow moved again with more determination, but Buckshot was there splattered out, blowing in her face saying, "Now what?" It was the same with three more cows as Buckshot mirrored their every move, conquering them one by one. It was somewhere between a thought and a thing, an ephemeral display of magic and myth, man and beast as art. Abbie was giggling, "Man, if he ain't something."

Jesse grinned. "He'd rather die than let a cow get past him." He stepped down and loosened the cinches. He walked to the colt's head and slipped the bridle while flared nostrils gulped in air. He stood in front of the horse and softly placed his fingers between the horse's eyes and circled them lightly, whispering, "You're a good boy. Yes, sir, you are a good boy."

Abbie watching wished he didn't see her as a kid, or worse, his daughter. Then she drove the thought away. She helped him carry his stuff from the truck into the house. Climbing the stone steps, she was talking back over her shoulder, "You gotta be dead. Three hours sleep. That's nuts. Couldn't wait to see me, huh?"

"That's right."

He walked her back out to the porch. "Thanks for not burning the place down." He put his arm around her and kissed the top of her head. Magician-like, an envelope appeared in his hand before her eyes. He watched her smile as she took out the card, somehow sensing it should be opened with care. It contained three golden aspen leaves that looked as if they'd been hammered out of a thin foil of the precious metal. She handled them delicately and said, " All right." She read the card, "Thanks for being so cool. Thanks for being my friend. With love, The Boss." She looked up at him with a trace of moisture in her eyes. Then again like magic he produced a black velvet jewelry box and handed it to her. In wonder, she opened it to find a pair of gold earrings shaped as small aspen leaves. "Oh, man…whoa…These aren't the real things. These are the real things. Jesse, they're beautiful." She flung her arms around his neck and pulled him down to kiss him on the lips. "Thank you. I don't know what to say."

"Say goodnight and drive carefully."

"Goodnight and drive carefully." She was heading back to town for classes in the morning. "And I wanna hear about the trip. Did you meet a movie star?"

"Yeah. Lassie." He watched her walk to the little VW bug and heard her yell back, "Thanks, Boss." She started the car and led a rising plume of dust down the drive out to the road.

He leaned on the log railing and inhaled the distinctive aroma of the Texas twilight, dun grading into blue. A high wind soughed out of the west and bore to him the sound of owl-talk from behind the barn. He sat in a rough chair and hung his heels on the rail. Holly Marie, not again. Buckshot, The Futurity. Damien had sat on this porch with him. He'd fallen off hanging by his knees from the rail, long platinum hair swinging from his upside-down face. He was ten years old, sixteen years before he died. One cannot be dead until all the things he changed and touched are gone. As long as there are memories, even the plaintive ones, there is no death. It takes a long, long time for a human being to die.

22

Looking for Light

Her grandmother's Victorian bed was piled with white lace-
trimmed pillows and a thick burgundy quilt. The sky through
the window was moon-bright with a thousand eyes. Naked under
the cool sheet, she pressed her hands prayer-like against her chest,
her hair spread, pale strands of cold gold, her eyes open. In the flick-
er of candlelit shadows on the ceiling, she had gone from meditation
to tracing a view of her life out of the shattered pieces of a fiery
mosaic. Then that lonesome leather cowboy from another planet
was grinning at her, giving rise to wonder and speculation. Her hand
moved over her belly to the moist warmth between her legs.

For the first time in her life she lacked direction, goal or purpose
other than to discover what lay ahead. She blew out the candle,
rolled to her side, shoved a pillow between her pulled-up knees, and
closed her eyes. Tomorrow, she thought, I will feel a horse against
my thighs.

She was watching the dawn lighten the sky when she heard Bear stirring and plumbing working. When he came down the stairs with his hair combed wet from the shower and the bottom half of a business suit on, she had the coffee going. She kissed him good morning. She fingered the starched shirt, "I guess you were planning on me feeding, huh?!"

His big grin, a little sheepish, "Would you? I'll cook some oatmeal."

She looked fourteen, Huck Finn in faded bib overalls and scarred up hiking boots. "Kinda nice to have me around, isn't it?"

He put his arms around her with his chin in her hair and tear-shine in his eyes. "Yeah," he whispered.

She slid open the barn door to the impatient shuffle and snuffle of horses anticipating feed. Bingo the goat sprang from the ground to the top of a fifty-gallon drum and danced a flamenco until Holly poured a portion of sweet feed on the lid which vanished like a teacup in a twister. She grained the horses and tossed flakes of hay. She unrolled a hose and filled the water buckets, then hauled it through a fence to the duck pond and let it run while she fed the ducks. She labored like a farmer, without a hint of the pampering she'd known.

Dance, a round-ribbed gray mare, was the gentlest and least intimidating of the three. She was soft-eyed, pretty-headed, and stood quietly while Holly groomed and saddled her. After weeks of idleness, an excess of energy pranced in her step anticipating a rider. Not without trepidation, Holly put her foot in the stirrup and eased lightly into the saddle.

She felt the mare's pent-up desire to uncork and spoke soothingly, asking her to be a good girl. She rode down the dirt road to a bridle path across the open pastures of neighboring property. Before long they both began to relax and come together. As she became aware of the distinct movement of the mare between her legs, she remembered Jesse saying that when you get good you'll know which of the horse's feet are leaving the ground and when, as if they were your own. Then you can place them where you want. She tried to feel the left front foot. That leather cowboy who had never even been to New York, smelled a subway, or haggled with a Parisian landlady; she wondered what he was up to right then...in Texas.

There was the wind-borne scent of sage and flashes of magpies on fence posts strung with wire. She thought of her brother Brad and his vivid presence in anything she had ever enjoyed. How desperately she missed him.

She was walking back to the house when Ray Cooper's pickup turned into the drive. Ray was a cowboy, an artist, and a craftsman. He was building a little one-room house for Holly to have to herself. No plumbing, no kitchen, but it would have electricity. They called it the Holly House, the size of a bedsheet, off to the side of the main house. She told Ray how much she loved the little porch he was adding, a great place to watch sunsets.

An old brick warehouse housed a video editing company. Holly Marie sat in the near darkness punching keys and twisting dials, gazing intently at the monitors. She stopped the tape, rolled it back and started it again. It was Jesse talking to Daniel, the cystic fibrosis boy. The camera had crept in to a close-up on Jesse. His tenderness and compassion clear as he placed his hand on the spare shoulder of the boy struggling for breath. Holly's throat tightened as she spoke aloud to the empty room, "Look at that...it's beautiful."

Later that evening, she showed it to Bear and Ruby. Each time Jesse appeared, they commented on his sincerity and how effective he was on camera. "Don't you think so, Holly?" Ruby asked.

"Yep."

Bear said, "He's a natural."

"He's very appealing. Don't you think so, Holly?" said Ruby.

"Yep..." and then almost to herself, said, "I didn't think he liked me very much at first."

Ruby's hand paused midway between her mouth and the bowl of popcorn Holly had made for them. "Why do you say that?"

"He hardly ever looked at me. Whenever I was around, he ignored me or looked away or talked to Larry or something."

Bear laughed.

"What's funny?"

"I think you just made him nervous."

"How? What did I do? I couldn't have been nicer."

Bear was still laughing. "He's a country boy. He's just shy, that's all. I wrote him a letter today to thank him for coming and all his help and everything. The tape is really great, Holly. You did a wonderful job. The CF people are going to be thrilled." He put his arm around his daughter and hugged her. "I'm going to give him a call and ask him if he'll sign a release so we can use him on the tape for promotion and fund raising."

Holly said, "When?"

"When, what?"

"When are you going to call him?"

"Oh, a day or two. I'll wait till he gets my letter. Why?"

"Nothing…" She shook her head and went to the fridge for a Coke.

23

Darkness

He put on a jacket and walked out to the porch and into the chill of the thick November night. Dozer rubbed his leg and flopped at Jesse's feet as he leaned against the post and looked to the north. The sound, Holly Marie, came softly, as his voice tried to find the wind that would touch her hearing.

Abbie was warming up a horse while Jesse struggled with an eight-foot length of galvanized pipe, plumber's goop, and a couple of wrenches to repair a leaky water line to a row of stalls in the barn. Ricardo returned from the post office with a stack of mail, dropped it on a bench, and came to lend Jesse a hand.

Two hours later, Jesse flipped through the mail to the letter from Bear and opened it. For the rest of the day, he imagined Holly watching him work and wondered what she would think of his way of life. For more than twenty years, the only love he'd known was that which he shared with his son. He could count the times in all his life he'd heard the words, I love you. He thought about that and what it would be like to hear, I love you, Jesse.

———◆———

Jesse could hear the smile in Bear's voice, "You were just sensational. You ought to be a movie star, man. Have you ever seen yourself on tape?"

"No...I don't think so."

"Well, it's great and I want to thank you for letting us use it. It's gonna do a lot of good."

"How are y'all doin' with your horses?"

"They'd been getting fat and sassy until you got Holly going. Now she's out there riding every day. She's even got me back to riding again. We're having fun. She's right here, I'll let you talk to her. Come and see us. Ruby sends her love. Thanks again."

The next thing he knew, she was on the phone. With her "Hello, Jesse...," the warmth of her breath was in his ear. Irises were blooming, school was out, and summer had arrived.

He said hello. While he was trying to think of what to say next, she said, "Everybody here thinks you ought to be a TV star. We think you already are."

All he could do was chuckle a little. "How are you gettin' on with your horses?"

"Pretty good. So far I haven't gotten myself bucked off. I keep trying to remember everything you told me. I think I'll need some more lessons."

What an invitation. He couldn't believe she'd said it. There's a line a man could do stuff with. "Well...we'll have to see that you get 'em." Oh, that was good. Real good. He wondered if his brain had gone soft from too much time alone.

"Yeah...Bear is yelling, 'come on up and visit.'"

"Well...thanks...I'm, I'm kinda stuck here for a while...but...that'd be nice. I'd like to do that."

"How is Buckshot doing?"

She remembered his name. Amazing. "He's doing real good."

"I know it's in December. What are the dates?"

How does she know The Futurity is in December? She'd never even heard of The Futurity until he told her about it.

He gave her the dates. She told him good luck, she was sure he would win and that Bear, Ruby, and she would have their Indian friends hold a ceremony to guarantee it. I'll send you a copy of the tape so you can see how good you are. You've got to promise to let us know how you and Buckshot make out."

He hadn't felt this light of spirit since high school. He sat on the front step of the porch and watched raindrops make craters in the dust. He twirled his spur rowel with a fingertip and said, "What in hell am I doin'?"

24

The Futurity

The winner takes home close to a quarter of a million dollars plus the fame, glory, and satisfaction that comes with it. Only sixty of the highest scoring horses out of more than six hundred entries get to compete in the semifinals.

By Sunday afternoon, Jesse and Buckshot had already won the first two go-rounds and were among the semifinalists. It was the eighth day of competition. Jesse and Abbie behaved like transporters of nitroglycerine, afraid to breathe, one bad move and their world would blow apart. Abbie remained grimly silent as if some wrong word might break the spell. Everyone was talking about Jesse and Buckshot and Dr. Walter Nalls' stud that sired him. The stallion's stock had already tripled based on what Buckshot had accomplished so far. Larry Littlefield had already interviewed him for his television show and writers for every horse magazine and local newspaper hounded him with tape recorders and scribble pads.

Jesse was thirteenth to go in the semifinals. The audience had adopted him and the blazing sorrel colt as their own. Jesse studied the herd and knew pretty much what he'd like to cut. But often, a herd has a life and mind of its own and your plan goes south.

When the colt pinned his ears, dropped to his belly in that big-cat crouch in front of the cow and said c'mon, try me, the audience went berserk. The cow leaped to one side attempting to charge by, but Buckshot moved so quickly he was right there in her face as if there were two of him and one had been there waiting.

And so it went with two more cows until the buzzer sounded. The crowd went wild, right through the announcing of the score. They knew they'd seen the best and the score confirmed it.

Jesse took Abbie in his arms as she came to them with a face about to explode off its bones. He noticed the tears in her eyes as he loosened the girth and handed her the reins. She walked the horse back to his stall, stripped him and made sure he was happy before she went back to join Jesse watching thirty-two more horses try to beat him.

None did. He and the copper-colored colt had won the semifinals. They would be among the twenty elite athletes to compete for the championship.

He was quiet, alone in his hotel room. He thought about calling Holly Marie but no, not until it's over. He opened his wallet and took out a flattened tinfoil square and unfolded it. He looked at the contents and then slowly picked up a small ribbon-tied lock of pale blond Damien hair and brought it to his nose, then to his lips. Then he put it back, folded the wallet, and put it back in his pocket.

25

The Finals

Holly Marie had sent him a small gathering of aromatic prairie grasses and wild herbs to bring him luck. They were pressed in a small plastic bag in the left pocket of his shirt.

He buckled on his spurs, swung his chaps over the colt's withers, and stepped up into the saddle to walk him toward the warm-up pen.

Abbie's thoughts were a ticker-tape checklist on a loop in her brain. She was sure she'd done everything in her power to contribute to the success of Buckshot's run. This was it. This was what he was bred for. Now all she could do is watch…and pray and jiggle her foot as she stood at the rail separating the judges' stands from the warm-up area.

Near the entry to the working area, Jesse sat quietly, Buckshot's neck extended and relaxed. They were ready to work. Blood raged through a tangle of twisted nerves, a heart pounded like a locked up beast while his mind remained a void enduring the chaos within that was Jesse Burrell. An unconcerned vacancy in his eyes gave the lie to the turmoil inside. There was one more horse before him, a daunting combination of spectacular breeding and a gifted trainer. He would be the last to go.

He was watching the finest of his peers, Bill Waterman, a two-time Futurity champion, the man who could dash his dream, ride like slow-moving water toward the herd. The two turn-back riders converged to encourage the cows to return to the herd, leaving Bill with the one they knew he wanted in front of him. There exists among good cutters and their 'turn-back help' an uncanny wordless communication that seems telepathic.

Bill wiggled in the saddle. His horse locked on to the cow, and the gleaming mahogany bay went to work. He and the horse had all the flash and the tricks to provoke a cow. The buzzer sounded, ending his two-and-a-half minute run. Bill patted him twice on the neck and turned him toward the exit. The announcer called the score. "Timothy's Smart Clock, ridden by Bill Waterman, gets a two-twenty-three-and-a-half which puts him in the lead, with one horse left to work." The packed coliseum rocked with screaming applause.

Jesse filled his lungs and blew it out, wiggled his feet in the stirrups, and tilted his head from side to side. He twisted at the waist from left to right, reached up and pulled his black hat down tight and squeezed the colt toward the herd. He focused on the cattle as he felt himself merge with the colt, sharing the same lungs and heart. A hushed stillness filled the coliseum as he entered the herd like a burglar with residents at home.

The colt squared off with his first cow, crouched like a lion and pinned his ears as if he just might roar. When the cow finally quit and Jesse turned back to the herd to cut another, the crowd roared. When the buzzer went off, Buckshot was demoralizing his third cow. The audience raged in appreciation as Jesse lifted the reins and reached up to apply that finger-tip, feather-light, lover's stroke to the colt's neck. He said something only the colt could hear.

The announcer's resonance filled the stadium. "The score for

Bueno Bar Tab ridden by Jesse Burrell is two-twenty-three-and-a-half." The sound from the audience threatened the foundations of the building. The announcer tried to speak over it. "Ladies and gentlemen, I believe that is the first time in the thirty-three year history of The Futurity that there is a tie for first place." The din continued as the microphone went silent with the promise of more to come. In less than a minute, an amplified click sounded and the big voice continued, "Ladies and gentlemen, there will be a work-off to determine the winner. The order of go to be determined by the toss of a coin."

Bill Waterman rolled his shoulders and rode into the herd. The glossy bay had all the chrome, a white blaze down the middle of his face, three white socks, and a glistening black mane and tail full and flying. His moves were quick with a lot of snap, giving the heart-stopping impression that he might be waiting too long to make them.

Their second cow wanted to be a runner rather than work in the center with quick changes of direction. Bill used his skill to head the cow, forcing changes while looking for an opportunity to quit and cut a better cow and still beat the clock so as not to have the buzzer sound while entering the herd. It's a better impression on the judges to end your run with your horse working a cow, not standing flat-footed in the herd. While those thoughts tugged at his brain the cow shot to the wall with the horse in pursuit and squeezed right under the horse's nose and back to the herd. And that is cuttin'…the worst happening to the best. Bill would get a score, but losing a cow is a five-point penalty. A serious blow. The judges gave him a two-fourteen.

Jesse joined the audience applauding a great champion as Bill rode out and stopped next to the judges' stands to watch Jesse's go.

Buckshot stood still as death, neck long and low, eyes soft, the merest flick of an ear showing he lived. Jesse pulled down his hat and picked up the reins. Instantly the colt came up on his toes and the force began to flow. Jesse squeezed him into a lope for about forty feet behind the stands and slid to a stop, hocks in the ground.

He spun him once to the left and once to the right. He lengthened the reins, stroked his neck and rode into the working area.

Buckshot splattered out in front of the cow and blew a blast of hot sweet breath in its face that scared the piss out of it and made it want to return to the herd more than anything in the world. And that was just the start. The cow turned inside out trying to get past Buckshot but never got to see anything but the fire in the colt's eyes glaring into its soul. Six thousand people screamed, whooped and hollered the roof off the place. Buckshot's dominance over the second cow, even bolder than the first, had the audience cheering every footfall. They knew they were watching the making of a myth. Jesse and the horse were one celestial creature.

The colt jammed so deep into the ground on a stop, that Jesse felt his boot touch the earth as flecks of dirt flew in his face. The cow lunged to the left. The colt's spine twisted under the saddle like a wrung towel as the front legs swept a fifteen-foot arc and he drove his full weight forward with the thrust of his hocks. This was the move that would win the gold. The crowd howled in joy at the perfect synchronization of the horse with the cow, foot for foot.

Jesse couldn't be sure later whether he actually heard a sound, or did he sense it? In the instant of that all-powerful thrust, his entire universe exploded like a cataclysmic collision of planets.

In the midst of that storm of hooves and hair and leather and sweat, the colt faltered and Jesse felt the pain, he felt the colt's valiant determination to continue. He also felt the limits of bone and flesh and heart and mind as the hip sank and a shudder iced his soul.

The cacophony of sound fell to a murmur, then deadly silence as Jesse lifted the reins and stepped off the colt. The cow ran to the herd. Buckshot stood quivering, wide-eyed. Runnels of sweat ran through his eyes and dripped from the soft muzzle to the red dirt. His left hind foot, he held limply off the ground. He would never know that the reason his leg could no longer bear his weight was a fracture of the third phalanx of the pastern, shattered like a crystal goblet thrown at a fireplace. And no power of mind or will, no matter how determined, could make it whole again. Six thousand devastated people sat stunned, having just witnessed the making and the breaking of a champion in two and a half minutes.

Abbie was at the colt's head, tears spilling as she wiped his face and whispered to him and cupped his eyes softly, murmuring hopeful comfort. A veterinarian quickly administered a shot of painkiller. Someone opened a back gate and beckoned as Jesse coaxed the colt to hop agonizingly out of the arena on three legs. One or two attempts at applause died quickly entombed in the solemn silence.

The veterinarian set up his portable imaging system to view the ravaged ankle. The pictures told a grim tale. Abbie stayed at the colt's face, whispering. After a brief somber discussion between the vet, Jesse and Dr. Nalls, it was decided that Buckshot could not be saved. Jesse grabbed his upper lip between his teeth and bit hard as he felt a sword slice through his heart. A pain-filled, "Oh, nooo…" escaped from Abbie. No time was wasted in administering the lethal injection that would end the life of Buckshot…the brave.

In Jesse, the rage howled in silence before turning to unwitting desolation.

26

A Tough Call

He walked into the bedroom with two inches of scotch and swallowed half. He flopped back on the bed and breathed deeply. Then he reached for the phone and put it beside him.

She knew what time it was in Texas. She'd been waiting. She had a phone next to her old Victorian bed. Naked, under a frilly sheet pulled to her chin, she had one arm under her head and her right hand between her legs. The half moon had just moved into the frame of the open window. As she turned her head, a soft breeze fluttered the curtain. The phone rang. She answered with buoyant expectation. Instantly, she knew something was wrong. Try as he did to get above the gloom, she knew. He started by saying, "Well, we didn't win…" But she knew it was more than that, much more. "Oh, Jesse, tell me…what happened?"

He couldn't remember anything she'd actually said but somehow found comfort in her heartfelt words. He could feel her sharing his anguish and like a mother's kiss on a child's bruise, it lessened the sting. She wanted to know everything. What happened, how it happened. He heard the pain ragged in her sweet voice as she said, "I'm so sorry," over and over. "It sounds so useless to say…I feel so badly for you."

He told her hearing her voice was a big help. Then he tried to lighten the mood, asking about her parents, their horses, and how the video was coming. The small talk wound down under the color of tragedy.

"Well, I guess I'd better let you get some sleep. I'm sorry I called so late…but it took us a while to…"

"It's not late. Jesse…I'm so sorry about Buckshot."

"Thanks. Anyway…I'll look forward to getting that tape and I am gonna send you a book on cuttin'."

After he'd hung up the phone, he poured another whiskey and put on his headphones. Bach was soothing but you had to be still enough to listen to get soothed. He took off the phones, rose from the bed, walked to the window and stared out at nothing. He looked up and saw the moon.

A cold loneliness crept about and invaded his being. And not Bach nor Steinbeck nor Patsy Cline, nor John Coltrane was going to take it away.

27

A Treasure Chest

As they stood in the barn near the stall where Buckshot had lived, Jesse wrapped his arm around Abbie while she sobbed and soaked his shirt. He cooked her dinner and they drank a little whiskey and he got her to giggle. Then they went out to the porch and he watched her walk to her quarters in the trailer. She climbed in and shut the door.

The United Parcel truck drove up to the barn to deliver a carton from Colorado. With a feigned lack of concern he took it into the tack room and placed it on the floor in a corner under a wall of hanging bridles. When he came out, Abbie's antennae were quivering as she brushed a horse as if to strip its hide. She had determined not to ask, kill her though it might.

That evening after she'd left for town he fetched the box to the house and placed it on the dining table. He opened his pocketknife and cut the tape. Beneath a layer of plastic peanuts, he fished out the boxed video. He scooped out more white pods and found a jar of popping corn bearing a hand-made label that said, "For pleasurable viewing, pop this, add butter, then sit back and watch the tape." He rummaged further and came up with a card. It read, "For Jesse dear, We are so sorry to hear of the great misfortune that has come to you. To lose such a treasured friend, such a valiant beautiful creature. One can only try to imagine. We hope and pray you will find another with which to share your love and your special talent. Holly has helped us to understand and appreciate the unique bond that you have with horses. We hope some day to see you work with them firsthand. Meanwhile, please know that we feel for you and our hearts are with you." It was signed individually, "Walk in love, Bear and Ruby."

At the bottom of the carton was one more box wrapped in kid's cowboy paper. He untied the grass twine. He was smiling at the whimsy and care that had gone into this treasure chest. Cramped in the box was a stuffed brown rabbit, more of a rascal than a bunny. One soft ear flopped forward over a twinkling eye. He wore a sly, mischievous grin. Around his neck, a small white folded card was tied with a blue ribbon. In the same careful script, it said, "This is Rabbie the rabbit. He knows you are sad and he wants to make you laugh and pretend you are happy. And then you will be happy. He has left his girlfriend to come and see you. Her name is Bunny Bunny. You might have to fluff him up a little after his journey." And then a simple one-line sketch of a bird in flight, a falcon, and beneath it the words, "Holly Marie."

He popped the corn and put in the tape. It touched him deeply to watch the kids so young, bent, and twisted before they'd had a chance to live. The boy he'd put on the horse, Daniel, expended more energy to walk twenty feet than Jesse would to unload a hundred bales of hay. He wondered if God gave them an extra measure of strength and courage, or did it come in the same package as the ailment? He looked at the wall clock and wondered if it was too late to call her. What would he say? He could thank her. Tell her what a great job he thought she had done with the tape. Just pick up the damn phone. He swore he'd do it in the morning. He wanted to think about it.

He held the book cover open with a pen in his hand. He clawed at his head as if the plowing would produce an inspired inscription certain to cause her to think of him as a person of value. At last the pen began to move. He drove to the post office, special. Then he went back to the house and stared at the phone as if it were a rattler.

Her voice like warm honey sweetened his mind. She was delighted to hear him tell what a treat the treasure chest was. "I thought the tape was really inspirational. It made me want to send you money."

"Well, thank you. That is very nice to hear."

"I was amazed. The way you put together the most beautiful moments out of the whole event. How'd you learn how to do that?"

"Oh, I've always been interested in film...and writing. I took some classes in New York."

"You've sure got a talent."

"Thank you. Did Rabbie cheer you up?"

"I smile every time I look at him. I've got him set up where he can keep an eye on everything."

"Make sure you keep him fed on that popcorn."

"Oh, I will. He's lookin' good. I sent you a book on cuttin'. When you get everything in that book down, you can teach me."

"That'll be the day."

"How are Bear and Ruby doing?"

"They're fine. I might be bringing Bear some business. One of the big car dealers who was a sponsor of the event saw my tape and was quite impressed. We had a meeting to talk about me creating a commercial for him. So I got Bear involved and it looks real good so far."

"That is wonderful. It's good to hear that things are working out for you." He was running out of talking steam and didn't want to keep her on the phone too long to where she might be wanting off and too nice to say so. "If...if...uh...if it's okay, I'll...call again and see how you're...doing...with the book and the horses and...everything."

"That would be nice..."

"Okay. Well...take care then. And thanks again for everything. It was really neat."

"You, too. Bye."

"Bye..." Whew. He felt as if he'd been holding his breath. Why did she make him so damn nervous? Anyway, he walked with a lighter step when he left the house to go to the barn. He tried to think about what she might be wearing and how she had her hair fixed. He tried to imagine her room as he stepped into the saddle and turned toward the arena.

———⋙◆⋘———

It was a girl's room with redwood walls. Ancestral portraits in antique silver frames, straw hats dangling ribbons on wood pegs, an old steamer trunk with brass hardware, miles of shoes and boots by European craftsmen, and a pair of worn, lug-soled hiking boots. Pale cotton curtains rippled in the night breeze. A candle flickered in an old pewter holder. Dried prairie flowers sprouted from a porcelain vase on the marble top of an old English chest of drawers. A silver hand mirror and hairbrushes had belonged to Grandmama. Bunny Bunny, Rabbie's girlfriend, sat next to the brushes with her back against the wall.

Holly had her elbows on the windowsill, gazing at the darkened prairie night, smelling the grass and listening to coyotes yapping on a hill. The wind had lost its warmth. She shut the window, pulled off her jeans and her brother's flannel shirt. She stepped out of lacy white panties and unhooked her bra. She stretched her arms over her head walking to the oak-framed mirror on the wall and looked at herself sculpted in the candlelight. With her left arm reaching for the ceiling, she stroked its length from fingertips to her shoulder. Trailing her fingers across the back of her neck under her hair and then down to her breast, she cupped its small weight and circled the pink nipple with her thumb. She stroked the flat smoothness of her belly till her fingers felt the soft fringe along the humid grotto. She rotated her head slowly letting it fall back and roll to the side feeling the silky stroke of hair across her shoulders. She shivered and turned to the bed.

28

Memories

He walked from stall to stall stroking and murmuring seductive whispers to velvet ears. He climbed slowly up the stairs to Zack's loft.

Dozer watched him lie back on the bed then flopped to the floor with a groan, fixing his head on a paw. Jesse closed his eyes and let his mind wander in the darkness.

The golden boy, Damien, was looking tarnished in the fluorescent coldness of the hospital room. The glow was gone. A complex network of wires and tubes crawled in and out of him to and from plastic cocoons and metered nests with blinking lights and numbered graphs. He was still as death but for the rhythmic hissing of the machine that moved his chest up and down in a parody of breathing. It was an image burned forever in Jesse's brain as he sat there. It had been five days with no change, not a blink, not a hair moving. Jesse had gently lifted an eyelid that seemed not fully shut and saw a pale lifeless pupil that had once been bright and blue. He borrowed scissors from a nurse and cut a lock of platinum hair, a final desperate clutch at something he could hold onto, evidence that his son had been here. He knew as he looked at the body on the bed that the spirit of Damien no longer occupied it. He kissed him anyway on the cheek and held the big lifeless hand for a moment and left the room. He had already signed the forms.

The scene played over and over in his mind. It would sneak up and assault him like a mugger by surprise. Often, he could cut it off and think of something else—fishing in a mountain stream, wild-flowers and log cabins, cold chicken, and music. But then he didn't ever want to forget his son, so he'd try to remember the good times, the laughter, the joys of firsts, the letting go as he found his balance on the bike, his first time driving the tractor. But this time he decided to let it play out. He wanted to feel the emotions rip through him, tear him up, and fling him about. He wanted to allow it to envelop him without resistance…like crawling into a python for a look at its innards.

Jesse's eyes were closed but he knew, at the same instant Dozer did. The dog made a sound, lifted his head, got to his feet and stared at the wall with that quizzical look and whimpered, wagging his tail. Jesse sat up and saw his son in the moonlight.

Jesse heard the words in his brain. "Dad…I'm all right now. I'm sorry. You couldn't have done anything more than you did. It was meant to be the way it was. I know you love me and I am with you. I love you, Dad."

"Oh…Jesus…" he hadn't breathed. "I love you, Damien. I miss you so much…" His heart drummed in his throat. He stood and extended his arm as his son began to vanish like a vapor in a breeze. Dozer whined and brushed against his leg. He reached down and stroked his head, then headed for the door.

Stars glittered in the black above the thick twisted cottonwood behind the barn. Moonlight filtered through the flutter of leaves overhead as he sat on the plank swing hung low enough for a boy's legs. He pushed himself in a slow circle, leaned his full weight back on the ropes, looked up at the swirl of stars, and felt his head begin to swim.

29

To Write a Letter

A pale rolling mist enveloped everything beyond a few feet from the porch. Light from the barn glowed dimly in the distant gray. Ricardo was up and beginning to feed.

He had been holding the pen poised above the pad long enough to have written a thousand words but the page was blank. He mauled his face, took a last swallow of cool black coffee, a deep breath and wrote the words, "Dear Holly Marie…" and then he stopped and pondered. The risen sun had routed the mist by the time he'd penned a page. He had read and reread, scratched out, and rewritten and even gone in to get a dictionary. He closed the pad, went into the house, scrambled eggs, and drank more coffee. Then he went out to work.

⇒•◦•⇐

Holly Marie had fed the horses, dogs, goat, and ducks before fixing breakfast for Ruby and herself. Then with a scrubbed face, worn jeans and a ball cap, drove to the post office to pick up their mail.

She took the brown paper-wrapped package from Texas up to her room and opened it. Inside, on the first page of the well-worn volume, were written the words, "There is a potent, influential energy that comes from within the horse and those who fall under its spell are the slaves of a grand passion." Beneath, it was signed, "Jesse," and the date. She smiled then read the words again saying them softly. She kicked off her boots, stacked the pillows and lay back on the bed and began to read Training and Showing the Cutting Horse.

⎯⎯◆⎯⎯

A big black Mercedes, miraculously glossy and clean, shunned by the red Texas dust that matte-finished everything under the sun, came to a halt near the barn. Dr. Walter Nalls stepped out as armored as his car with an aura of repellent that rendered him impervious to dirt and dust. He could have sliced open a patient with the crease in his Wranglers. Dr. Nalls specialized in facial reconstruction. He'd spent five years putting together a Mexican boy's face that had melted like wax from a barbecue accident. He did it quietly without payment.

A client and friend, he owned Bueno's Big Bar, the stud that had sired Buckshot. He took Jesse aside and said, "I'm going to make you an offer you can't refuse. I want you to breed San Mamacita to Bueno again and get you another colt. A present from me."

"That's a mighty generous present."

"Think of me as a generous man."

"I do. And you're right."

"About what?"

"I can't refuse. Thanks." He reached out and shook the doctor's hand. Walter clapped him on the shoulder.

That night he read his scribblings in the notepad for the tenth time and made a few more adjustments before he closed it and went to bed. The next morning he was on the porch with coffee and the pad to greet the sunrise flaming across the green-sweatered hills. He read the letter again, rubbed his hair and pulled his nose. Then he went into the house and sat at a gnarly-legged table with stationery and copied the letter from the pad as carefully as he'd ever done anything. Then he read it again. He blew out a deep breath thinking this is insane, tear this up, boy, right now, while you still have a chance and nobody knows to what extent you have lost your mind. But he didn't tear it up. Instead, he read it one more time.

> Dear Holly Marie,
> I hope you won't find any offense in the clumsiness of this attempt to communicate with you. Here is what I'm thinking. Life is short. Sometimes real short. I know you know that. And it's the thought that I could be dead before I get embarrassed that gives me the courage to try to say what's really in my mind and my heart. Please know that there is no reason to feel any discomfort of any kind. There is no pressure in any of this, only an easy offer of friendship.
> You stepped out of Larry's house to the porch where I stood with a bunch of unshaven Texas toughs and I swear I couldn't believe my eyes. I did an actual double take. There I was, having a pretty good time, I thought. Then came you...in pale blue silk and a black hat, and everything else ceased to exist. Then it hit me that you were the daughter that Bear and Ruby had spoken about with such love and pride. Ever since that moment on the porch, you have been in my mind. I have tried to push you out when I think about convention and that I shouldn't allow myself to enter-tain any thoughts of you whatever. But you have been so kind and talking with you makes me feel so damn good. I thought I'd say to hell with convention and the fact that I've

got boots older than you are and invite you to come visit and have some free riding lessons.

There's a private guest room with its own bathroom and great big ol' padlocks on the inside of all the doors. Hell, I'll even give you a loaded gun.

I just realized that for all I know, you might be engaged to be married. Or maybe you are married. Have you got a husband tucked away somewhere? Anyway, I'm sure there's a line of admirers from Kiowa to New York and Europe seeking your attention. So, if accepting this invitation is not something you want to do, I'll understand. I might blow my brains out, but I will understand.

If I never hear from you again, just getting to know what little I have of you has enriched my life. Please be at peace with this and let me know what you think. If you decide to accept, it would be my great pleasure to send you the plane tickets. All the best to Bear and Ruby.

I've got a love-sick Rabbie here who misses his Bunny Bunny. So if for no other reason, say yes and bring her with you to mend his ailing heart.

Yer saddle pal,

Jesse

He folded it carefully and slid it into an envelope. The post office was next to the auto supply and a small grocery store. There was a mailbox in front. He walked up with the envelope, and like teasing a dog with a biscuit, waved it above the box but didn't put it in. He turned away, went into the grocery store, bought some beer and pretzels, a couple of cans of green chilies, some beans, and a package of tortillas. The letter was in the pocket of his shirt. He put the groceries in the truck, went back to the mailbox, and stood there with the letter in his hand. He pulled open the chute door but still didn't drop the letter. Suddenly, a quick waft of Damien's cologne was there. He felt a force like a vacuum suck the letter from his grasp. Down it went. He stood in wonder for a moment, then smiled, walked to the truck, and drove back to the ranch.

Abbie was going on about, "…I mean, what a pain in the ass…the guy's a nitwit. I hate it when I'm smarter than the teacher…I wasted the whole damn day yesterday. I don't know what the hell I'm gonna do with that degree anyway. It's only good if you wanna teach. I don't wanna teach anymore. I should've gone to vet school. Make just as much money as a brain surgeon and you don't have to listen to any bullshit from your patients. I met a polo player. His daughter's in one of my classes. He wants to learn about cutting. I gave him a card and told him to call you. His name is Kevin Bradley. Big bucks. You could just tell. I'll bet you he calls."

"How much?"

"Five bucks."

"Deal. Tell you what. If he becomes a client, I'll give you ten percent of everything that comes in through him." Jesse settled a saddle on the back of a bay gelding.

" All right! I get enough of that going, I'll shine the school…and when you die you can leave me the ranch."

"I'm probably gonna kill you first." Jesse stepped into the saddle and turned the bay toward the pasture.

30

A Stallion's Work

Jesse had raised San Mamacita. He had shown her as a three-year-old at The Futurity where she finished third. He last bred her to Bueno's Big Bar four years ago, which produced Buckshot. Once again, handlers prepared her for covering by the big sorrel stud.

Her shoes were removed. She was ovulating. To determine her readiness for covering, a "teaser" stallion was used to flirt with her over a five-foot high plank wall between them. Bueno was far too virile and excitable for such a task. He would have climbed the wall or gone through it ejaculating on the way. She proved her readiness by standing still, almost squatting, opening her vulva spasmodically, and oozing fluid.

They quickly dressed her for the mating. A thick leather protective neck covering was strapped in place. Bueno, in his exuberance, would bite a mare's neck with enough force to snap a bone. Abbie stood at her head in the large breeding stall while Jesse buckled hobbles to her hind legs to prevent her kicking at the stud.

A chilling shriek pierced the air and sent a shiver down Abbie's spine. It stood the hair on the back of her neck. The barn vibrated with his approaching presence. Prancing unshod hooves struck the bricked barn aisle with the threat of an invasion. He screamed again, a trumpeted whinny announcing the arrival of a demon from hell. Sideways, he came, cantering in place, pounding the ground, arching his neck. A handler on each side stepped gingerly along. One held a long line with a chain through a bit in the stallion's mouth. He came glowing in a dark wet sheen, all nerves and muscles quivering with one fierce desire. The palpable heat rising from his hide shimmered like rippling light on a road. He threw his head side to side tossing foam and snorting rumbles from deep within where his blood surged. Each foot he held suspended in the air, as if he were intended to be more above the ground than on it. Then it dropped to stave holes in the earth.

At the entrance to the breeding stall, he stood straight up on his hind legs pawing at the air and trumpeted loudly to the heavens where the rigid scepter of his royal maleness aimed. Like oiled bronze, fifteen feet tall, he came to her walking on his hind legs and snorting all the way. A handler had to pull him down to the ground before allowing him to mount her. To let him descend from such a height would've risked injury to the mare. A trembling mass of power, grace and strength, he rose and wrapped his legs along her sides, lunged like a shark for the shield on her neck and poured his fire into her soul.

Jesse, Walter, Abbie, and the handlers stood silent. Finally, Walter said, "He knows his job."

Abbie said, "Awesome."

"And he does it just for room and board," Jesse said with a smile.

31

From Polo to Cuttin'

Santa Rosa International was an offshore drilling company with a net income of over one hundred million dollars a year. Kevin Bradley grew up in it. He owned the best horses, hired the best pros and worked as fiercely at polo as he did his business. He was just past fifty and fitter than most at thirty. He sat easily on a seasoned bay mare next to Jesse on his roan as Abbie settled the herd. He had a pleasant soft way of speaking. "It was a little over a year ago. One of my best horses too. We were taking the ball to goal, flat out. She just collapsed under me. We cartwheeled through the air. I ended up with a broken leg, fractured ribs, and a cracked skull."

"And you're still playing?"

"Yeah, but not for long," Kevin said, "if I want to stay married. Carley says if I don't quit, she'll quit. I'm excited about this."

Jesse asked Abbie to ride into the herd and demonstrate how it's done. They sat their horses, watching, as Jesse explained what she was doing and why. She cut three cows, then quit just right and rode toward them stroking the horse's neck, her face reddening.

"What do you think," asked Jesse, "ready to give it a try?"

"Yes, sir."

"Just ride in there and have fun. She knows what to do."

Jesse talked Kevin through entering the herd and setting up a cow to cut. He had a sense of cattle, how they think and move in relationship to a horse. He got one set up just right.

"Now just drop your hand on her withers and let her work."

The mare locked on to the cow, splattered out, and quivered. Kevin laughed as he focused on the cow and the smile never left his face.

Jesse and Abbie applauded as Kevin, tanned face beaming, rode toward them. He was giggling like a boy. "I have been riding horses all my life and I have never…had this much fun on a horse. She is amazing. Thank you, sir."

Jesse shook his hand. "You rode her just right."

Kevin engaged Jesse in a walk toward his truck. In fifty yards, he asked fifty questions and ended giving Jesse his card. "You're sure that mare is not for sale?"

"I'll ask…but…I doubt it. We'll get you fitted on something you'll like just as well. It'd be good for you to ride a few other horses. Get a feel of different ways of going before you make a decision."

"When can I come back?"

"Whenever you want to."

"I'll call you later today. Damn, this was fun. That Abbie is quite a young lady."

When the fancy Texas Hauler cranked up and started down the driveway, Abbie was back at the barn getting a horse ready for their next client. Jesse took a five dollar bill out of his pocket and folded it in the palm of his hand and walked back to the barn. Abbie turned to him all aglow. She had her hand out. He slapped the ready five into her palm. "Plus ten percent. He wants me to find him a horse and he wants to start taking lessons immediately."

"Yeow," she said, and gave him a high five.

32

Yes

Eighteen days. Not a word. He'd come to hate going for the mail. He knew he'd been a fool. She was not about to dignify his outrageous presumption with a reply. He was getting black-hearted.

He needed a food supplement for the pregnant mare, San Mamacita. Cullen's Feed wasn't far from the post office.

The return address on the package said, H.M. Bassett, Double Rainbow Ranch, Kiowa, Colorado. He drove home, eyeing it on the seat as if it contained a bomb.

He smuggled it into the house like contraband, took it into his bedroom and shut the door. When he pulled out the crumpled tissue paper, a two-inch cube of pinewood like a child's block fell to the bed. He picked it up. On the side facing him, a feather had been etched into the surface with a wood-burning tool. He turned it slowly to the next side. There, rendered in a few simple lines, was the graceful, soaring image of a falcon in flight. He moved his thumb over the surface, then turned it again. Burned in on the next side was the word, "Jesse," and a small star next to the name. He smiled and bit his lower lip. He turned it to the next side. Burned in script was the single word, "yes."

He looked for a note. There was none. He picked up the block of wood again and read all its sides and when he was sure he was reading it correctly, he let loose the yahoo that had been welling within. It surged to the surface in a full-throated, stampede-starting howl that was heard by Ricardo in the barn.

Good God Almighty, she said yes. Now what? He turned the wood block over in his hand to the image of the feather. Of all things, why a feather?

He thought about the wheat-colored hair, the ivory skin, and her wildflower fragrance enveloping his senses as they rode together on that Colorado day through the postcard of the Rockies. She is a big city sophisticate, lived all over the world, been everywhere, done everything. What am I going to do to entertain her? You dumb old son of a bitch, what the hell have you gotten yourself into now?

He walked around in circles scratching his head, trying to decide what to do first. Go out and ride, pretending everything is normal. Go out and tell everyone the most beautiful woman in the world is coming to visit him. Call her. Yes, he had to call her and tell her he'd received her yes and how happy he was to get it. He stood there and looked at the phone with his heart drumming like he was about to bungee jump off a bridge.

All of Colorado's sunshine was in her voice when she answered, "Good afternoon."

She made him smell smoke from a fire that was not yet lit. "Good afternoon."

"Oh, hi. How are you?"

"I am real fine. I just picked up my mail. I've never been so happy to receive anything in my life." He heard her light chuckle, the ripple of a mountain brook.

"That's nice. Thank you."

"What made you put a feather on the block of wood?"

"I don't know. It just came into my mind to do it. Why?"

"Just that feathers have a special significance for me."

"Maybe I knew that."

"How?"

She laughed like music. "I don't know."

"When can you come?"

"When would you like me to come?"

"Any time from this moment on. And stay as long as you can."

" All right. Let me see when I can and I'll call you back, okay?"

"Yes ma'am. That will be just fine." A fever surged through him as he asked about her parents and the horses and doing the commercial for the car dealer. He closed his eyes and tried to see her face as she thanked him for the book on cutting.

"Where is that quote from, the one you wrote on the inside?"

He chuckled as he said, "Me."

She was silent for a moment, then she said, "It's really neat. How did you come up with that?"

"I don't know." He felt his face redden and laughed.

"I was curious. I'm always trying to figure everything out. Especially where creative stuff comes from."

He waited a minute to see if she was going to continue, then said, "Thank you for saying yes."

"Thank you for asking me."

When he walked out the front door, he nearly fell down the steps.

33

Kevin Buys a Moon

After half a dozen lessons on several different horses, Kevin Bradley wrote a check for seventy five thousand dollars and became the proud owner of Merlin's Moon. And Moon became the newest resident at the Lazy JB.

Kevin stood there stroking Moon's gleaming hip and smiling like a boy at Christmas. "I've owned hundreds of horses in my life and I swear each one is just as exciting as the first."

The rest of the day Holly Marie was in every thought.

He went to bed that night without having said a word about her to anyone. He wondered when she'd call, how long before she'd be in his house...and how long would she stay.

34

A Shopping Spree and a Bet

He was reaching for a saddle in the tack room when the phone rang. It was Abbie's job to answer it. She moved to get it. Jesse picked it up. "This is Jesse." Abbie continued selecting bridles and wondering what in hell was going on with him. He seemed weirder than usual lately. Her antennae were up and her ears were on.

"Hi. How're you doin'?" His face lit up and went to full glow in a second. "Great," he said and listened. "Oh, great. Yeah, that'll be fine…yep…" he listened for a longer time and tried to inconspicuously turn away from Abbie's unveiled scrutiny. "Sure, that'll be fine. I'll be there. Thanks…me too…bye." He scribbled on a pad, folded the scrap into his pocket and grabbed a saddle. He walked out smiling to himself, and put it on a horse.

Abbie, consumed with curiosity, made every effort to appear unconcerned as she hung the bridles on the saddle horns. She had her back to him when she heard him say, "Her name is Holly Marie. She's from Colorado. She's got a hump on her back and an eye in the middle of her forehead and she's coming to visit. She's half my age. It may be the dumbest thing I've ever done in my life but I'm excited about it. I'd be grateful if you'd help me get the place ready for her…make her feel welcome."

"Holly Marie, huh…bet I'll hate her."

"How much?"

"Five bucks."

"Hey, your ten percent of Kevin has made you a wealthy woman. I'll bet you a hundred you don't hate her."

"Five bucks."

"Okay, big spender, you got a deal."

They drove to San Antonio and went on a spree. She picked out thick towels, luxurious sheets, a real bath mat, fancy soaps, and aromatic bath oils and candles. Abbie had slandered his curtains as having been there since Geronimo ran amok. Frilly white ones would brighten the room. "And you really need to get a new bedspread. That old Navajo rug smells like a herd of buffalo. God knows what's living in there. Of course, maybe she's not gonna spend much time in the guestroom. In which case, you need to get a bedspread for your bed." She pursed her lips, a dare to respond. He just shook his head.

She was checking her list when he asked, "Should I get some of this room spray? Says here, wildflowers."

"You'd need a case. Hell, it's a ranch. No need to make it smell like a whorehouse."

35

Getting Ready

He got out of the shower, clipped and filed the nails on his hands and feet testing for rough edges that might offend female flesh. He trimmed nose hair and snipped an edge along his sideburns and shaved with care. He put on pressed Wranglers and a starched white shirt. He buffed his favorite trophy buckle and pulled on his best boots. He stood in front of a mirror. He was trim and fit, hard as rock. His chiseled face was lean and lined, taut and tanned. Silver streaked his light brown hair. His eyes gleamed with purpose. I may be a little long in the tooth but hell, I look pretty damn good. That lasted about ten seconds before panic grabbed him around the throat.

He stood in the doorway looking around the guestroom for the tenth time. It was bright and clean. He'd remembered a neckerchief she wore, covered in sunflowers. She said she was partial to sunflowers. He'd put a bunch in a vase on the nightstand next to the bed. He checked the bathroom one more time. He tugged at the new shower curtain and smoothed the folds. There was a knock at the front door.

He called out, "Come in."

Abbie entered saying, "I'm outta here. Looks great. Hope she appreciates it. If she's got any complaints, I'll be justified in hating her. So does work go on as usual? Am I supposed to be here tomorrow or are you gonna lock the front gate?"

"Hey. I don't even know this woman. She's coming here as a friend. That's all I know."

"Yeah...right."

"You be here. It's a work day...what time will you be here?"

"One-thirty. You better get going. If she's as ugly as you say, they might drop a net on her as she gets off the plane. And if she's not, she might just turn around and go back if you're not there."

"Thanks. Thanks for the help."

"See yah..." She smiled and looking like a waif waiting to be claimed, went out the door.

36

Arrival

Though his heart would have had him pressed to the barrier, he stood off to the side, so he might see her before she spotted him. He tried to calm a rampage of emotions.

Taller, leaner than he remembered. In her brother's dark blue blazer and jeans, she exuded the quintessence of female sexuality. Wearing her black cowboy hat, a huge duffel slung over one shoulder and a black leather knapsack hung from the other, she marched with purpose, expecting to be found. Had he not been there, she might have marched straight to Mexico rather than appear disappointed.

He stepped in front of her smiling, reaching for the heavy bag saying, "Hi...you look great." The entire county of San Antonio agreed, demonstrating with craned necks and naked stares of admiration, envy, and lust. She relinquished the bag and stepped in sync beside him with that heel-springing gait. He wanted to kiss her, just on the cheek. But instead, as he walked beside her, his arm had

encircled her waist. He felt a vibrant coil of heated energy surge
from the core of her on a faint scent of musk.

Behind the elegant, self-assurance, moved a braided twist of
apprehension and doubt. She was constantly in motion between the
two extremes, seeking a truth she could trust. They'd both reached
deep for the courage to be bold. He to ask. She to say yes. She
scanned the spinning bags, grateful for the task. He studied her as if
to disassemble her molecule by molecule and put her back together,
remembering where the pieces went.

She moved a slender arm slung like a whip, strong as a dock-
hand's, snagged an enormous black duffel bag from the carousel.
"That's it," she said on the move. He tried to take it from her. She
said, "I've hauled this all over the world. I don't think I could walk
out of an airport if I weren't carrying it."

When they got to the truck, vacuumed and washed, but never-
theless, a truck, he apologized. "I thought about renting a limo but
I figured it'd be too much of a fall back to reality."

"I like trucks." She smiled, flashing delicate teeth, and climbed
in. He shut the door for her, walked to the other side and fixed himself behind the wheel. He looked at her, bit his lower lip and smiled.
"It sure is nice to have you here."

"Thank you." She had a way of making you feel you were
hearing the words for the first time. Darkness descended as they
pulled out on to the road to Bandera. A melon slice of moon was
rising south.

Dozer and Blizzard were there to greet them in the warm night.
Holly dropped to her knees and got right in their faces. "And what's
your name?" she said in a child's voice, ruffling the big dog's face.

"That's Dozer."

"Is that because he likes to nap?" She pulled his loose jowls into
a wide grin. "That's a smoogie face."

"No...my son Zack...he found him on a construction site. It's
for bulldozer."

"And this guy?" She was scratching between Blizzard's ears

while still tugging on Dozer's face.

"That's Blizzard…cuz he blows like snow through everything."

"We've got two big goldens, brother and sister…" she turned back to Dozer telling him about the goldens. "They're smoogie, too." She stood up and helped Jesse with the bags.

He led her to the guestroom where on the door hung a sign he'd put up after Abbie had left the house. It said, "Welcome, Holly Marie." When she thanked him, he grinned and turned away like a schoolboy who'd just asked for his first date. He put the bags in the room, showed her the bathroom and said, "Unpack, take a shower, do whatever you like. Just be at home. I've got some food going, so whenever you feel like it we can have something to eat." Then he turned and left her alone to settle in.

Every romantic impulse that had ever existed and been entombed under centuries of disuse had been, in the past days of anticipating her arrival, unearthed and set free. He had lit the fire, opened the wine, and turned on the music, Mozart, to love by. Scented candles shaped the shadows on the walls.

She came like a whisper into the room, in a warm glow, on a vapor of perfume. A tall, lithe, wraith in a sheer, flowing frock. Her hair was piled and twisted, speared by a thin long makeup brush holding it in place. A cameo profile smiling, turned and came to him. He took her hand and led her to the sofa. They sat sideways, facing each other watching the fire play over their skin. She pulled her knees to her chin and looked over them at Jesse. Her feet were naked on the cushion, just a reach away. She smiled, bejeweled in the fire-light, blue-gray eyes beneath lowering lids. The soft flesh at the corners of her mouth lifted the pouting lips. "This is nice…peaceful."

Slowly, he extended his hand toward hers. "I can't believe you are actually here…in my house…sitting across from me on this sofa. I can see you, I can smell you, I can hear you…" as he reached her hand, she opened it to accept his touch, "…and I can feel you. So I guess you must be here."

She laughed, "I think so."

131

He eased his hand around in hers as they explored their palms and felt the tingling thrills that fingertips sent scooting down the backroads of nerves. The essence of his being seemed to flow down into that moist palm. The fire crackled and the music lulled while they spoke the small talk of finding their way to a measure of ease.

As she brought her wineglass to her lips, the tip of her tongue glistened in the flickering light.

He listened as if his life hung in her words. She spoke to him with an ease she'd never known before, describing feelings she'd never been able to voice. Till now. And how good it felt.

There was something in the way he asked that unleashed a purging. She took him from New York across the continent of Europe to Asia and back to New York and the death of her brother by an act of random violence. Her naked honesty freed from him a flock of feelings of his own.

Her eyes glimmering, she stopped to breathe and empty her glass. She reached up and pulled the makeup brush that held her hair. She shook the honey-hued mane loose and let it fall around her neck. She tucked her silent chin, hair veiled across her eyes. He watched and barely breathed. Her voice came softly out of the shadows, an alien sound from another time, a distant, melancholy plea for understanding. "He was so much more than my brother. We were like twins. We knew what the other was thinking…" She cut herself off, took a huge breath and blew it out. "Wow. You're a good listener."

"You're a good talker." He realized its potential as an insult and laughed with her. "I mean it…you tell it good. It was good for you to tell me about it. It was good for me to hear it." He paused.

"I can't believe I did that."

She shook her hair out of her eyes and leaned toward him. Her breath perfumed the air. My god, he thought, I could fall into those eyes and never find my way out.

"You use your eyes to search out other people's thoughts rather than reveal your own," she said looking deep into his eyes.

"I'm not real good with talking about how I feel…I'm trying to learn. Doesn't come easy."

She smiled, smoothing the rutted road of his life. Her toes stuck out from the hem of her frock. They were slender, white and pretty. His fingers floated and lit, stroking from the creases to the tips. He did it just once and slowly withdrew his hand.

"Show me your horses." It was a whisper.

The night was star-bright, quiet, and cool. Blizzard and Dozer walked with them as the horses nickered and snuffled. They stopped at each stall. Holly stroked the velvet muzzles above the half-doors. Jesse named them and told her about each one. She ran her fingertips over a brass plaque on a stall door that read, Bueno Bar Tab. "Is this where Buckshot lived?"

"Yep."

"And who is that guy?" referring to the brown and white overo gelding standing in the corner of the stall.

"That's Concho. He's kind of wary. Belongs to a lawyer. He got him in a settlement. Instead of money. Pretty nice horse. He likes women."

It was past midnight when they climbed the steps to the porch. His hand touched the arch in her back as he opened the door for her to enter the house. They stood in the middle of the living room. Looking at each other. Jesse turned to the fireplace to move the embers around as if it were necessary. "Do you have everything you need?"

"Yes. Thank you."

"Well…you know where the kitchen is…sleep as late as you want in the morning. I'll be down at the barn or in the arena. Sure is good to have you here."

"Jesse." She stood tall across the room. Her hair, shining amber in the candle glow, the pale flowered frock draped along her slender form took his breath away. "Thank you for the sunflowers. They're beautiful. That was very thoughtful. And thanks for listening to me talk your ear off. It felt good."

He smiled and nodded. "Goodnight, Holly Marie." It felt good to say her name.

"Goodnight, Jesse Burrell."

He watched her go and stood there thinking, I could have…just walked up and…kissed her…Jesus…the thought made him nervous. He blew out the candles.

He was naked on his back in bed, staring at the ceiling, an arm slung under his head. A warm demon of desire curled in his loins now began to stretch and waken with a purpose. He let his mind run and saw himself pulling on his pants, going to her door, knocking softly. "Come in," she says. He sits on the edge of the bed and looks down at her face, framed with the fan of fine-spun hair and her bare white star-lit shoulders saying she is naked beneath the sheet. In silence, they look into each other's eyes. He leans down and softly kisses her yielding lips as his hand slips under the sheet…

That was as far as he let it run. He turned on his side, pulled his knees to his chest, closed his eyes and wondered what she was thinking.

37

A Yogi in the Dark

He rolled over and squinted at the red numbers saying 5:00 a.m. He hadn't slept. He dragged himself out of bed and cat-footed around the place like a burglar. There was enough distance between the kitchen and guestroom to run water for coffee and clink a cup and spoon. He stuck a banana in his shirt pocket and carried the cup through the living room, glancing at her door, shut. He eased open the front door and closed it quietly behind him. It was still dark. Ricardo's rooster yet silent. Suddenly, a sense of a presence sent a shiver along his arms as he turned quickly to the right. There in the darkness on the floor of the porch was a large living thing, undulating slowly like a seal. It said, "I couldn't sleep."

"Damn." He laughed. "You scared the hell out of me. I thought you were a mountain lion…"

"Sorry." She uncoiled and came to a sitting, cross-legged pose. She was wearing a leotard.

"What are you doing?"

"Yoga."

"Yoga. Never known anybody that did yoga. What's the difference between yoga and yogi?"

"A yogi practices yoga. I used to teach it…but then I got away from it and…since I've been back in Colorado, I've been trying to get back into it."

"So you are a yogi…practicing yoga."

She smiled and nodded.

"Mind if I watch?"

"No. I'm almost done."

Uncoiling her legs, she moved smoothly stretching out on her stomach and reaching with her arms like a waking cat, on a thin rubber mat. She flowed from one graceful pose to another, breathing like the hissing of a giant reptile. He sat with the cup in his hand, his chin slack in silent awe.

She finished as the rooster sounded and a hint of sunrise began to lighten the horizon. From sitting on the mat, in a blink, she was standing tall, straight. She smiled in a tranquil face.

Jesse said, "That's amazing. The strength it takes to do some of those things."

"I'm pretty strong." Grinning, she made a fist of her right hand and punched the open palm of her left with a resounding smack. "So don't mess with me, boy."

"I won't. How about some coffee?"

He was waiting for her in the living room, looking at the shelf where Rabbie sat, Bunny Bunny now at his side, his arm around her shoulder. Holly came from the bathroom looking like she'd spent her life on the ranch. Cowboy hat, Wranglers, a wrinkled cotton work shirt, and roper boots. Her face scrubbed pink, no makeup and blazing blue-gray eyes. She came to his side, looking at the paired rabbits, pushed out her lips and said, "They're happy now."

Ricardo had groomed the front yard, with special attention to the flowers. Jesse introduced her. He bowed slightly, saying, "Con mucho gusto."

She responded in perfect Spanish, telling him how beautiful the garden was. He was instantly enslaved. Jesse asked, "How'd you get to be so handy with Spanish like that?"

"I went to a school in Mexico for a while, when I was thirteen. I also worked in Spain."

"Boy, I need you around here. I barely get by in English."

Chauncy, the goat, showed up in the barn. "My mom's got one just like him, Bingo. Only he's white. He thinks he's a dog."

"Chauncy thinks he owns the place."

"So does Bingo. Must be a goat thing."

She watched Jesse work. He moved with practiced purpose to the light musical clink of spurs as he walked. All smooth and flowing, the lifting of horses' feet to clean their hooves, the pull of his jeans against the tightened muscles of his thighs, the supple power in his shoulders as he swung the saddles lightly to their backs, the easy, soothing murmur as he walked behind them, constantly touching and stroking them, letting a tail slide through his hand and at the same time telling Holly what was going on. He showed her a point above the hoof that, when massaged for just a minute, could calm a nervous horse. As he put the bridles on, he told her the easy way to slip the bit into the horse's mouth and how a bit should fit. She stood beside him as he handed her the reins. A humid scent blended with her light perfume and enveloped him like a warm breath and let loose inside of him a yearning. He tried to think of something else as he led his horse out of the barn.

They trotted under white clouds across green pastures, Blizzard at their feet, snapping at grasshoppers spurting from the weeds. He watched her posting easily at the long trot. "I still think you're suckering me, you look like you've been doing this all your life." They found the herd and gathered them up, Blizzard loving his job. Darting here and there, nipping heels, flattening like a rug but ready to spring at errant feet.

She was riding the lawyer's paint, Concho, a cow-savvy little bugger who knew his way around a herd. A high-headed heifer tried to break away in front of Holly. The paint instinctively leaped to cut her off and damn near put Holly on the ground. "Whoa!" she hollered as she grabbed the horn with a white-knuckled grip and managed to stay aboard.

Jesse laughed. "Good job of keeping the forked end down. That's the main secret of being a good rider, keeping the horse between you and the ground."

Pale and wide-eyed, she smiled, saying, "Yeah, I can see how that would be important. And just when I had you believing I could ride."

At one-thirty, Abbie's bug chugged up in a flurry of dust. She hopped out and hustled to the arena. Holly was coming down along the rail at a dead gallop. Jesse stood with his arms along the top rail watching the horse gather speed. She sat up and sunk down slowly saying whoa as she lifted lightly on the reins. The horse melted into the ground and slid to a beautifully balanced stop.

Concentration furrowed her brow as she walked the horse along the fence. Suddenly the smile broke through the shining face and beamed at Jesse.

Jesse was grinning. "Good job," he chuckled. "That was a good job."

Abbie was standing there smiling. She came forward as Holly stepped down. "Looked cool to me." She squared off in front of her, almost a foot shorter, and thrust out her hand. "Does this mean I'm out of a job? Hi. I'm Abbie."

Holly beamed her klieg-light radiance as she bowed and took Abbie's hand. "Abbie, I'm so happy to meet you. I've heard a lot about you. I'm Holly."

Jesse watched Abbie melt under Holly's sincerity. "I don't know how much you can rely on what he says. He told me you were ugly and spastic. Nice guy." He smiled at them yakking away in the tack room while he hosed a horse's legs with cool water.

As Abbie was getting ready to leave for the day, she said good-bye to Holly and told her it was really nice to meet her. She reddened with surprise when Holly spontaneously embraced her and said, "Thanks for all the help, Abbie. Will I see you tomorrow?"

"Yep, I'll be here." As she turned and walked by Jesse, she muttered out of the side of her mouth, "Looks like you lucked out. She's really neat." She stuffed a five dollar bill into his hand and headed toward her car.

38

A Kiss

He wore soft, baggy slacks and a white shirt with the sleeves rolled up. He was standing in the kitchen, slicing peppers and mushrooms. He'd poured a shot of Lagavulin and was sipping as he worked.

She'd been in the bathroom a long time. John Coltrane's mournful, lonesome sax saturated the house.

He felt her presence and turned as she came into the room. He was sure that if he blinked she would vanish, that some act of God would remove this golden moment, the reason for his continued existence. She was as perfect as a snowflake. The tawny hair hung in shimmering coils around her face. The curving, provocative mouth was painted red. The long, fragile, innocent dress, lavender with delicate pink blossoms clung to the slow curving of her flesh underneath. A lacey border of slip hung just above her slender feet thinly strapped in bare sandals. She smiled a radiant tenderness that made him believe that all was well. "My God," he said softly. He knew in that moment he had fallen hopelessly in love with Holly Marie Bassett. And he knew that he had never before in his entire life felt anything even remotely close.

His voice was a hoarse whisper, "You are the most beautiful...elegant...graceful woman I've ever seen." He was entranced.

She realized the sincerity in it. This cowboy, this half-horse creature of the earth who listened to Mozart and Coltrane and had books of poetry next to a catalog of tractors, was coming to her. His brown hands were reaching for her face. As gently as he'd held an angel's feather, his fingers touched her cheeks. He looked into the silver-blue depths of her soul, tilted his head and brought his lips to her mouth.

The kiss was wet, long, and hot, down to his soul. She brought her hand up his back, along his neck, sliding her fingers into his hair, feeling the hardness and the heat of him through the flimsy fabric and knew that she loved him.

It might have been easy to go on, to let his hands roam and clutch and claw and take her to his bed, but this was not a moment to let easily pass and become something else. They separated slowly and took the time to breathe. A warm tide of blood had rushed into her cheeks, her neck was flushed, and the pupils of her eyes were as big and black as a cougar's.

"Is garlic all right with you?" he said, lost in the cougar's eyes.

"I love garlic. It purifies the blood."

"Would you like some wine? Or whiskey or beer? Or Coke or water or..."

"Wine...thank you."

When he handed her the glass, he reached out and let his fingertips trail lightly down her cheek and across her lips.

⸺◆⸺

Empty plates had been pushed back on the low plank table in front of the sofa where they sat sideways as they had the night before. Flamelight from the fireplace played across their faces. He knelt on the cushion and took her up into his arms and she flowed into his embrace. He felt the softness of her breasts against his chest as he stroked her naked slender arm. He stood, taking her up with him and held her close as he kissed her neck with small, light, sucking kisses up to her ear where his tongue flicked along its rim and her hair fell across his face. Then he took her hand and led her to his bedroom.

From the first moment of their meeting, she had positioned herself to know this half-man, half-beast with the searching eyes, and yet had armed herself to resist if he advanced. She had thought about him almost all the time, swinging back and forth between desire and curiosity and a need to preserve her isolated self. But now a strange and sudden thing had happened. All the armor and practiced coolness had dropped away from her and crawled back to their source. He seemed to have an uncanny instinct that told him just how far to go and exactly when to pause and wait and let a thing settle. It was the way he related to horses and dogs, to let his desires become their idea. He had swept her walls cleanly away.

Silver skeins of moonlight washed across the bed. She raised her hand slowly to his face and trembled as he stroked her arms and neck, then one by one undid the tiny buttons down the back of her dress. The frock slipped to the floor. Jesse felt that he had never seen a woman, before this moment. Her breasts, perfectly petite, rose lightly, powdered pale pink, on the faint sibilant intake of her breath her cocoa-hued nipples swelling.

He placed his hands just above her hips and sat her on the bed. Kneeling between her legs, he put his lips lightly to the top of her breast and like the flutter of a moth, circled slowly, the nipple waiting. A longtime, slow moving river of soft kissing.

He rose above her on the bed, arms and legs like braided ropes, molded by the mellow shadows of the moon, looking down at her. "I can't stop looking at you. When I'm close to you, I can't see you so well." Slowly he lowered himself between her legs and taking the

143

band of her panties in his fingers, slipped them down.

He wondered if there were words to say the things he felt. He wanted her to know him. If he could open his body, she would see all the hidden things in him; things he didn't even know were there. He cupped her hips in his hands and lifted the hillock to his face.

On the edge of a precipice crumbling underfoot, she tumbled into space, spiraling down, leaving herself behind, and falling toward a Holly Marie she had yet to meet.

She saw him as a centaur as he rose above her and came down inside her with a gentle power that possessed and took her to the land of myths and magic where only legends dwell. He pressed against the length of her and felt her legs quiver against his thighs.

Deep inside her, his long, unconscious quest came to an end. His loneliness vanished like water spilt on desert sand. She wrapped him in her arms and pulled him into her and her into him. And in that last convulsive throb of consuming ecstasy, with the wick of her mouth between his lips, he poured milk and honey and foaming champagne into the warm sweet delta tide and knew he would never be the same again.

They lay entwined like tossed silken scarves. Her head cradled in his shoulder, he breathed into her hair. "I love you, Holly. I didn't know that such a feeling could exist..." She felt him shake his head as if to deny it. "I've loved you from the first moment that I saw you...two thousand years ago." He kissed the corner of her parted lips.

He was deep inside her again when all motion ceased. They lay absolutely still and focused all their energy to the place where they were joined. They put their breath together and laced their fingers and held right there for the time of two lives. They were silent but for catches in their breathing and moaning kitten sounds from Holly's open mouth.

They made love the whole night through, talking, dozing, waking, whispering, and feeding from the centers of their souls.

Ricardo's rooster trumpeted the dawn. Jesse woke inhaling the musky fragrance of their brewing in the night. Her breathing had the rhythm of sleep as he turned and cupped her perfect breast, the nipple, a berry between his fingers, instantly began to swell. His passion stirred. Soon they were lost in the pungent heat that, like a summer haze, had wrapped around them.

In the riverstone grotto of his bathroom, she stood under the water-spray while he covered her with lather and sat on the floor to do her feet. The water cascading over them, he looked up from where he sat and opened his mouth to catch the stream flowing from the delta. She shoved her fingers in his hair and pulled him to her.

39

Chaps

On an old cast-iron griddle, she made the best pancakes he'd ever tasted. He stuck his belly out, patting the exaggerated fullness as they walked to the barn. "Gonna let you ride a different one today. Got to keep you on your toes."

They were ready to mount up when he said, "Wait a second, come with me." He took her hand and led her to the end of the barn and up the stairs to Zack's loft and let her in. It was warmer and slightly musty, having been shut for a while. "This was were Damien stayed…when he was here." He walked to a window and opened it. A pair of chaps hung from a peg on the wall. "Try these on." She hesitated with a look of doubt. "He would love it if you wore them." She started to buckle them around her waist. He was still pretty waspy when I got them. They might be just about right."

He knelt to fasten the zipper at the top of her thigh and felt the heat coming through the denim beneath his hand as he swept it up to caress her butt. He stood and pressed her to the wall. He kissed her long and deep and told her that he loved her. He moved his hand to just beneath her breast. "I want to make love to you right now."

"No...no..." she giggled. "Let's wait...let's wait...we've got to ride...it'll be fun to have to wait." She puffed out her breath and led him to the door.

He smiled, groaning, checking her legs. "Pretty good fit. Just need to punch a hole in the belt."

"You're sure?"

"He's laughing right now. I guarantee it. If he could see your butt, he wouldn't sleep for a week." He shut the door behind them and stroked his finger down her spine as she went down the stairs.

She could still feel his hand under her breast and the fingers down her spine as she watched him swing slowly into the saddle. She realized she was wet.

She loped the mare around the arena while he told her little things about horses. "They're as different as people are. If you listen, they'll tell you who they are. Then you'll know how to get along."

He noticed the shine on the pouty lip. "This mare is a little more aggressive than Concho. Her turns'll be a little quicker. She's got more snap to her. Just relax, trust her, and have fun."

She nodded her head. Her tongue was sticking out and her eyes in a squint, focused on the herd.

"Put your tongue in your mouth. If you bite it off, Blizzard'll eat it before I can get to it."

She'd given him her camera. He talked to her as she entered the herd. She cut a cow like a longtime hand, and then she let the mare go to work. He clicked off a half dozen shots of her doing just right.

She rode out of the herd breathing hard, looking a flushed fourteen. Fugitive wisps from the thick braid were wet against her neck. It struck in him a tender lusty thought.

He was grinning and shaking his head. "I've seen people who've been riding cutting horses for ten years not have the feel that you've got. You ride that mare better than her owner does."

"Thanks," she said breathlessly.

148

Dr. Walter Nalls arrived in his dustproof aura in a sparkling white pickup. "Passing by. Thought I'd stop and see how the mare is doing."

He shook Holly's hand and was instantly charmed. When no one but Jesse could see, he raised his brows over widened eyes and nodded with appreciation, admiration, and approval, all in one look.

But for Dozer, at their feet like a dropped coat, everyone had gone and left them alone. They sat on the porch, the sun seeping into the distant dun grass. The sky like the shimmering inner surface of an oyster shell darkened as night began to fall. A meadowlark flitted to a fence post and gurgled coupled notes. There was rustling in the grass, the warbles of the doves and crickets in conference under the porch. Ribbons of lightning curled down in the distant blackness and rain began to pelt the roof like tossed pebbles. She sat in a wicker chair, he at her side in one of plank and twisted willow limbs, silent in the thoughts the rain inspired.

40

A Sad Tale

The driving rain quit the laundered land and left it smelling of leaves, of wood, and of grass. The moon wore a veil of lingering clouds. Her hand moved to the arm of his chair. Her voice seemed to emerge from the night itself. "Do you think you could...tell me how he died?"

He took a deep breath and hummed it out. She could see him pull his upper lip between his teeth and move his jaw side to side. Then, as if to throw the phrase away for lack of import, he said, "It was drugs." It seemed that might be all he would say, but then he went on. "He had the disease. For ten years, I tried to save his life. Had him in every rehab place in the state. He tried. I guess he just didn't...I'd put him in the front door and he'd try for a while...and then he'd go out the back window. He was sixteen when I realized he had a serious problem. I remember I sat him down and told him if he didn't get his life together, he'd either end up in jail or dead." He tightened his jaw and bit down on his lip.

"Was it an overdose?" She asked as softly as a breeze.

"No. Not really. It might just as well have been. I don't really know. All I know is what the paramedics told me. He was with some friends, I guess they got some bad stuff and it made him sick and he…and…and…he choked…they got him to the fire station and then they left. Nobody knows who they were. I tried to find out. I talked to the paramedics. They said their concern was the patient, not who brought him there. I said what if there was a crime involved? They said, we're not cops. That was it."

"What drug was it?"

"Crack cocaine."

She wanted him to talk about it. She sensed in him the desire and thought it might serve him well. "What did the paramedics do?"

"Well…he was unconscious. They put a tube in him to get him breathing and got him to the hospital. The doctors said he was in a coma when he arrived. His brain had been deprived of oxygen for some time." He went silent and stayed that way for a while. "They put him on life support. When I got there they had him wired up like Frankenstein, tubes and IVs and…his chest was going up and down, but you could tell it was mechanical. That's the way he was for seven days. One doctor wanted to pull the plug after two days. Another said no, and that there was still a chance…and that's the way it went, back and forth, day after day. It's over. No, it's not. It's over. No, it's not. I just sat there praying and talking to him. I sat on the bed and kissed his forehead. It was cold." He went silent again. "I had the feeling as I spoke to him, that he'd already quit that body. That's when I went and got a pair of scissors and cut a little lock of his hair. It was short then. When he was a kid he always wanted it long. I don't think he liked being in this world all that much.

"I'd seen him about a week before. He was working. He liked lifting weights. He looked really healthy. He'd met this wonderful girl, Melinda. Clean as a whistle, hard working, came from a real nice family in Houston. She was crazy about him. And he was nuts in love with her. I thought she'd be the saving of him for sure. Thing was, he could make you believe anything he wanted you to believe." Jesse made a little sucking sound with his lip before biting it again. He stood and walked to the edge of the porch, leaned against the post. He held his hand out and let a drip from the roof splat in his palm and brought it to his face.

Her voice filled the space behind him as she placed her hand on the back of his neck. "Why don't you go take a shower? I want to get pretty. Maybe we could watch a movie. I could make some popcorn."

He was still looking up at the moon. "I don't have any popcorn."

"I brought some."

He turned around and wrapped her in his arms and kissed her softly, long and tender. His fingers in her hair, he looked into the lavender shadowed eyes as if to seek the answer to a puzzle. "You brought popcorn with you?"

"Yeah. It's a special kind that I bet you don't have in Texas."

41

An Italian Movie

Marcello Mastroiani and Sophia Loren cavorted in a lavish bedroom in nightclothes while sub-titles spelled their spirited repartee. Holly dug into the huge wooden bowl of popcorn with thin apple slices spread on top, then passed it to Jesse. "This is so neat. What's a Texas cowboy doing with all these foreign films?"

"I guess I was just born curious...specially about folks who aren't Texans."

The phone rang. He let the machine answer. It was Walter Nalls calling to invite Jesse "and your charming young friend, Holly Marie, to dinner at our house on Sunday. Helen is looking forward to seeing you and meeting Holly Marie. Hope you can make it. Let us know."

Jesse looked at her. Sunday was to be her last night in Texas. "Looks like you being here is giving me a social life. I don't want to share you with anyone on our last night. Do you have to leave Monday?"

"I could put it off till Tuesday. I have to be there Wednesday."

"I don't want to think about you leaving." She folded in his arms, stirring the hellfire of lust in him as he lifted her hair and put his lips to her neck.

With a click, Marcello and Sophia vanished, so did Holly's gown and the ribbon from her hair. He kissed the delicate shoulder and slipped his hand in the small of her supple bare back and lifted her hips to pull the lacey panties away.

He looked down at her face, lovely and soft, in the spun gold cushion of hair. She felt the strength of his body and the powers of his soul consume her. She turned her head toward the window and the night.

The pale angle of her jaw and neck like desert-bleached bone caused a thing in his throat. He spoke to her only with his love as their bodies came together with a fierceness, thighs pounding, her legs clenched around him, their breath chirped and moaned. He could feel her nipples against his chest. He filled his hand with the lushness of her hair and lifted her face to his mouth. She murmured a small cry and thrust her hips against him. She locked him in her arms, her body quivering, a fiery glow rising in her cheeks, she crushed the air from his lungs and drew from deep within his willing seed.

Enlaced among the twisted sheets, her head lay cradled in his shoulder, her hair along his neck. She moved her face to his and felt a drop fall to her skin. She rose up slightly and kissed the corner of his eye and thumbed away the tear-track on his cheek. She had not intended to love him. There was much about the uniqueness of him to create an interest but she had no thought that he possessed an influence that would master her and take her feelings from her own power and lock them up in his. She realized that every good, true feeling that she had was somehow joined with him.

42

A Yoga Lesson

The thin murmurs of ranch life began in the dark with a blast from rooster lungs. Holly gave him his first yoga lesson, with poses and stretches to ease his back. Afterwards, she sliced bananas and strawberries with orange wedges and brought them to the table. When she offered the fruit, he took her hand in his, kissed her fingers, and marveled at the perfect whiteness of the nails, almond shaped, shiny and thin at the tips. She shivered and touched his face. Then she smiled and said, "We cremated my brother. What did you do?"

It took him a minute to shift gears. She had a way of coming from unexpected places. "I'd thought about that…it met with too much resistance. He's buried not too far from here. I'm glad. It gives me a place to go."

"Would you take me there? I'd like to see it."

"Would you?"

"I would."

43

Three Stones for a Spirit

She scanned Holy Rood through the open window like a search-light at a prison break. He pulled up under a tree. She stood there and inhaled a silent, imperceptible yoga breath. "It's a beautiful place." He took her hand and led her through the grass between a row of graves. From thirty feet away, she pointed to the place where Damien was buried and looked at Jesse. He said, "Yes."

They stood side by side and looked at the stone. She knelt down and he walked off to sit cross-legged in the grass and watch. He felt as if she'd known him as she prayed her silent prayer. She stood and picked up the leather bag she'd unslung and took out an elk-skin pouch as Jesse came to her side. She pulled the drawstring and extracted three small stones. Putting them in his palm, she said, "I brought them from the high plains where our Native American friends live. They've been blessed. I'd like to leave them on his stone…if it's all right."

"It's all right."

As she moved to place them there, he said, "What made you bring them?"

"To put them here."

She took his hand. They stood in silence. The mystery of the place sounded softly in the whistle of the wind through the tall grass and the moan of interlacing boughs. Damien's scent was there. Before he could turn to see if Holly was aware, Zack was standing there, looking at them with a twinkle in his eye. Jesse looked at Holly. She knew he was there and that Jesse was seeing him. She squeezed his hand and followed his gaze. Jesse saw him raise his hand and describe a little arc with his forefinger as a cool adios. Then he was gone.

———✦———

A Mexican guitarist strummed while they studied the menu, a huge salt-rimmed Margarita in front of Holly and a shot of Tequila and a beer at Jesse's place. He put the menu down and looked at her. "Sometimes…I see him. I mean I really see him. Not just in my mind. He's standing right there in front of me. I know it sounds loony."

"Not to me."

"Have you seen your brother like that?"

" I was three thousand miles away when he died. He came and stood right in front of me just before I got the phone call telling me what had happened. I've seen him several times since."

"Damien has spoken to me. Not words from his lips…but…I don't really hear them with my ears. But they are thoughts…and they come into me somehow. Do you know what you want?"

"A burrito."

On the way home, the warm dusk had deepened into amorous darkness. He reached across and stroked her shoulder. "How do you feel about sleeping out under the stars?"

44

Sleeping Out

The moon rode the rim of distant hills. The soft swish and clomp of hooves moving through the grass and striking the earth had a rhythmic soothing pulse.

A lone cottonwood loomed at the top of a small rise. They stood down under its filigreed canopy, pinpoints of starlight blinking through the leaves. He hobbled and stripped the horses, and then rolled out their bed. She opened the saddlebag of treats while he gathered the makings for a fire. The flames sawed in the light breeze as he walked up to the tree and sat on the bedroll beside her.

In the darkness of the land, the flames dwindled to a glow, seething over the coals like some maverick force that had burst through a rupture in the shell of the earth to reveal the fire burning at its core.

His hand slipped along her neck under the soft lean jaw and turned her face to his. The sweet scent of musky perfume and her own odor of warm vanilla filled his senses. He brought his lips as close as he could to hers and yet not touch. He held them there, exchanging their breath, feeling the tingle as his mouth filled with liquid desire. And then he kissed her. He whispered into her mouth, his lips brushing hers, "I can't believe this is really happening to me."

Teasingly, slowly, as if to use up the night, they peeled away the coverings of their flesh. Naked among the nocturnal creatures of the hills, they coupled, beasts seeking knowledge reserved for higher beings, and howled at the stars, abandoned by the moon. Their pounding hearts pulsed as one with force enough to tilt the planet off its course. Jesse thought in that spasm of ecstasy that his life would be the price. And if so, so be it.

Her legs twitched as she lay in his arms and wiped her lips against his shoulder. A small shiver rippled through her. He turned and held her close against his chest as she wiggled into place.

He had never known such a joyous sense of being alive as this woman inspired in him.

He knew it could not last. They whispered small things in the rustle and stirrings of the night and the burble of the creek until they slept.

45

Doctor and Judge

W alter Nalls excused himself to answer the door, leaving Jesse
and Holly with his wife Helen at the bar. Superior Court
Judge Lamar McCarthy and his polished wife Leona stepped into
the foyer. Lamar was big, six-three and two-twenty. He wore a
white orthopedic collar Velcroed around his neck, and his right arm
was in a cast and sling.

"Good Lord," said Walter, taking Lamar's offered left hand,
"What happened to you?" Then he quickly took Leona's hand
and kissed her on the cheek. "Hello, Leona. Good to see you. You
look lovely."

"Thank you, Walter." She stepped around them to enter the living
room as she said over her shoulder sarcastically, "Tell him, cowboy."

Lamar had a quick humorous wit easily replaced by a stoic, dig-
nified demeanor. Raised in Texas, around horses and cattle, there
was a rough side to him that really wanted to be a cowboy or forest
ranger. He wore fine flannel slacks, alligator boots, and a silk shirt

but would have been just as happy in denim and Pendleton wool. He could trade his robes for Wranglers, get on his good sorrel head horse, and rope a steer with the best. Leona was his opposite, a parlor woman to the manor born, with a taste for fine antiques, jewelry, and designer clothes. Her face wore the placid expression that comes from the constant gratification of whims and ceaseless catering to vanity. She endorsed his hunting and fishing, the ropings and cattle gatherings that took him away with the boys. She loved him coming back and making love to her like a john with a whore. She also loved the fact that no one would ever have guessed.

As they followed Leona into the living room, Lamar said, "Pour me a Jack and water and I'll tell you the tale." He was laughing already.

Holly had instantly captured Helen in her web of charm and with her, the all too-willing Lamar. Leona decided that this woman was far too young, too beautiful, too charming to be real and too intelligent to do anybody any good. And she, Leona, would somehow prove her case.

Walter handed a glass to Lamar. "So, tell me."

Lamar took a hefty swallow of bourbon. "Well, I was up in Montana, fishing. The guide was a salty old son of a bitch. Had an odd assortment of critters around his place, llamas, mules, peacocks, a few cows, and some horses. We'd packed in for about three days. We're coming back, riding past a field with a bunch of cattle in it. Mommas and a few calves. We're riding along a fence. Suddenly, out of a thick patch of trees, comes a-charging this bundle of blackness. I thought it was a damn bear at first. It was a stud colt with his ears pinned and his teeth bared like a barracuda. This son of a bitch looked like he was gonna tear something up. There wasn't a white mark on him anywhere. Soot black. He dove into those cows, separated a calf and proceeded to cut that calf like nothing I've ever seen. It looked like he was gonna eat it. I just stood there and watched. It was awesome. Like he just came out of nowhere with a terrible urge.

"The packer said he was out of a mare he'd bought in a truckload of half-wild mustangs out of Nevada. He didn't know she was pregnant. He'd turned her out for the winter and when he went to gather her up, he found the colt at her side. Said he was a damn savage from the first moment he saw him. Said he'd tried to break him but he just wasn't worth the time or the trouble. He was convinced he was possessed by Satan. 'Even his color,' he said, 'look at him, black as sin.' I asked him what he was gonna do with him. He said he had a rodeo stock contractor was gonna take him and make a bareback horse out of him."

Lamar took another slug of Jack and went on. "Well, like I said, I'd never seen anything as athletic as this little bugger. There was just something about him. So I bought him and had him shipped to my place. He tore up the guy's trailer who brought him down." Lamar was amused by the memory. "Anyway, I thought I could get something done with him. Keeping him in a stall was like trying to cage King Kong. So, the other day I had him in a pen and the son of a bitch took a run straight at me and turned me ass over head. When the dust settled, I had a busted wing, a helluva crink in my neck, and a hostile wife." He looked at smug Leona and giggled like a boy. "Tell them what you said, sweetheart."

"I said, Lamar, I don't give a damn what you do as long as it doesn't kill you. I like having you around, seldom as it is, and I don't want to be deprived of that pleasure by something that ought to be in an Alpo can. You get rid of that horse or I'll get rid of you. That's what I said."

"So what did you do with him?" asked Walter.

Lamar grinned. "I've still got him."

Leona pronounced a death sentence. "He's got three more days. If he's still there, I will take my twelve-gauge and deliver him to his maker."

Lamar, wearing his silly grin, said, "Are you referring to me, dear, or the horse?"

"The choice is yours, cowboy."

Walter lifted his martini, saying, "Before you can him, maybe you ought to have Jesse take a look at him."

Lamar went from chronic big grin to dead serious magistrate. "Tell you what, Jesse, you come over and take a look at him. If you want him, you can have him. In the interest of preserving my marriage, I'll just give him to you." He looked to his wife for approval. Leona's face creased in a wrenched grin.

Jesse thought for a moment. "I'll come take a look at him."

Throughout the evening, he had been attentive and overtly affectionate toward Holly. She touched him in loving intimacy, and lavished him with private smiles and glowing eyes.

The real purpose of the dinner was to scrutinize, opinionate, and evaluate the new female import from Colorado. The mystery of Jesse's love life had long been the object of curiosity and speculation among the hill country women. Those interested for themselves and those with friends on the hunt. Who was this beautiful young thing staying in his house, sharing his bed? She was clearly intelligent, elegant, forthcoming, and apparently dig-proof. Leona's attempts to provoke were met with aloof serenity, self-confidence, and the dazzlingly bright smile. Helen liked her immensely.

46

Let's Go Look

She came into the candlelit bedroom in a rich parade of hair and perfume. At the candle, she lit a stick of incense and fitted it to the holder she carried.

Jesse stretched on the bed. "Did you bring that with you?"

"Yeah. Since I first left home. Makes a hotel room seem nicer."

He reached up and took her into his arms, easing her to the bed. He sat up and crossed his legs under him. She was propped against the pillows. He looked at her with a longing so intense that her breath caught in a little gasp. Slowly, she leaned forward and put her lips sweet as lilies of the valley against his. Her eyes closed. He felt her fingers in his hair as he wondered how this would end. How would he endure her leaving?

They slept in the lingering vapors of amorous twinings till Jesse woke in the still dark with that awful sense of dread. Tomorrow morning, he would drive her to the airport and when he got back to the ranch, she would not be there. She felt him shift and turned her sleepy face. "I didn't hear the rooster," She whispered.

"He hasn't said anything yet." As the words left his lips, the rooster sucked in, lungs full, he blasted his alarm to the hills. "Until now…"

They sat on the porch in silence with cooling coffee cups and watched the sun like a busted yolk oozing along the eastern ridge. He felt her turn to look at him. It took a while before she said, "Hey, Mr. Desperado, Mr. Outlaw Jesse James, you've got work to do. You better git to gittin'." She stood up. "C'mon, hurry up, let's go…"

He locked his fingers across the top of his head and watched the yolk become whole as it rose above the ridge. "Let's go look at that colt Lamar was talking about."

47

His Honor's Place

Six thousand square feet of two-story limestone mansion housed Lamar McCarthy, the intrepid Leona, and their nine-year-old daughter Sarah.

Jesse had called Lamar before he left for court and arranged to deal with Miguel, his barn manager, who wore a black twenty-past-eight mustache and led the way with a no-breed blind mongrel at his heels. Ten years earlier, they'd forded the Rio Grande together eluding the Border Patrol in the pitch of night. The mutt had been with him ever since. Miguel now had papers, thanks to the judge. The mutt did not. They walked up to a fenced pen big enough for a horse to get to running in it. He was standing under the shed roof at the end, alert, armed, ready for war. Feral instincts had warned of their approach. He was on his toes, shifting from foot to foot as if the earth might give way beneath him. From a hundred feet away, his energy was manifest, wild, twisting, coursing through the network of bone and muscle cloaked in black velvet.

Jesse's practiced eye scanned him from feet to withers and nose to tail.

As if to say, you want to see something, take a look at this, he shook his head, blew his nose, shoved his hind feet into the ground, and lunged forward. He galloped the length of the fence and instead of turning at the corner, drove his quarters into the ground, slid fifteen feet in a dust storm, rolled over his hocks and took off in the direction whence he'd come and continued around the pen at neck breaking speed. He circled it four times, then ran to the center, skidded to a stop, and stood, looking at them, hardly breathing, as if to say, "You want more?"

"I've never seen a horse as black as that," said Holly. "He's beautiful."

"He sheds out, he'll look like a polished boot." Jesse hadn't taken his eyes from the colt. The colt hadn't taken his eyes from Jesse. "The judge didn't lie. He's got some moves to him."

Miguel said, "He's muy fiero, Mr. Jesse. He don't like people too much." As if to prove Miguel's appraisal, the colt exploded from absolute stillness into violent motion, charging straight at them from fifty feet away, like a Spanish bull at a matador. He came with such velocity they backed away from the fence as if he might come through it or sail over it into their faces. He screeched to a stop, wrapping them in a cloud of dust. When it settled, he stood there with eyes blazing through a scrim of forelocks, focused on Jesse.

Jesse held his gaze, feeling the heat that emanated from him and said to Miguel, "You don't have a round pen here, do you?"

"No, señor. We got no round pen."

Meeting the black's fixed gaze, Jesse said, "You reckon we can get him in the trailer?"

"They got him in one to get him down here, Mister Jesse." He was smiling at the obvious. "He didn't like it too much."

"I'll just bet he didn't."

They finally got him loaded with some coercion in the form of ropes, a blindfold, and muscle. Miguel would be gimpy for a week having suffered the indignity of a hind foot slamming his thigh like a battering ram yet leaving the bone intact. On the way home, sporadic spells of silence were shattered by unshod hooves hammering cushioned walls. Holly said, "Are you sure he won't break a leg or something?"

"He's too surly to hurt himself. If he does, we'll feed him to the dogs."

48
Round Pen Reasoning

They pulled into the driveway at the Lazy JB, ominous quiet in the trailer behind. Jesse backed the trailer up to his round pen. He got out and opened the door to the eight-foot-high walled pen to form a funnel when he opened the trailer gate against the pen. From the outside, he untied the ropes that held the colt against the trailer wall and set him free. In a clatter of hooves, the black shadow bowled out of the trailer into the pen, dragging rope behind. Jesse shut the pen door and parked the truck and trailer in its place.

Walking back with Holly at his side, carrying her camera, she said, "What will you do with him now?"

"Well, we'll start with kindergarten and see if he's got any sense at all or if he wants to be a retard and end up in a can."

"Can I watch?"

"You can stand on the platform on the other side of the pen and look over the top."

The pen was a circle, fifty feet in diameter. The walls were inch-thick plywood panels bolted to six–by-six-inch posts. The bottom half of the eight-foot wall was lined with three-quarter inch-thick rubberized conveyor belting. It was a combination combat zone, therapy room, and padded cell.

Jesse secured the door behind him. The colt in the center thirty feet away turned with fury in his eyes and froze. He flattened his ears and showed a rim of white glaring at the top of his eyeballs. His nostrils stiffened wide. His mane and tail were twisted, tangled into witch's knots. Jesse could smell the wildness of him. He lacked the scent of leather and cultivated grain. Jesse held a long, soft ranch rope, coils in his left hand, loop in his right. They stood sizing each other up. Jesse tried to read the colt to anticipate his first move. Neither flinched. The colt was a stallion, a dominant monarch with a troubled childhood who saw Jesse as a challenging interloper to be vanquished, run off into the hills with his tail between his legs. Jesse meant to show him there were other ways to go.

He shook out the loop, feeding rope, increasing its size as he swung it over his head in a buzz of nylon against rawhide. He took a step forward, the rope whirring. A move that would have sent most horses into flight. The soot-colored colt reared up pawing the air and came down charging, ears pinned and teeth bared, straight at him. Jesse had thought he just might. He was ready. He stood his ground. At the last possible second he stepped aside and snapped his wrist, and like the crack of a bullwhip, the tip of the loop popped the colt across his nose and stung him good. He bawled and bucked, clacking his heels high in the air. Then he whirled and came again, with the same result. He stopped and shook his head saying that didn't hurt, but still thinking about this creature in front of him and trying to figure how to deal with him. Jesse took a step toward him. He backed, still considering. Jesse had the loop laid out behind him.

The colt decided to try again and made a move. Jesse swung the loop up ready to pop. The colt stopped. Jesse advanced, swinging the rope. The colt decided departure might be an answer and took off around the pen on fire to get somewhere. Jesse stood in the

center swinging, feeding rope into the loop as the black head tossed
toward the wall looking for a hole to freedom. He bucked and
lashed out with powerful kicks and galloped through the deep sand
on his way to nowhere. Mounting fury was being fed by frustration.
He'd begun to breathe deeper now, sucking air into the gaping fun-
nels of his nose as Jesse stepped in front of him popping the rope
and forcing a change of direction. He dug in and whirled around his
hocks, and spurted away with such intent, he tried to climb out of
the pen by diving up the eight-foot wall and hanging his forelegs
over the top. He scrambled with hind feet not meant for wall climbing and fell back with a heavy thump, landing on his side in the
sand. He got up galloping, panicked, lost his balance, flipped ass
over head, and came up running, breathing harder now.

Jesse jumped in front of him again, forcing him to turn away and
flee once more. He quit swinging the rope and just stood there
watching the colt run. The colt began stealing glances at him and
then he'd look away at the ever-present wall, then back at Jesse who
began to murmur soothing sounds of greeting. He flicked an ear in
acknowledgement although continuing his run.

Jesse stepped toward the path the colt would take but not so
quick to force a turn, more to arrest forward motion, saying whoa
as he came. The colt began to slow. The furious pace in the deep
sand had taken its toll. Rest was becoming a good idea. Jesse continued his seductive whoa, offering a soft place to sit, relax, and talk
it over. The colt quit the gallop for the lope and then the lope for
the trot and finally a wary walk, never taking his eyes from Jesse. At
last he paused. He turned and faced the foe, his ribcage bellows
pumping, breath rifling in and out of flaring wells, sunlight glistening on his soaking black hide, veins pulsing underneath, eyes burning, aimed at Jesse.

Jesse let the rope slip from his hand to the ground, moving
slowly toward the quivering colt. He stopped, extending his hand,
palm down, in a gesture of friendship and peace. A step closer, his
hand a foot from the charcoal muzzle, air pumping warm from

nostrils now tense. An inch closer, he reached. The colt flung his head, froth fleeing his lips, and turned away from this god who was trying to get inside him. Jesse supported his desire to leave, chased him away and picked up his rope, swinging the big loop and tossing it easily out at the colt running. He kept flicking half-hitches softly, smoothly, over the colt's head, around his neck, across his butt till the rope draped the horse like a string of pearls and he trotted easily under the ornament.

Ten laps later, Jesse offered again a place to sit and rest, saying whoa, easy boy, easy now, dragging the words out long and slow and stepping easily ahead of him to encourage a willingness to stop. The colt was looking at him now, flicking an inside ear.

In five minutes, he'd gotten to where the colt was standing still, letting him stroke his face and rub his neck and wipe away the sweat dripping from his lips. The mouth began to soften; the ears were tuned to him.

He snapped his fingers in a steady beat while he stroked and rubbed and leaned against the colt. Then he stepped away and beckoned the colt to follow, snapping his fingers. And as if on a lead, he did, his nose a foot behind Jesse as he walked a figure eight, trailed by the colt festooned in rope. Jesse murmured reassurance as he took the rope and slowly unwrapped the colt, letting it drag over and around the sensitive parts. He fondled the coils and brought them slowly up to the colt's nose. He snapped his fingers and rubbed the slick neck with the back of the hand holding the rope that flopped against the wet hide. When he got near the tender underbelly, where the lion rips first, the colt thought seriously about leaving town. But Jesse had sensed it and backed off till the colt was ready to trust him there.

In less than ten minutes, he could flap the rope anywhere on the colt's body while he stood like stone. He snugged his loop around each ankle separately, and led the colt in a circle by the roped foot alone.

When he eased the saddle down on the Navajo blanket, the colt bunched his back but he never moved. Jesse talked him into a soft acceptance of the girth pulled around his belly. He leaned against the colt, denying he was wild and dangerous and stroked him as if he were a friend in grief.

He stepped away from the colt who started to follow but Jesse pushed him off and sent him around the pen at a trot to get the feel of the saddle on his back and the stirrups flapping at his sides.

He held the lead rope in his left hand, standing close to the colt's shoulder, right hand on the saddle horn, he raised his left foot to the stirrup and tested his weight in it, the colt looking at him and fixing his legs to accept the weight. He stepped off the ground, standing in the one stirrup, ready to bail if the colt exploded. He eased his right leg over the saddle and lowered his seat till the colt was bearing his weight. The colt's feet were rooted in the ground. Jesse knew he could uncork at any second. He was the kind that if he panicked would dive to the sky, flip his belly to the sun and come to earth upside down on top of you. He gently pulled the halter lead bringing the horse's head to the left. He moved his left front foot and then the right. Jesse squeezed his legs and the colt walked off as quiet as a kid's pony carrying a friend he'd never had.

Jesse didn't try to guide the colt but let him take him where he wanted to go. In that moment, came the mutual acceptance, the genesis of an inspired relationship.

He opened the door to the pen and invited Holly in. She seemed mesmerized as she walked up to the colt. She stroked his face and gazed into his huge brown eyes, the rage gone and in its place, the world seemed to exist. "That was the most amazing thing. I can't believe how you did that. You got him to trust you."

"He's a pretty good boy. He's just scared. I don't think he's got a mean bone in him." He reached and rubbed the once clenched muzzle between his hands and felt it soften like dough before it's bread. "We just might suit each other. What do you think, boy?" He traced a circle lightly between his eyes, then stroked an ear. "We've got to come up with a good name for him." He was looking at Holly. "You do it. You name him."

"I'll have to think about that."

Holly was holding the lead rope at the wash rack getting show-ered with over-spray as Jesse wielded hose and sponge, flushing dirt and sweat from the seal-smooth hide. The colt seemed content with the attention and his very first bath. Maybe this wasn't such a bad world after all.

He found Chauncy, the little black goat and put him in the arena with the colt. The colt arched his neck and stiffened with nos-trils flaring. He lowered his head as if to bite or strike the little guy. Holly said, "He could kill that goat in a second."

"Chauncy's quicker than a mongoose. He'd have hell trying to get a piece of him." Just then, the colt's ears came forward as he sniffed the goat and determined he was not a threat. The goat walked around the colt to check him out and finally walked right under his belly and out the other side. The colt pushed his nose against the goat's ribs and a friendship was born.

49

A Last Night with Peppermint

He'd been thinking maybe tonight they would just hold each other and talk or not talk —just be with each other. She was lying there in pale moonlight and candle glow like a portrait from another time. He could feel the steamy warmth of her radiating from the bed to where he stood. The curving ivory shoulders, her bosom rising above and beneath Irish lace, a slender arm under her head, the golden shimmer of hair spread across the pillow, a curl rested in her armpit. Her eyes were half closed; a distant smile gave no clue of its cause.

He slipped under the covers and moved his arm across her breasts. He was full of the feel of her flesh under the thin sliding gown as he drew it up and down. An unspeakable passion began to swell in him. He turned her face to his as his hand traced her thigh beneath the film of fabric and kissed her parted lips, tasting the peppermint candy that she pushed into his mouth with her tongue. He lifted the gown over her head and draped it to cover his face and wrapped it tight, a mummy mask, and bent to kiss her belly through the cloth across his lips, then moved to the soft moist mound and slipped away the gown from his face. He felt himself drawn into a wilderness of danger and enchantment. Her fingers moved in his hair, clutching at his brain.

She seemed as light as air, his hand beneath her back, the other on her breast, a leg over his shoulder, as he pushed against her with all of his being until with a stifled cry he ceased to exist as Jesse and became Holly Marie. She pulled him to her and said his name, "Jesse, yes…yes."

50

Soot

He loaded her bags in the truck. When he came back into the house, she was looking at a framed, black and white photo on the wall. It was Zack, two years old, on the black horse, tucked into the saddle in front of Jesse and holding the reins in fingers articulate beyond his years. She felt him behind her. "He's holding the reins just the way you do." He took a deep breath and on the exhale, said, "Yeah…" He was a little surprised to find his eyes instantly wet.

"It's a great picture," she said, aware of its effect. She moved to gaze at the others, his mother and father, a grandmother, two grandfathers, uncles and aunts and cowboys and old men with moustaches. She wanted to imprint them freshly in her mind to take the memory along. There were none of Jolene or any other woman. A slim history of a man alone.

They walked to the barn where she said adios to Ricardo and Blizzard and Dozer, the horses she'd ridden, and the pregnant mare San Mamacita, and then to the arena where the black colt stood looking at them with curiosity instead of suspicion and rage. Chauncy was three feet away like a small shadow of the coal-black colt.

She hung her arms on the top rail, looking at him and said, "Soot. Lamar described him that way. I think it's right. I think you ought to call him Soot."

"Soot. I think it fits him. Soot it is. Hey, Soot." The colt flicked his ears, shook his mane and moved his feet but stayed where he was.

"They respond to you in a way I've never seen. Why is that?"

He shrugged, "I don't know. Maybe they sense that I'm not trying to steal their fire. I just want to share it a little."

"Are you trying to steal my fire?"

"No ma'am. I want to keep your fire burning right where it is."

51

Departure

Flight 2452 was ready for general boarding. They got up and walked toward the entrance to the jetway. He took her in his arms and held her so tight he thought he might hurt her. "I feel like I've got a bowling ball in my throat. I love you, Holly Marie."

"Thank you." She smiled in that perfect politeness. "You be a good boy now."

"Holler at me. Let me know you got there all right. Thanks for coming."

"Thanks for the riding lessons."

He stepped back. "Bye."

She backed away toward the entrance, smiling a sad smile and raised her hand. Then she turned and was gone.

Cedar-stake fence posts sutured the road-scar through the wind-tortured skin of the earth. He felt his guts were about to spill out onto the floor of the truck. He'd been transported to places he didn't know existed. But where in hell could it possibly go from here? He still didn't know how old she was. There were times she looked fourteen. She lived more than a thousand miles away. He had no idea what she wanted for her life. He knew damn near nothing about her except she'd lost a brother she adored, had been a successful model, had neat parents, and was possessed of a unique intelligence. Why in hell would she be wanting to have anything to do with him?

52

First Grade

He avoided the house when he returned home and headed instead for the arena. The arena was big enough for the colt to make things unpleasant if he didn't want to be caught. Jesse had a carrot in his back pocket. He walked easily toward the colt, projecting an expectation of good behavior. Anything less would cause suspicion. He murmured his seductive patois and held out his hand in greeting as he got closer, slowing as he read the colt's attitude. Ears flicking. Nostrils wide, slightly tense, a ripple of sound, not quite a snort. Jesse stopped, then moved to his right. The colt shifted to face him. Jesse was three feet away. He stayed there talking easily, calling him Soot. He kept his hand extended and moved a foot closer. It seemed the colt might leave, so Jesse remained where he was. Then he backed a step and beckoned the colt to come to him. After some consideration and after listening to Jesse, he took a step to him. Jesse backed another step and waited. Soot took another step and another until his nose met Jesse's hand and the soft stroking that followed.

He slipped the halter over his head, gave him the carrot and led him out of the arena to the round pen.

The saddle was on the ground in the center. The soft ranch rope beside. He shut the door and took off the halter. The colt stood there. Jesse gently pushed him away and whooshed him into a trot around the pen. He picked up the rope and swung the loop easily around his head in rhythm with the cadence of the trot. What tension there was evaporated quickly, and soon Soot began to lick his lips and look at Jesse for instruction. Jesse stepped in front of him and he easily turned around and went the other way settling back into the cadenced trot, Jesse chatting to him all the time.

He loped him in both directions without him panicking and running off, and when he finally stepped forward and said whoa, the colt stopped instantly and turned to face him. He walked up and stroked his face and neck, telling him what a good boy he was.

"Pretty neat." Abbie's head just barely cleared the top of the wall.

Jesse looked up at her and smiled.

"I've been watching."

"For about five minutes," he said, letting her know he missed nothing.

"Right. He's a handsome devil."

Jesse smiled. "Get on Roanie. I'm gonna ride this guy in here for a few minutes and then take him into the arena and move him around a little."

Side by side with the colt along the arena fence and Abbie on the roan, they moved at a long easy trot. Jesse picking up a light feel on the reins, guided the colt into the corners bending him and lining him out on the straightaway, teaching him with gentle tugs to follow his nose.

Forty-five minutes later, Jesse had stripped him off and was running his hands over legs and ankles, tendons, and pasterns, and massaging the pressure points above the hooves. He stood up and stepped back, taking a hard, cold look. Abbie was saddling Kevin Bradley's horse but watching every move Jesse made. He ran his hand along the sculpted hip. "It's hard to believe this guy is out of a mustang mare. Anybody'd swear he was pure quarter horse. Look at that hip. Hocks set low. Short cannons, even the jaw." He took a deep breath and blew it out. "Man, I'm afraid to think about what I might have here."

53

A Lingering Scent

The sun was gone, leaving a soggy night. He left the porch chair and entered the house. It felt empty and cold, though the night was warm. He stood in the doorway to the guestroom, the bed where she slept the first night, made, the flowers beginning to wilt, the scent of her lingering in the air. He sat on the bed and bent to smell the pillow where her head had lain. The scent was stronger there. He stood up slowly, looked around, and breathed it in. An envelope, pink, was tucked under the edge of the vase. He unfolded the note walking into the living room and sat on the sofa. The same scent wafted from the paper. He brought it close to his face till it touched. Then he held it far enough away to read.

Dear Jesse,
    I did not know if you wanted me to change the sheets.
I slept there but one hour as I tossed and turned the night
thinking of you. I thrived with your care and love. I feel as if

a fine powder has brushed against my skin like fairy dust on the petals of a rose. Your touch has reminded me of the essence of my nature...the softness that comes with being a woman.

   Thank you,
   Holly Marie

Beneath her name, she'd drawn in simple black strokes, a falcon launching toward the heavens.

Sunk deep in the sofa with his feet on the table, he read the note again, this time aloud and then again. Then he refolded it, slipped it back in the envelope, took it to the guestroom, and put it back where he found it. He filled his lungs with the perfumed air and left the room closing the door behind him.

Stretched on the sofa, scotch in hand, trying to separate thought from feeling, mind from heart and soul. Yes, she cared, he could believe that. Now what? Why not just take it as it comes? What if there isn't anymore? A new agony rose. As he tried to strangle it, the phone rang. The hollowness was gone when he heard her say, "I'm home."

"I wish you weren't. My house feels like a dungeon."

"I had a wonderful time. The first thing my parents said when they saw me was, 'You look great.' I looked in a mirror. They were right. They're yelling down to say hi and thank you for taking such good care of me."

She asked about Soot. She said she was tired, hadn't slept at all last night, thinking about leaving.

He asked if it would be all right if he called her.

She said, "You better," and wished him sweet dreams, "Goodnight, Jesse Burrell."

"Goodnight, Holly Marie..." His conscience and reason almost betrayed him. He damn near said, "I love you..." but did not, and felt he'd been dishonest. His bed, cold and empty, offered little comfort that night and short fits of troubled sleep.

54

Porch Talk

An alfalfa-scented breeze blew across the high plains around the Double Rainbow Ranch and along the second story porch where Holly and Ruby, in wide-brimmed straw hats adorned with fake sunflowers, sat watching a reddish gold ball sliding toward the horizon west of Pikes Peak.

"I thought I was dead inside. He woke up something in me, Mom, and he did it without trying. I wish you could have seen him with that wild colt. It was magic, sometimes I still don't think I really saw it."

"Oh, sweetheart, I'm so happy you had a good time."

"I want to see him again."

"Well, Holly, invite him to come here. Your little Holly House will be finished in a week or so and you can stay there...or whatever...Bear would love to have him come. It'd be so good for him to have a male friend to hang out with. And he could help you with the horses..." The small hoof-clatter on the slatted wood floor and tingling bell preceded Bingo, looking for attention. He pushed his horns against Holly's leg. She scratched between the horns and he pushed harder. "Manners," she said and shoved him away. "So you think Bear would like to have him come visit?"

"He'd love it. While you were in Texas, he talked about Jesse, how much he liked him."

"I'm gonna do it." She raised the Coke can to strawberry lips and said, "Look," as the sun threw a last bloody glance at a world of purple and gold under billows of white. Bear's car came crunching up the gravel drive between a pair of pastures. The mother and daughter, who looked like sisters, stood up.

55

Soot on a Cow

Two days were as long as he could wait before he called. "You should do a video about training horses. I could help you put it together and shoot it and Bear could market it." She was full of ideas. She extended the invitation to the Double Rainbow.

"Wow. Would I like to do that." His heart pounded at the thought. "This place would disintegrate in two days if I left right now. But I'll sure put my mind to it. I know you've got things to do there, but if you find you've got time to come back to Texas before I can come to Colorado, even if it's just for two or three days, I'll send you the tickets. I miss you." It was out of his mouth before he could help it.

When he'd first put Soot in the smaller pen, the colt trotted its fence with anxious mutterings and much tossing of his head. Then Jesse put Chauncy in with him and all was well.

The colt nickered as Jesse walked in to halter him. He had progressed so much faster than any horse he'd ever trained. Jesse had but to ask and the colt would oblige. When Lamar McCarthy called to ask how Jesse was getting along with "Satan," Jesse said, "Well, I haven't canned him yet." He wanted to brag on him but knew he wouldn't.

Abbie had brought in the cattle and bunched them at the end. Jesse rode slowly into the herd, feeling the energy within the colt focus with aggression on the herd. He rode him two-handed in a side-pull, a simple rope noseband hung from a headstall with a rein attached to each side. A good tool for tipping a horse's nose in the direction you want to go while saving his mouth. Jesse wasn't looking for anything fancy from Soot, he just wanted him to nose around in the herd and get the feel of cutting a cow easily, without pressure and driving it away from the herd and maybe keeping it out there a little. He pushed a fat heifer out from the herd about twenty feet. Soot was on it like a shark, his connection absolute. The heifer made a move toward the herd. Soot dropped to his belly like a panther, pinned his ears, and threatened to eat the cow.

Biting isn't allowed in a cutting contest. Soot was aggressive enough to try it and Jesse knew he'd have to be quick to discourage attempts to chew on a cow and still not inhibit the colt's natural keenness. As he thought about it, the cow changed direction and before Jesse could even think to guide the colt, he'd swept an arc and dove into the cow's face like a hell-born fiend. The cow shrunk back as if it might cry. The colt's move was so quick, Jesse had to adjust his seat to catch up.

They worked four head. The colt was scary spectacular. Jesse took him off to the side and stepped down to loosen the cinches and stroke him. He wanted to leap in the air and click his heels together. Instead he whispered something private in his ear, like lovers in a crowd.

Abbie was beside herself. "Am I dreaming or did he really just do that?"

Jesse blew out a breath and just shook his head. He led him to the fence. Abbie got off her horse and followed. Her face beamed excitement. "He is unreal."

Jesse, with a serious face deep in thought, pulled the saddle from the colt's back. "I know I'm asking the impossible, but I want you to not say anything about this colt...to anybody. Let's just keep him our secret weapon for a while...for as long as we can, anyway. Okay?"

"My lips are sealed."

"Wire staples and duct tape couldn't get that done."

"Hey. Hey."

"Excuse me. I lost my head. C'mon, I'll buy you lunch."

56

Candy and a Clydesdale

He pulled up to the mailbox. His spirit lightened when he spotted the red, white, and blue priority mail package. Along with a stack of envelopes, he put it on the back seat.

"A package from Holly?" She said it with a sly grin.

He reached out and grabbed her neck in his huge hand and shook her head gently. She let it roll from side to side, frizzed curls flopping around her face and laughed.

———✥———

It had cooled some as the sun went down. He fell into the sofa with the package on the table in front of him. He sliced through the tape and pulled out handfuls of Styrofoam nuggets. A disk of glycerin soap with a miniature Clydesdale imbedded fell out. Then a bag of popping corn, a package of licorice twists, foil-wrapped homemade chocolate chip cookies, and something in pink paper tied with blue ribbon. It was an eagle feather wound with a leather thong at its base and a note in her unmistakable script.

"My family and I want to honor you with this eagle feather for you truly soar and carry our hearts on wings of strength. Guaranteed to be tornado proof and good medicine for new beginnings...life."

And next to her name, the signature black shadow sketch of the raptor lifting off. Probing more Styrofoam, he retrieved a jeweler's box, containing three unique stones and a note, "Collected while Gumping on the high plains. They will bring good luck." The last thing he pulled from the package was a neckerchief, blue and white checks with a blaze of sunflowers. It smelled of her perfume. He tied it around his neck and got up and walked around the room with no direction. He reached for the phone, picked it up, then put it back.

57
A Short Night

He slipped into the rumpled sheets. Okay, I've got this colt.
This son of a wild mustang bitch could do it. He could go to
The Futurity. He's got it. There isn't a hole in him. And if Tom
Cruise were a horse, he'd want to look like Soot.

And then there is Holly Marie Bassett...

The sun was still on the other side of the world when he stepped
out on the porch knowing they'd all be asleep in Colorado. He went
to the barn, straight to Soot, and stood there looking at him. The
colt came to him and looked back.

He decided right then, seeing deep into the soft brown eyes no
longer filled with fear and anger, that Soot would go to The
Futurity. The black shadow, the ignoble urchin with the looks of a
movie star and an uncanny athleticism could walk away with the
gold. With The Futurity only eight months away, he would have to
pay a penalty nearly doubling the twenty-five hundred dollar fee.
Five thousand dollars, money he didn't have.

———❖———

"What's Gumping?" he asked, grinning at the sound of her voice.

"Well, you remember in Forest Gump how he was always running everywhere?"

"Yeah."

"Well, I've taken to walking everywhere. I call it Gumping. Bear wants a stone fireplace. I told him about yours. So we're collecting rocks. The other day I was about two miles from our house dressed like a goofball. I'd found this neat rock. I was carrying it in front of my belly. It was huge, and I guess I had a bemused look on my face. I was in another world, just walking along carrying this thing. Suddenly, a huge fire truck pulls up along side of me. Scared me to death. I thought I was being busted for stealing a rock. One of the guys asks if I'm all right. I said, 'Yeah, I'm fine.' He said, 'Oh, well we just got a call that there was a strange looking woman walking along the road and someone thought you might have a problem.' I said, 'No, I don't have a problem.' They kept looking at the rock I was carrying, the whole time. I said, 'Thanks very much for your concern.' He said, 'Okay, ma'am.' I know he thought I was nuts. Then they drove away. Can you believe that?" She was giggling. "So when are you coming to visit the Double Rainbow?"

"You really want me to do that?"

"Of course."

"Your father's not gonna be waiting for me with a shotgun?"

"Yeah. I'm setting you up for an ambush."

"I'm gonna do it. I can only come for a few days, though."

"That's about all we could take of you."

He chuckled with her. "You're probably closer to the truth there than you think. I'm gonna take the black colt to The Futurity."

"Really? That is great. He's doing good?"

"He's pretty cool. We've got a lot of work to do, and only a little bit of time."

"You'll do it. So when are you coming?"

"I'm gonna work it out. Anytime is okay?"

"Anytime."

She told him to look for something else in the mail. At first, the thought excited him. Then he became convinced he was out of his mind. It had happened when she came through the screen door at Larry Littlefield's ranch the first time he saw her. He loved her, first sight, last sight, every sight.

58

Soot Shines

A cup of corn oil in his grain each day had brought the sun-dulled black hide to a luster a seal would envy. Jesse smiled in the sensuous pleasure of his hands running over the slick colt and thought of Holly with a maddening tenderness and a rage of passionate desire that made everything else pale.

There was joy in the intricacy of the relationship between him and the black. He felt that somehow his son's spirit was a part of it, part of the colt. When he was on the colt, it felt as if he had his arms around his son. He wouldn't be telling that to anybody. Well, maybe Holly.

He'd brought twenty head into the arena. Cattle, the horse, Blizzard, and the man. As he nosed the colt into the herd, he crawled under the horse's skin and felt the intense desire begin to quiver in his flesh. He hunted cattle like a lion. He was born wild and Jesse loved the wildness of him. Soot was bored with slow cattle. If one showed no real desire to return to the herd, he sank on his hocks and danced in front of it, drawing it to him. If he forced it to make a move, he'd recklessly blow by it just enough to let the cow think it had a chance to escape, then he'd crack over his hocks and be right in its face, sinking into his stop, utterly victorious, the cow defeated. Jesse couldn't help but think the colt had done this all before, maybe in another life.

59

Entry Fee

Kevin Bradley's wife Carley, a soft-spoken, southern belle from Atlanta, could ride a horse. She grew up showing jumpers that her construction mogul daddy purchased on the expensive advice of fashionable trainers.

After an hour of watching from the fence, at Jesse's invitation, she put her foot in the stirrup and climbed aboard her husband's horse. Kevin smiled up at her. "Carley, I know I'm making a big mistake. You are gonna love this."

Jesse rode around with her while she got the feel and explained the difference between riding a cutter and a jumper. Before she could think about it, he said, "Go cut you a cow."

While Abbie put the finishing praise to Carley, Kevin and Jesse walked toward Kevin's truck. "I knew it," said Kevin. "You better go ahead and find Carley a cuttin' horse. Don't say anything though, I want to surprise her."

Profit on a horse for Carley, plus training and boarding fees—

minus, of course, Abbie's ten percent—would cover the entry fee for Soot at The Futurity.

60

A Maiden Voyage

It was a little practice cutting, a chance for Kevin to wet his feet, for Carley to sit on one of Jesse's horses and watch. It was a good opportunity to introduce the spooky Soot to the noise, the action of cars, trucks and trailers jammed in a parking area, loudspeakers, being tied to the trailer with other horses, not too close to mares, of course. He was all flicking ears, flared nostrils, and wide-eyed.

When everyone had finished and were wetting their throats and replaying the events of the day, Jesse spoke quietly to the owner of the arena. Minutes later, he rode the apprehensive Soot into the arena and let him slowly walk around the fence as if it were a minefield, sidestepping away from the light flap of hung banners advertising feed and trucks. He rode him back and forth in front of a banner till he'd touch it with his nose and not jump back. He loped him around to loosen him up and then eased him into the herd and cut a cow. The place was mostly empty when he started. When he finished, it was mostly filled.

That night Lamar McCarthy called. The word was out that Jesse Burrell had him a colt. Excitement bubbled in Jesse's belly, a huge grin ripped across his face as he quietly said, "He might turn out to be all right."

"All right?" Lamar had his big laugh going. "I hear he's a god-damn scorpion. I hear you're gonna have to wire his jaws shut to keep him from eating a cow."

"Who told you all that?"

"Everybody." Lamar was tickled. "You son of a bitch. I'm coming out to your place tomorrow. I want to see him."

61

His Honor Takes a Look

He stood on the platform and watched Jesse work the colt afoot in the round pen. When invited, the colt followed Jesse wherever he walked, head down, eyes soft, neck relaxed. Jesse stopped and turned to rub Soot's face then he looked up at the judge. Lamar's jaw had gone slack till he saw Jesse's eyes. He shook his head and laughed. "I'll be damned."

Jesse bent at the waist, his hand extending toward the colt's front foot. The colt lifted his foot and placed it in Jesse's hand. Jesse stroked his neck and put the foot back on the ground. The judge said, "I'll be damned."

At the arena, one arm hung on the top rail and the other tilting a beer, Lamar watched Jesse on the colt circle at the trot. Reins seemed unnecessary. As if guided by one mind, they moved without effort, diagonally across the arena, fore and hind legs crossing one in front of the other. Then they eased into a lope, a circle to the left, a lead change, a circle right, then a gallop down the rail to a sinking, drop-dead stop, then a spin left and right and then…stillness.

The judge muttered, "Son of a bitch," and shook his head. Jesse was smiling thirty yards away and a mile wide.

Jesse cracked a beer and brought another for Lamar. They sat on a stack of hay bales. The judge said, "I tell you, if I didn't see it with my own eyes…"

"Tomorrow, I'm gonna enter him in The Futurity."

The judge just shook his head like a dazed person. "You better…" Then he woke up laughing and said, "Jesus Christ! Am I gonna have to buy a ticket to see that son of a bitch that broke my arm cut a cow?"

62

A Ride to the Airport

Abbie had the driver's seat in the dually jacked up as far as it would go. For Jesse, being chauffeured was a treat. When he teased her about her aggression, she said, "Hey, I'm just a peewee in a little car. I'm always looking up at everything. You know what that's like? This makes me feel like Michael Jordan. I can kick some ass, man."

She gave him a hug at the curb and said, "Tell the ugly wench I said hi."

—————⟡—————

The Denver International Airport looked like an overblown Saudi monarch's palace, a mammoth white tent with spires poking in the sky.

Standing there backed away from the crowd and leaning against a column, she was a tall, lean bundle of incongruity that somehow came together as an identity of its own—denim bib overalls, hiking boots, a lace-trimmed T-shirt, a ball cap with shining sequined stars, ponytail out the back, the summer-bright smile in wide red lips and those icy gray-blue eyes sparkling. As free as a child at a carnival, she was slowly waving a pinwheel with gold and silver blades that spun a tornado of joy filling him from head to toe.

He dropped his bag at her feet and took her in his arms. He smelled her neck and felt his heart beat against her chest. He stepped back and gently held her face and kissed her lips softly. He felt her hand against the back of his neck as she pressed against him and murmured, "Welcome to Denver."

She held his hand as they walked to the baggage claim, heads turning as they passed. She seemed to notice nothing but him.

"Bear's car had a dead battery so he had to take Starbuck. So I've got Olie May. Bear offered to take her but I couldn't let him arrive at the office in Olie May. There she is. Hope you don't mind."

Olie May was a twenty-three-year-old Chevy Nova, once bronze, now a canvas for spray can art, a circus car. An American flag across the hood, stars and a quarter moon adorned the roof, the number 39 on one door, and 19 on the other, a carved pumpkin face smiled from the trunk lid she unlocked. "She sat in the yard for years not running, so whenever anyone got the urge we painted on her, thinking we'd get her towed away. Then one day a friend of Bear's came over and fiddled under the hood and no one could believe it, he got her running and she's been running ever since."

Once in the hotel room, Jesse slipped the bellman a fiver, shut the door, and slid the bolt. When he turned, the simple fact of her standing there took his breath away. She looked so beautiful to him it made his jaws hurt. He pressed her against the wall and kissed her long and deep, soft and wet until they were naked on the bed and making love in the late afternoon.

They lay in each other's arms and legs like twisted vines, every nerve steeped in the feel of their flesh. He turned to look at her. Eyes closed, her tongue moved, an unconscious exploration of her swollen lips. She moaned and turned to crawl against him. He held her close and closed his eyes. And like a bloodhound trailing a fugitive came a dreadful sense of doom hard upon the heels of his joy.

They awakened hungry in the dark. He kissed her everywhere at once and wished he had a thousand mouths to taste the all of her. An exquisite spring blossom, she stretched her tendril limbs and leaped into life, off the bed and into the shower, calling him to join her. They soaped and stroked and giggled and groped and hugged and kissed with water and shampoo cascading between their lips.

He wore pressed black Wranglers, sharkskin boots and a crisp white shirt. He put on his tweed sport jacket, as she appeared fresh from the cover of Vogue. He'd only seen photos of women who looked like that. He hadn't really thought about them actually existing. The long black-stockinged thighs under the flared hem of ethereal skirt flow. And here he was taking her to dinner, having just made love to her. Good Lord. Somebody jump up and poke me.

The car, Olie May, was already famous. The attendant smiling broadly as he held the door for the beautiful woman, said, "Don't forget. You ever want to sell her. Just let me know. I'd sure like to have her." Holly's smile damn near made him trip over his own feet.

They made love again that night in the light of the candles she had brought and the wisps of incense smoke and slept deep in the bliss of it all.

The next morning while he showered, he was sure he smelled waffles. He walked out of the bathroom still drying his hair and found her in the living/dining room at the bar, fridge door ajar, wherein she had stored the fixings, setting the table while the waffles were cooking.

He couldn't believe his eyes. "Where did you get the waffle iron?"

"I bought it yesterday."

"And you brought all that stuff with you?"

"Yep." She had real maple syrup and fresh strawberries and brown sugar.

"Man. I have died and gone to heaven." He came up behind her, slipped an arm around her waist, lifted her hair, and kissed the back of her neck.

They drifted through the western art museum across from the Brown Palace Hotel, reading the hand-scrawled notes by Charles M. Russell on his drawings and his letters with little illustrations sketched in ink. They drank cappuccino and ate chocolate-covered biscuits in a café. Afterwards, they returned to the hotel and took the clothes from each other's body and stood naked at the window overlooking the city and made love while watching pedestrians below and office workers out on smoking breaks.

They got dressed, keeping the scent of their love about them, and walked the mall on Sixteenth Street, hand in hand, browsing bookstores and gift shops. On the red brick street devoid of cars, draft horses stood between the shafts of carriages for hire. There were Percherons, a Clydesdale, several Belgians, and a dark brown and black giant with a white blaze down his wide face. Jesse was stroking his cheek as he called up to the woman idly holding the reins. "Is he a Shire?"

She was surprised. "Yes. How did you know?"

"I like horses," he shrugged.

"Most people think he's a Clydesdale."

"Yeah…" He stroked his head. "He's a nice boy."

Holly watched the small exchange. She began to cherish hopes she wasn't sure she should.

They had Guinness at a pub and walked to the theatre complex and bought tickets for that night's live performance of Shakespeare's The Taming of the Shrew.

They walked back to the hotel with their arms around each other's waist. "That was just great," he said. "That's the first time I've ever seen a Shakespeare play. That was one tough woman."

"I could take her."

"I just bet you could."

The depth of his feeling, the extent of the joy of being with this woman, was the most fearsome thing he'd ever known. He'd lost whoever he thought he was, and found himself feeling, doing, and saying things he'd never even imagined. Her head in the crook of his arm, her hair against his lips, he whispered, "My love for you has taken me into a wilderness…I am lost."

"Are you scared?"

The only sound in the candlelight was the whisper of their breathing. She listened and waited.

"Some." He turned and pressed his mouth gently against her breast and his hand found the special hollow in the slope of her back. She arched like a drawn bow and pressed his head to the perfumed softness of her flesh.

63

A Drive in Olie May

He shut the trunk, paid the kid who coveted the car, and hopped in. He touched her leg as she fed Olie gas and peeled away from the hotel as if they'd just robbed it. He smiled and cinched his seat belt a notch tighter.

Sixty miles later, at way more than a mile-a-minute, in the high plains of central Colorado, she wrenched the wheel of screeching Olie May and bounced on to a dirt road in a storm of dust and gravel, ignoring Jesse's chuckle. Three minutes later she hurled the car right into a long dirt driveway and began blasting the horn repeatedly. Two golden retrievers came bounding out of the tall grass and down the drive to meet the car churning up the hill. Before it was parked, Ruby was out the front door waving a big warm smiling welcome. She was at the car as they got out and wrapped her arms around Jesse as if he were long lost and highly prized. The big dogs waggled as Holly got in their faces fussing and pulling, slapping their sides, and introducing them to Jesse.

Bear was in the barn, grooming and saddling horses. With a big, twinkle-eyed grin, he came forward and greeted Jesse with a bear hug. Damn, this family made him feel good. He liked Bear before he ever met Holly Marie. But that was before he was sleeping with her, before she had taken possession of everything he thought he was and turned him inside out.

They rode down the dirt road to a bridle path that eased around and alongside the neighbor's fences. High cotton clouds hung in the bright blue, rimmed with light. Lodgepole lupine, larkspur, Indian paintbrush, and golden daisies rippled in patches of red, yellow, and purple.

Ruby had stayed behind preparing dinner, served by candlelight in the redwood house on an oak table set with elegant antique plates, ornate silver, and fine linen. They held hands and said a prayer for those they'd lost and they who thrived and eyes got moist. Bear raised his crystal glass to thank Jesse for being there.

64

Holly House

The "Holly House," not much bigger than the bed of a pickup was crammed with a small desk, a tiny table, a stool, two lamps, a thin chair, and a narrow bed. All antique heirlooms. The walls were hung with old portraits, family photos, and a painting of an English cottage. A small stained-glass window had been fixed in the top half of the door.

The high plains wind had whipped up, stirring the branches of aspen and pine that circled the little place where Jesse and Holly cuddled under the cool sheets. He felt the need to whisper as if the P's, as she referred to her parents, were a thin wall away. Her prairie-scented hair lay lightly on his chest. "That was a great dinner. I feel like I'm gonna explode."

"Pork roast. Mom's favorite thing to cook. Bear loves it."

"They make me feel…right at home."

"Well, what else? Why wouldn't they?"

"I was really nervous about coming here."

"Why?"

"Why?" He laughed. "You know Bear and I are at least the same age. He's probably younger than I am."

"So?"

"So...," he laughed again at her dismissal of his concern. "There are those who would call this robbing the cradle."

"And there are those who wouldn't."

"How old are you?" He just spit it out. Though dreading what the answer could be, he was glad he finally did it.

She smiled coyly. Years of conditioning would not allow a quick and honest answer, although she knew she wouldn't lie to him. "Models never tell their age. Let's see...I've lied about it so much, I have to think. How old do you think I am?"

"Twenty-four. And if you tell me I'm right, I'm leaving."

"I'm...let's see...twenty-six. You believe that?"

"I hate it...but I believe it. Man, I'm in despair."

"No...I'm...let's see...I'm thirty-three. I'll be thirty-four in January."

"Are you putting me on now?"

"Nope."

"What year were you born?"

"Nineteen seventy-one."

"I don't believe you."

"Yeah, I am thirty-three."

"Show me your driver's license."

She reached across him for her jeans on the floor and for the second that her breast was in his hand, he didn't care if she was nineteen. She opened her wallet and handed him the license. He smiled, reading the truth. "I swear, sometimes you look fourteen. Thirty-three. Well, at least I'm not double your age." He found her breast again and her lips and then, in the wind-sound, that wonderful, rare, nectared space in her for him to live before he died. She held him inside her with a pulsing desire that throbbed between them.

65

Flight 1239

It was ten at night when they parked Olie May. He'd arranged to get the last flight. It seemed minutes ago that she stood there with the pinwheel in her hand wearing the summer smile. Now they were saying goodbye.

"Flight twelve thirty-nine to San Antonio is now boarding all passengers," said the speaker.

She opened her arms to release him. He felt as if he were being ripped from a Siamese twin. He touched her face. Then he kissed her lips and backed away slowly to the jetway entrance. She came forward as if tethered to him twenty feet away. He eased into the current of the boarding and just before the bend, looked back. She stood as close as she could with her hand raised and a pensive look of untold dramas on her beautiful face. He raised his hand and smiled, backing, till the bridge wall took her place.

He rolled up his jacket and stuffed it under his head against the window. He closed his eyes, his brain riveted on Holly Marie driving Olie May at seventy-five back to Kiowa in the dark, and a good chunk of it on crooked roads. First, he thanked God for the blessing of meeting her and then he asked Him to please keep her safe. He asked for His guidance in what to do about this impossible thing that had grown and deepened, giving him a reason to want to be alive.

66

Doing the Job

The Bluebonnet Stakes at Brenham had a cutting event for every level of skill. Jesse and Abbie hauled six horses two hundred miles. Soot was along for the seasoning. Chauncy, the tranquilizer, rode in the trailer at the colt's feet and kept him as calm as a meditating Buddhist. Walter Nalls, Kevin Bradley and Carley, Daryl Ann Henley painted and perfumed, and the lawyer, Derrick Le Fevre, owner of Concho, the paint, were waiting nervously.

At the end of two days, all was festive. Kevin had won the novice class and was threatening to levitate. Carley fell in love with a flaxen-maned sorrel mare called Swinging Lena, owned and trained by the legendary Leon Harrel. Kevin asked Jesse what he thought of the horse. "She's won a bunch. She was trained by the best. I think Carley would get along with her. Thing is, I expect Leon is kinda partial to that mare."

They slipped away from the revelers. Kevin relentlessly wielded his powers of persuasion on Leon, got the mare bought, and arranged to have her waiting for them at Jesse's place when they got back.

They had purchased champagne and invited everyone to the Lazy JB to celebrate their victories and witness Carley being presented with Swinging Lena.

A fire swayed in the big stone pit beside the barn. Patsy Cline's plaintive lament, "I Fall To Pieces" wafted in the soft spring night. Kevin asked them all to gather in the barn. He disappeared for a minute and returned leading the gleaming copper mare with the platinum mane and tail. He locked his eyes on his wife and led the mare straight to her and held out his hand with the rope and said, "She's yours."

Carley's eyes filled with tears as she bit her lower lip and smiled while the barn echoed with applause as she put her arm around Kevin and kissed him murmuring "thank you" in his ear. She wiped her eyes and began to move her hands slowly over the sleek shining hide. "She's gorgeous." She looked at Jesse and said, "Now I've got to learn to ride her."

While they washed down pizza with hundred-dollar champagne, Jesse eased away to the house. He called Colorado to tell her he missed her, that he couldn't wait to see her again, that he thought about her all the time, that they needed to make a plan. Suddenly, everything in his life seemed incomplete without her, the urge to go to her almost impossible to resist. The instant he hung up, he resented having called and wished he could unsay what he'd said. He suddenly had a sense of what it must be like to be addicted to a drug you know will destroy you.

He fixed a smile and went out to join the party. Daryl Ann swooped like a peregrine at a field mouse and handed him a glass of champagne, "Where have you been hiding, you villain?" she asked, her breath warm and sweet with wine. She stepped on his foot and pressed down to hold him there. He smiled, a little embarrassed, though the group was closer to the fire and they were in the shadows and enough wine had flowed to soften sensibilities. "I have it on excellent authority that you've been entertaining a creature from Colorado. And that she has actually shared your roof and heaven knows what else. And that she's quite beautiful. And I have been deprived of the pleasure of meeting her." She reached up and slipped her fingers along his neck, into his hair and crawled around to his ear until she had his lobe in a pinch. "And that she's practically a bubble-gummer. You are an outlaw son of a bitch." She pulled his ear, fingering his neck. "So take me to your tack room and show me your tack. If you don't tell, I won't."

He wore an inscrutable face as he whispered, "Daryl Ann, you are a truly enchanting woman. I know I should leap at the opportunity to show you my tack, but I have taken a vow of celibacy for an indefinite period of time. And I'm keeping it."

Painted lips parted and she flung her head back shaking her hair as she laughed. "And I am joining a Muslim convent in Istanbul." She slowly drew her fingertips down his arm.

"That's my story and I'm sticking to it."

"Well," she smiled with wicked eyes and licked her lips, "as long as you're having fun, I'm on your side." She linked his arm and led him toward the fire. "If she ever gets kept after school and you want someone to play with, call me."

67

Cuttin' in Colorado

A broiling Texas summer could challenge the fortitude of a Zulu.
Holly was in Colorado where it was cool. There were cuttings
in Colorado. He could haul the horses and the clients could fly in
and out. He called her. She said, "Yes, I could do that. It's about a
five-hour drive from here." He had a big smile when he hung up
and lightness in his heart.

He needed to have Abbie stay at the ranch with Ricardo. He
called Billy Diggs to see if his son Mason wanted to go to Colorado.
For Mason, it was a dream come true. If his dad had said no, he
probably would have run away.

———◈———

A Rocky Mountain summer storm had blackened the sky and
salted the ground with hailstones steaming now in the bright
sun. At the walk approaching the herd, his level of intensity

matched the horse perfectly—relaxed and keenly focused. While the cow tested the horse, Jesse seemed weightless, in a trance, without effort, an element of the fierce encounter taking place. When it was done, he leaned forward to whisper something private to the horse and rode out with a smooth single stroke along the horse's neck as the crowd applauded. With Holly Marie watching, he had won the class. He muttered the words, "Thank you, Lord," even though in his heart he figured the Lord didn't have time to be concerned about a cutting in Colorado.

He slid the security latch and crushed her against his chest, his mouth at her neck, the taste, the smell, the golden silky feel of her moving beneath his hands, his mind lost all thought. She played the macho aggressor, tearing at his clothes and shoving him toward the bed as he laughed and surrendered to the startling yoga-power behind the push and fell back on the bed. She flung his clothes to the walls, knelt above him and then became still, looking down. In the slow, graceful arc of a swan, she lowered her head, her hair whispered over his chest. He reached for the buttons on her blouse. She whispered, "You're not supposed to do that. It's not very nice." She wiggled her shoulders and freed her arms from the sleeves. Her pale skin was almost blue in contrast to the black lace bra. He freed the rosy buds and draped the bra across his eyes like flyers goggles, then reached up to hold her in his palms. "When I'm not with you," he whispered hoarsely, "I think I've only dreamt you."

"My body's been dead for years. You make me feel alive again."

Each time they made love, each time he saw her face, it was as if it were the first. In the leaping light of candle flame, she stretched beneath him, alabaster white and rose pink, arching her back, reaching her arms above her head like a goddess emerging from the sea. He moved from where he knelt to lie beside her and take her head to his shoulder. He whispered, "I love you. My God."

Her voice came from another world. "I love you, Jesse."

He turned and looked into her face as if to verify what he knew he'd heard. She was smiling, though in her eyes a distant sadness smoldered in the gray. The words he'd waited to hear seemed to have come on an ominous wind.

A small childhood scar under her left eye, an infinitely poignant imperfection in her flawless face, caused a heat to rise at the sight of it, and the tiny blemish twisted his heart.

He awoke in the morning with his head beside hers on the pillow, sunlight shining through the golden down on her cheek. She blinked and said, "Good morning."

They started the day with waffles and omelets. Daryl Ann Henley had been scarce the day before but plentiful at the moment. There was language in her hips as she swiveled between tables, a handsome buffed cowboy in tow. She stopped, flashing Vegas neon, and greeted Jesse, who stood up and introduced Holly. She introduced the cowboy and leaned slightly toward Holly. "I've heard a lot about you. You've been the buzz of the hill country. It's so nice to meet you." A diabetic might have been in peril with the sugar content, but she made it sound sincere. "I guess we'll see you all later. Bye." Smiling, she touched Jesse's shoulder and led the cowboy away.

68

A Beast of Pain

It turned out to be a really good idea, coming to Colorado. The Texans were smoking them and loving it.

Kevin insisted everyone join him and Carley for dinner. Beyond Holly's charm and manners, Jesse became aware of a distance, a silent distraction, that only he could see. He leaned to whisper in her ear, "Are you all right?"

Though she said she was, he knew she was not. He'd seen the slightest tremble in her chin, in spite of her effort to control it. All he could think about was getting her out of there and sorting it out.

When they finally got to their room, she walked to the window and leaned back against the sill as if she might collapse. Her face was white and tense. He walked to her. "Holly, what is it? What's wrong?" She had fallen into a well of silence. "Tell me, what is it?" She seemed incapable of speech. Her eyes had grown dark in the shadows. She bit her lip and shook her head from side to side as if to free herself. Her chin began to quiver, followed by a torrent of tears spilling from her eyes and a woeful, wrenching sobbing as he wrapped her in his arms to prevent her from crumbling into fragments of herself.

What began with reddening eyes, a trembling chin, and the most heartrending effort to contain her pain, had become a full-blown storm of tears and, choking sobs—the unmistakable sounds of the most profound grief. This was a raging beast of pain. She had become a little girl with a dead puppy in her lap. So loudly did she wail, he was sure there'd be a knocking at their door.

He brought her to the bed, loosened her clothes, and held her head next to his heart, stroking her hair as she breathed easier. At last she whispered, "I'm sorry."

"It's okay…" He continued stroking her hair.

"I haven't had a chance…to cry…for my brother. I took care of so many things, all the details…the organ donations…his ashes, I carried them in a taxi…my parents. I took care of everybody, everything…except me. I haven't had a chance to cry. I've kept it inside for so long. We were like one person. He was funny, he was kind, he always put other people before himself…it's just not fair. I don't know why now…what it was about today that triggered this…" She wiped her eyes and sniffled through a wet laugh. "Maybe because I'm enjoying everything so much. We always shared our good times, maybe that's why I miss him so much today. Our house is so small. I don't want to make my parents sad…so I keep it all to myself." She turned and looked up at him with swollen eyes. "Thank you for letting it be okay."

Her tender complexion was blurred and inflamed, more beautiful than ever. He wanted to make love to her. The raw lips, the wet, matted eyelashes, the pink nose drew him to her and she opened her arms to take him in. "I love you, Jesse."

He was only half-asleep, aware that she was not, when he heard her say, "How do you feel about having a child again?"

"I can't even imagine it." He was stunned by the question and spoke into the pillow.

His answer pierced her heart like a lance of ice, as unexpected as if it had been hurled out of a bouquet of roses.

He realized only as the words had left his lips, the brutal bluntness of their force. He propped on an elbow and saw on her face how hard they'd hit. He knew he'd spoken the truth but wished he'd done it better, or not at all. "It's just that...I don't know, I love kids. But since Damien died, I find it difficult to think about babies...birth...Sometimes I can't even look at a baby. I don't know how to explain it. I wish I could." He was lost in frustration, wanting her to understand, not knowing how to get it done. "When you lose a child, even if he's an adult, you've lost your baby. That's how you first knew him. The baby always exists as long as the adult is there. When the adult dies, the baby dies, too. It's like losing two people. I guess a baby, somehow for me, represents the potential for..." he shook his head as if to deny what he was saying, "the most deeply hurting pain."

"It can also be the greatest joy." It came softly from a long narrow hallway in her mind.

"That's true...I know it is..." His voice trailed off. He said no more. Nor did she.

After a time of silent separate thought, he sensed the chasm between them though they were close enough to feel the warmth of each other's blood. He drew her into his arms and whispered in her hair, "I didn't mean it to sound the way it came out."

She breathed in and released a small murmur of response.

69

A Parting

The mountaintops stood behind them, islands in the morning mist. He leaned back against the fender of her car and held her close between his legs. She forced a smile as he touched her face and tugged her collar up around her neck. He kissed her soft and slow, until he felt her lips give in, he whispered, "I love you…go." He guided her into the seat behind the wheel and shut the door. She rolled the window down and looked up at him. "Drive careful," he said and leaned in to kiss her one last time. He stood up and looked into her eyes trying to read the silent mystery there. Something had been damaged and he knew it, but he didn't know how to fix it.

She drove away with her arm out the window, fingers formed in the sign language symbol of love, waving gently. He watched until she vanished at the end of the street. He blew out a breath and headed toward the trailer and his truck. This was a woman of many shades and hues and beneath the external tranquil beauty, churned the groans of roaring wind and rain. Children, that was an important question she asked. Even though he'd known this could never work, he'd told her he loved her, again and again. How could he not have…even if he had known it couldn't last.

Mason had the horses booted for travel, and lined up on both sides of the trailer. Jesse clapped the boy on the shoulder and said, "Come on, let's get some breakfast. Then we'll load them up and hit the road, Jack."

"Jack?"

"It's an old song."

"Huevos rancheros," the pretty college-girl-waitress repeated Mason's order as she wrote it, smiled and turned away.

Mason stared at his orange juice. "She sure is a real nice lady."

Jesse looked after the waitress. "Yeah…."

"I mean Miss Holly."

"Oh…yeah…"

70

Texas

The buoyant bright light of Abbie bounded off the porch behind the dogs. She hugged him while telling nonstop everything that transpired since he left, even though they'd spoken nearly every night.

He was in the saddle at seven. The colt was on the muscle. Jesse gave him his head, and he snaked it to the ground as he galloped off slinging his hind feet to the sky, clacking his hooves together applauding the day. His body cracked like a lash at the end of a whip as he bucked. He knew that Jesse was right with him, sharing the celebration of his wild spirit. Minutes later, they settled down to the business of working cattle. If anything, the colt had gotten better and smoother, as if he'd been training himself.

Mason called to thank him for the great trip. "I talked to my mom and dad. They know I'm serious about wanting to work with horses and maybe be a vet and they said it'd be okay if I wanted to ask you if I could come and help you out for the rest of the summer. You wouldn't have to pay me or anything. My dad said it'd be all right. I...I could ride my bike over..."

Jesse sat on a horse with a smile on his face, "Come on," he said.

The boy wasn't sure he heard right. "Are you serious, sir?"

"Yes, sir, and I'll pay you, too. I was just thinking about how I need to hire another hand."

"Gosh, that's great. Thanks. When do you want me to start?"

"When can you?"

"I could start right now."

"Come on."

71

Instinct Will Not Be Denied

In the tiny Holly House, she sat at her desk trying to put thoughts in her journal, hoping that giving them form in ink would make them clear. Her heart still held the sting of his feelings about children. She wanted to find the truth of what she felt. She'd never thought much about having children. The idea of children was always so connected to a man, a father, a husband, and until the Texas cowboy, she had never met that man. But now with the loss of her brother and the finding of Jesse, something had begun to brew. She knew that a child wouldn't bring her brother back, but the thought of creating a human being out of love seemed a very appealing thing. If nothing else, she needed to know the possibility was there.

Worn weary with a lonely three-day struggle to resist the urge to call, he punched out her number. The sound of her hello brought scant relief. He had to see her face, touch her skin, smell her hair.

It was resolved that she would come to Texas in ten days and videotape Jesse training. He insisted it would be a business venture. She would be paid outright or participate in a percentage of the profits from its sales, whichever she preferred. The last words he spoke before easing the phone to its cradle were, "I love you." Every time he said them, he felt they'd escaped against his will. There was something about this love that was stronger than he. It made him uneasy.

72

Colorado Sunshine In Texas

She arrived overflowing with ideas, a storyboard, a script complete with camera angles, ways and places to advertise, and a marketing scheme. He smiled, sitting next to her on the sofa at the big table, a bottle of wine between them. "You've done a hell of a lot of work. It looks so professional. Where did you get all that information?"

"I studied a little. Some from experience. A lot from Bear. I put it together on our computer."

"I can see the whole thing." He leaned forward and kissed her into a slower pace down a different path. He whispered thank you against her lips and felt the change as she softened under his touch and slipped her arms around his neck. She seemed to constantly create a universe wherein all was new, the tantalizing tilt of her head haloed in gilded strands of light, the smoke that veiled her mystifying eyes, the bone-china paleness of her skin, whose purpose was to take him from himself.

———⊰•⊱———

Abunch of friends and neighbors came to the ranch for a potluck screening of the finished product and cheered when it was over. Jesse had to deal with a ceaseless barrage of gibes about being a movie star. He gave total credit to "my writer, my producer, my director, and my cinematographer, Holly Marie Bassett." She bowed elaborately to applause, cheers, and whistles.

73
A Chasm

In the warm pink evening, a red-hot ball of sun slid down the sky for a last bloody glance at the day. Ribbons of clouds purple and white streamed along the rim of the hills. Dozer lay at Jesse's side, enjoying the probing fingers in his scalp. Holly pointed her wineglass toward the sky where a hawk wheeled on motionless wings, scanning the pastures with laser eyes for a dinner of flesh.

The hawk squealed and spiraled tighter, once, twice, then folded his wings and plummeted like a rocket. He disappeared in the distance behind the barn. "Dinner is served," said Jesse.

"What do you suppose it is?"

"He's got a good choice on this menu, prairie dog, field mouse, squirrel, and there's Bunny Bunny."

"That's not funny." But she smiled anyway. They fell silent as the sun sank behind the jade and garnet hills. He looked at her profile and wondered what was in her mind. He wanted to come right out and ask her, what does she want. What does she see for her life?

How does she feel about the difference in their ages in terms of the future? Where does she think this can go? Had she thought about it? Something was occurring, a change, an uncertainty. They surely were not focused on one thing together. They hadn't talked about anything like that. Then the voice within went silent. He reached across the small distance between their chairs and touched her arm. She smiled and put her hand on his.

74

Fury Unleashed

The fan above the bed churned the steaming stillness of a summer morning that would soon become a torrid afternoon. "Maybe you could keep an open mind." She was sitting up in the bed, not looking at him, knowing she had his attention.

"About what?" He said it even though he knew.

"Having children."

He breathed in tensely through a bitten lip. A sudden rush of anger filled him. Couldn't she understand what he'd tried to explain about his feelings regarding children? Couldn't she at least give him some time, a chance to think about it? He wanted to scream out, "No, I don't want to keep an open mind. I am not prepared to even consider what it takes to bring a baby into the world and keep it safe and raise it up to be a decent, worthwhile human being. And I'm too damned old. No!" is what he wanted to say.

This is it, he thought, I've known it from the start. The end is here. She has the right, of course she does, to be fulfilled as a woman; and a lot of women feel that comes with bearing a child. He was not about to try to talk her out of that. Instantly, he saw her clearly: full-ripened, round, blooming pink and peach and lily white, glowing in exquisite loveliness. No way could he discourage that or even try. He loved her so and knew she deserved happiness and wanted her to have it.

Her eyes began to fill as she listened to his silence. He stood and went to the window. Her eyes would not release him. "You won't answer me. You won't say anything. You just stand there like stone." She sprang like a leopard from the bed, naked but for his opened shirt flying like a cape as she lunged at him, tears splashing her darkened cheeks. She rammed her palms into his chest and shoved him back along the wall. "You said I mean more to you than the blood in your veins. You said you loved me." She screamed at him, "But not enough to have a child with me." She beat at his chest. "Why don't you hear me?"

He offered no resistance, stepping back with the blows. Her rage appeared from out of nowhere, without a cause from him that he could tell. An anger of such dimension demanded an attempt at understanding. Still, he had no voice. "Look at you," she spat the words, her face scrunched and furrowed in frustration, red and white and glacier blue, "you're so tough..."

"I'm not tough. I don't know what to say. I'm trying to understand. I want to be honest with you. I don't know what you're seeing...or what you think you're seeing."

She continued to shove at his shoulders till he locked her wrists in an iron grip and she thrashed like a netted tiger. He could feel her breath on his face inches from her tightened lips and glaring eyes. "You think you're a brave, macho cowboy, risk your life to save mine. It takes more courage to risk something you have to live with, something that forces you to rethink your beliefs. You're doing what you decided was best for you yesterday. You might be wiser today. You need to come out and see."

"You need to quit screaming in my face. I can't hear what you

246

want me to hear."

"You don't want to hear anything." For a moment her energy waned and she seemed to melt in a pool of tears. Like a mournful child's lament, she said, "I want my brother...I want my mommy..."

"A child isn't going to bring your brother back..." He knew it was stupid as the words left his lips and wished he'd remained silent.

She instantly flared anew, "I know that!" She screamed. "I never even thought about having a child until I met you. I wanted a child with you. You. How stupid I am." She slammed her clenched fists against his chest. "Do you want me to leave?"

He stood stunned in disbelief. Minutes ago, he was bringing her breakfast and kissing her neck. Now a beast he didn't recognize was snarling in his face. He tried to think, to gather his wits and not react with anger but so relentless was her assault, he could not.

Reddened and trembling, she repeated her demand with a challenge in it. "Should I leave? Is that what you want?"

A rope twisted in his guts. An instinct lunged forward, he heard himself say, "Yes. Yes, I think you should. You're far too unhappy to stay here. I don't want to be the cause of such unhappiness. I'm feeling real bad right now."

"Okay. If that's what you want." She turned and blew into the guestroom.

He stood there looking at the floor, shaking his head, his heart pounding unreliably. He muttered, "I don't believe this. Yes, I do. Just as well." He felt the air being crushed from his lungs.

The ride to the airport was a torturous experience, thick with storm-clouded thoughts racing without direction on violent winds of emotion. Anger, shock, insults battered reason, love, and compassion. A thousand thoughts and feelings raged within the confines of the Ford. A hundred impulses to speak were crushed by confusion, stubbornness, and pride. And so they rode in silence. There was no turning back.

He watched her vanish in the jetway and thought he would die right there where he stood. He lacked the strength to turn around, to walk to the truck. He drove in a world obscured by torment. By the time he got home, he was exhausted from trying to put the pieces together, to somehow come to terms. His brain was fried, his heart shattered. He went straight to the house and shut the door. He flopped on the sofa and put his feet on the table. Amid the chaos that churned within, his own existence came into question as something unreal as if he had not actually lived this life but had died a long time ago and has ever since been a being with no history and no thinkable future.

It was only midday. There was work to be done. The phone rang. It was Abbie calling from the barn. She wanted to know what she and Mason should do. He told her and said he'd be there pretty quick. He went to his bottle of scotch and pulled the cork, looked at it, recorked it, put it back, and walked around in a circle like a dog choosing a spot to lie down. He went to the kitchen, poured a coffee, placed it on the counter and stretched his arms to the ceiling and let out a bellowing roar that would have sent a lion cringing. It penetrated the thick walls of the house and traveled to the barn where all labor ceased. Heads turned, they looked at each other, and then resumed their tasks.

Everyone gave him the berth granted a leper. Abbie, nearly disintegrating with curiosity, spoke not a word. He rode six horses, working their butts off. When he got to Soot, a softening calm overcame him. Soot was not a guy you could be on edge around. He stroked the black's face whispering something salacious to him and led him out of the barn. The colt was beginning to look more like rubbed ebony than soot.

He cut three cows and then schooled the colt on his turn to the left. He wasn't quite as pretty going left as he was to the right. Jesse helped him find it, then ran his hand along the sleek black neck and whispered lavish praise. He gave him the full length of the reins and the colt stretched his neck long and low and shook his mane. Jesse just sat there quietly, part of the horse.

75

The Real World

He crawled out of bed, a wreck in a storm of passion. The dogs greeted him on the porch to escort him to the barn. Dozer ambled at his side, tall enough to have his head scratched without a bend from Jesse. Blizzard scooted ahead.

He was reaching for a saddle when the tack room phone rang. "Jesse Burrell."

Larry Littlefield said, "Butch Logan told me they ran your video at the magazine. Said it's real good. Congratulations, boy."

"Thanks."

"Holly Bassett did a good job for you, huh?"

"She did a helluva job."

"So everything is looking pretty shiny."

"Everything is looking pretty shitty."

"Why? What?"

"She was here. We had a fight. She's gone. It's over."

"What did you fight about?"

"Damned if I know."

"I hear you got a colt."

"Where'd you hear that?"

"I hear everything. Some folks have a pacemaker, I have a telephone. Hear you got a good one."

"He's a wild little bugger. If I can just stay out of his way and let him do it, he's got a lot of natural ability."

"I want you to win that damn Futurity this year."

"I want me to win that damn Futurity this year."

"Well, good luck, son. I'll see you. Hey. I was you, I'd patch it up with that little gal. She's a dandy. You were probably an asshole. Adios."

Like patches of black crepe tossed in the wind, the ravens swirled as he stepped from the truck. Holy Rood had been recently groomed. Flowers formed in clusters against the moist green lushness. The gray stones sparkled in sunlight.

He looked at the name carved in stone and knelt on the yielding sod, feeling the wet come through to his skin. He bowed his head, closed his eyes and began to pray. He hoped, when he opened his eyes, to see his son. He wondered if he'd ever be there again. The thought scared him and the emptiness within grew quickly vast and desolate. He breathed deeply and slowly let it out as he lowered his face to the cool wet grass and wept into the earth.

76

A Date

Every time the phone rang he wished it had never been invent-
ed. Why should she call? He'd practically kicked her out. It's
over. It is what needed to be. But it shouldn't end ugly.

Everybody had asked about her saying how much they liked
her. She's such a wonderful, warmhearted person. Where is she?
And when is she coming back?

Kevin and his wife Carley were just pulling out the driveway
after a schooling session. Jesse leaned against the fence as if he didn't
know what he was supposed to do next. He could not have told
how long he stood there before he heard Abbie say, "Hey, Boss."
She had come up behind him and stood there with her impish grin
and bright eyes looking up at him.

"Yeah."

"I never ask you for anything, do I?"

"Are you kidding? You never stop. What do you want?"

"I want to take you out to supper."

He grinned at her for a long time. She stood there smiling. Then she said, "There's a great Cajun band playing at the Yellow Rose. I want you to hear them. And I don't want you to say no. The food's good, too."

"When?"

"Friday night."

"You got a deal."

"Cool." She brightened even more and bounced away.

⟫•⟪

The Yellow Rose was upscale country western, stripped pine logs with high cathedral ceilings above a raised dance floor and a sound system to rattle the heavens. It was packed, but Abbie knew the host and had taken care of everything. They sat in a booth not far from the dance floor. A beautiful, black-eyed, black-haired Mexican woman with satin cinnamon skin served them. She flashed a smile that would make a bishop kick a hole in a church window.

Jesse didn't know when was the last time he danced. He didn't know if he ever danced. But, by crackie, Abbie got him out there and they whirled and twirled and he laughed. He knew that she'd thought up the whole thing out of pure love and that the restraint she exercised to keep from asking what had happened with Holly damn near killed her. It made him feel good to know that this little package of perpetual energy was a part of his life. He looked across the table at her and knew that he loved her.

Jesse had spotted them at the bar. Coarse and loud, they were looking his way over the shoulder of a flossy, painted tart in a skirt tight enough and thin enough to count the stitches in her panties. They were dickheads on the prowl, damn near drooling down the front of her tube-top while eyeballing Abbie forty feet away. He could feel the birth of a problem. Sure enough, here comes one of them. A big stupid cocky grin pasted across the front of a head bearing a brain as dense as the iron he pumped to produce biceps like legs dangling from a tight black T-shirt. His buddy was watching back by the bimbo. He wheeled up to the table without a glance at Jesse, spread his legs, and leaned down in Abbie's face, startling her. Smiling mockery and breathing beer, he put his damp hand on her wrist and with counterfeit politeness, said, "May I have this dance?"

Abbie moved her head back to avoid his breath. In a tone of absolute dismissal, she said, "No, thanks. We're talking." She turned away, assuming that was it.

It wasn't. He tightened his grip on her wrist and tugged, "C'mon, let's dance."

"Hey. I don't want to dance. Thanks."

"Yeah, you do." He pulled harder.

"She said no," said Jesse quietly.

He glanced at Jesse, "I'm not talking to you, dad." He turned back to Abbie and hauled her halfway out of her seat as she struggled to wrench free of his grasp. From where he sat, Jesse's clenched fist came up like a hammer between the husky's legs, slamming into his sack and lifting him a foot in the air where he howled and doubled over. As his face plummeted toward the table, Jesse cupped the back of his head to accelerate the impact. His buddy was flying to the fray, diving over his collapsing pal with outstretched claws aimed at Jesse's throat. Jesse's hand closed around his bottle of Coors and shoved it into the flyer's gut to his backbone. The guy crumbled, harpooned across the table, slick with beer and blood.

Abbie's manager friend got them out before the toughs recovered. "If it comes to anything, I'll just say you threw down some cash and left. I don't know who you are."

He rolled the window down and let the warm night blow in a soothing balm. Abbie was silent. Suddenly, he laughed. "You sure know how to show a guy a good time."

She hadn't been breathing for a while then exploded with a giggle. "Is there something about me that brings out the killer in you?"

"I was wondering the same thing. Maybe it's the hair." He

reached out and ruffled her head. "Thanks. I had a great time. Sometimes it's just so good to kick somebody's ass."

———>•<———

The sparkle of a billion stars brightened the Colorado sky. Holly lay in her bed, rigid, awake, her slender arm across her eyes to shut out the terrible beauty of the night. Unbidden, his face was there, the sound of his voice, his big, brown, long-fingered hands fluttered, detached, in the darkness behind her eyes. Such as that would not be shut out with the folding of an arm. Yesterday's dreams blooming with promise now lay fallow. Her love shivered in her heart like a child unsheltered in the cold. She was filled with yearning and hopelessness. She longed to be dead.

77
A Stroll Through Austin

Taxes were the issue this time. Jesse would rather have strolled barefoot over hot coals than sit across the desk from his accountant, watching him fingering his computer as easily as Jesse worked his reins. He left after a torturous two hours, having placed a Band-Aid on the Titanic and trying to ignore the battering sea.

He couldn't remember when he was last in Austin and if ever he'd walked the streets alone. He looked in store windows and bars and restaurants. He stopped at a shop window and looked for a time, then switched focus to his face in the glass and wondered who he was. He entered the shop. When he left, an hour later, he clutched in his fist, a small, wrapped parcel.

Gut-shrunk and wolfish, he walked into Callanan's. The bass was grilled to perfection and two pints of stout put a polish to it. A sharp loneliness came upon him. His head went down and he wondered what she was doing right then. The longer she was gone, the greater grew the emptiness.

The fan-stirred air blew warm across his skin. The seeping scent of honeysuckle through the parted curtain drifted in the room. What am I to do? The answer was prompt, filled with dread. Leave it alone. Don't call. It's done. But then came the weakness that said no, I can't do that. I cannot toss away this thing of beauty as if it had no value. But then another voice told him that he could, he should, he was too old, and she needed things he couldn't give or wouldn't give. He left his bed and went to the porch.

He curled his arm and leaned his face against the rubbed surface of the cedar post and wished for a way to be shut of it all. But wishing ran before memory as he heard the screen door clack shut in the Colorado afternoon and saw her smiling, walking in ripples of pale blue silk among beards and spurs, denim and flannel. He felt again the harsh beating of his rapid heart followed hard upon by damn near every moment he'd spent with her and every thought and feeling he'd ever had, until his brain became a bowl of cold Quaker Oats. He went back to bed.

Deep in the night, he suddenly turned and sat up. He rubbed his face and stared as if at some threat. Then he reached for the phone.

Since he'd watched her slender grace round the bend in the boarding bridge and disappear, a fever of loneliness had seeped into his bones. She had given him the power to live again. Now it was gone.

He touched the numbers. Bear's recorded voice answered.

"It's Jesse. Is anybody there?" Stupid question. I'm waking the whole house up.

"Hey," she said. If smoked honey made a sound, that was what he heard. "What are you doing? Besides waking up the whole house?"

"I can't even begin to understand what happened. I only know

I've never been so unhappy."

"Well, I've been having a great time. Dining and dancing, doing the town, burning up the streets of Kiowa…" Her voice grew small and sad. "Having a big time…"

"I love you, Holly. I need to see you. We can't leave it like this. Meet me somewhere."

"Where?"

"Wherever you like. You name it."

"I've always wanted to go to Santa Fe."

78

Taking a Risk

Flame-light flickered a warm glow on thick, white walls of adobe. Mesquite burned in a corner igloo. They sat on a deep Navajo rug. She looked across the top of her clasped knees into the shadows of his mind.

He stared at his right foot as if the secrets of the universe were in his big toe. "I'm a desperate man. I come here ignorant. I never did think I knew much of anything. Now the only thing I know is that I don't know nothing." He lifted his eyes to hers. "Except that I love you. I guess I came here to tell you that I shouldn't be here. It could never work. I'd be jealous of every man who looked at you. I'm not that good a fighter. You'd probably end up a nurse, taking care of an old geezer dribbling on hisself and wishing you'd never met me. If we had a child, I'd be going to his soccer practice with a walker. You might even end up murdering me and going to the gas chamber."

She rolled the wineglass along her lip and peered across its rim with silver-ice in her eyes. A soft smile curved in silence. Then she said, softly, "If you're afraid of love…you're afraid of life. If you fear life, you are already mostly dead. You're this rough tough cowboy outlaw bronc rider who's done a bunch of dangerous stuff, but have you ever really taken a risk?"

She continued to speak gently. "Nothing is permanent, Jesse. Everything passes. That's what you're afraid of, the passing. So you don't get involved. I understand that. But when I'm with you, I'm not afraid."

"Why?"

"Trust. I want to get close to you quickly, to experience as much of you as I can before it's gone."

"What's gone?"

"You, me, it, us. I could die tomorrow. I could die right now, in the next ten seconds. It happens. We know that. My brother and Zack were younger than I am. If I died before you, then all your arguments are invalid."

In that moment, as the words left her lips and the sweet scent of crushed lilac and Holly Marie came to his senses, he knew certainly that he couldn't live without this woman as long as he believed she wanted him. The dark places in his mind filled with light. An enormous spine-bending burden lifted and ceased to exist. "You are a silver-tongued devil…" He reached into his pocket and took out a ring and placed it in her palm. "I love you." She held the ring to the firelight. An opera of dazzling facets sparkled as his heart-powered mouth began to babble. "It's an antique…platinum…from the twenties. The blue on the sides are sapphires, kinda like your eyes sometimes…and the rest are…little diamond chips around the…the big one, the huge one, the monster." Then he started to laugh at himself. "Everything loses its meaning without you…and I want to ask you to marry me."

"When?"

"When get married?"

"When do you want to ask me?"

He laughed. "Now. I'm asking you now."

"Asking me what?"

"Will you marry me?"

She dropped her eyes and said, "Jesse, I would like more than anything in the world to be able to say yes. But I can't. I can't turn off my desire to have a child. I want it so much. It would be a compromise I know I couldn't live with."

"I've thought about it. A lot. I've been stuck in a rut for so long it's come to seem normal. I'd forgotten what it's like to have a new thought, a new feeling, see things in a different way. You've made me realize that. So I'm turning loose all my old rules and beliefs. I want to start out clean and new with you. I just want to see where you take me. Please be my wife."

"You mean that? You'd be happy about being a daddy?"

"Yes, ma'am."

"Then I'd be happy and proud to be your wife. But first you have to ask Bear."

"Okay. I'll ask Bear."

"I'm serious. You have to ask Bear." It was something she'd thought about ever since she first knew what it meant to be female, a man asking her daddy for her hand in marriage. "Jesse, this is the most beautiful ring. She held it between her thumb and forefinger. He took it and slipped it on her finger. She held her hand to the light and whispered, "A perfect fit. I can feel the love in it. Do you know whose it was?"

"No. There were three I liked. All different but from the same era. I closed my eyes and had the man put each one separately in my hand. I just held them. This one said take me and when I opened my eyes, it was the one I liked the best." He took her in his arms and eased her down to the thick rug and nuzzled his lips in the fragrant softness under her hair. Her pale arms laced around his neck, she slid her leg between his knees and said, "You're a Goofy-head."

"Are you really gonna be my wife?" he whispered in her ear.

She pushed her lips to his mouth. "Yes," she murmured.

79

High Plains High

Bear was putting the fluff to the gray's bedding with a rake. Jesse had his arms hung across the back of the mare, his fingers absently massaging her side. "So, Bear, this may not be the best news you've ever heard. Hopefully, it won't be the worst. But if it would be about halfway tolerable for you and Ruby…I would like to ask Holly to marry me. I love her more than I can say. I'll take real good care of her, the best I can in every way."

Bear looked slapped. He leaned on the rake as he absorbed what he'd just heard. A huge grin began to spread across his bright face till his teeth sparkled in the morning Colorado light. He laughed and said, "Hey. That's great. I know she loves you. We all do." They came together and Bear locked his bear arms around Jesse in a bear hug.

An hour later they were all sitting on the porch in the purple of the evening admiring the ring and talking about a wedding.

80

Larry's Porch

It was Holly's idea to marry in the place where they met. There were still a few hours before the ceremony. Larry and a band of outlaws sat with Jesse on the bunkhouse porch torturing him. Larry glanced at a pickup coming at the far end of the drive. The truck jerked forward then stopped, then jerked forward again, meandering from one side of the road to the other as it made its way toward them. As it got close enough to identify its occupants, one could see arms waving wildly and big upper body movement on the part of the passenger. Larry said, "Oh, shit. I don't believe it. That crazy bastard…" He stood shaking his head and laughed.

"What?" said Jesse.

"Fred Langston. This guy is something else. He's got a mechanical arm and leg. No foot. He carves his own pegs. He drives a tractor. Takes a truck completely apart and puts it back together. He can climb a ladder faster than a fireman. Cat is his girlfriend. She's blind. Can't see a damn thing. He's got her driving that truck."

Just then the truck swerved and came to a cushioned halt against a yielding scrub oak. They were too far to hear but when they got out to switch places, it was clear they were laughing hard. Fred backed the truck out of the bush, drove up to the house and left Cat to go in on her own while he marched his particular mechanical leg-swinging gait to the bunkhouse porch and smiled at the men laughing and said, "What?"

Someone handed him a beer and asked if he wanted a shot of tequila to wash it down. Fred used his prosthetic hook to pop the can and replied, "Oh, my God. If I have a shot of that, it'll make me want to bring back stuff I never even stole."

When someone asked what the hell he was doing having a blind woman drive his truck, he scratched a cheek constantly furred with a white stubble and said, "She usually does pretty good, but we got to laughing. You know, most times I forget she's blind. I mean, she doesn't act like someone who's blind. I saw a woman one day showing her photographs and Cat just stood there like she was seeing them. I don't know what the hell I was thinking of, but one time I asked her if she didn't think I ought to change a light bulb that was burnt out. She said, 'I don't give a damn if you change the light bulb, I'm in the dark all the time anyway.' Hell, I like her though. I tell her I'm young and good lookin'."

Larry had gotten hold of a cream-colored carriage from a friend who showed driving horses. It was fittingly elegant, festooned with flowers artfully applied by volunteers led by Larry's wife, Rosie. Larry had hitched one of his golden Belgians to carry the bride and her father to the congregation that spilled from the porch to the grassy knoll around it. Jesse and his best man, Larry, looked like the Earp boys in their black suits and white shirts as they waited for the carriage to appear.

A halo of light at the end of a beam lancing through the trees outlined the carriage coming over the rise. The big Belgian, proud of his task, stepped out smartly and headed down the gentle green slope to the side of the porch. A plain but pretty woman with long dark hair and drooping eyelids filled the air with enchantment from her violin. Holly's beauty always took Jesse by surprise. A fairytale princess at her father's hand, she descended from the carriage. Jesse's heart pounded the air from his lungs. She was all in pale, dusty beige like white gone old. A broad-brimmed straw hat, the veil sashed with silk at her neck. Behind the symbol of concealment, he saw her eyes blaze like diamonds in the sun and the pink of her lips smiling softly in the shadow. He knew the flowing folds of her dress cloaked a tumultuous heart. Bear brought her forward in the rustle and scent of silk and civet, a living portrait of feminine elegance, grace, and beauty.

When he heard her say I do, a flood of tears rushed to the rims of his eyes. He bit his lip to lock them there.

They spent the night in each other's arms in one of the cabins, whispering child things and declarations of passion. The next morning, Larry drove them down to Colorado Springs, put them in his twin-engine Cessna, flew them to San Francisco, bought them lunch at an Italian place near the wharf, then kissed them goodbye, flew back to Colorado, and rode four horses before walking up to the house, with his cell phone to his ear, to wash his face for supper.

81

The City by the Bay

They walked the hills, rode the cable cars, and climbed the broad
gray steps to the Fairmont Hotel. They tumbled on the bed
next to a cart with caviar, smoked salmon, triangles of toast, lemon
slices, bits of eggs, chopped onions, and black pepper. They clinked
their glasses and emptied them and kissed each other's lips wet with
wine. She took the bottle and laughed wantonly as the champagne
foamed over the rim of her glass and onto the rings on her fingers.
She flicked her tongue over the platinum and diamonds and refilled
Jesse's glass. She reached her champagne hand to his face and slipped
a finger in his mouth and poking at the inside of his cheek, said,
"You're a Moolie Monster."

"What's a Moolie Monster?"

"You are." She was naked now, before him. And once again, as if
he'd never seen her, he was struck by the mystery of her, the wanton
sensuality. Her beauty seemed to recreate itself right before his eyes
each time he looked at her and snare him heart and soul.

He slipped his hand around the soft slender column of her neck. "I never get used to looking at you. I feel I have this great treasure in knowing that all I have to do is turn my head and I'll see that carved nose and those smoky eyes." Suddenly amused, he chuckled.

"What?"

"I was just thinking that sometimes I think that because I love you, I should be able to sing...perfectly." He reached to touch her skin.

They flowed, melting into each other, smelling and tasting the beauty, drinking the spilling love running like a river through the glory of it all. In a hoarse whisper, she said, "Yes, Jesse, yes...come to me now...take me now." Explosive ribbons of his seed swam in her juices, circled slowly, and stayed to see what might occur.

82
Back at the Ranch

Abbie was waiting at the gate watching the passengers disembark. Jesse saw her coming forward, all fluffed hair, wide smile, and bright-lit eyes. "Hey, Boss," she said, going right past him to Holly who dropped her bags to free her arms for the embrace she knew was coming. "Howdy, Mrs. Burrell. You look great. How does it feel? You look great too, Jesse." She grabbed one of Holly's duffel bags and slung it on her shoulder.

"It feels wonderful. It's so good to see you."

"Thanks. I hope you got a lot of pictures."

Noon was yet to strike when they unloaded the truck midst fussing dogs and congratulations from Ricardo. Mason came shyly forward saying congratulations. Holly climbed the porch steps carrying the last bag. Jesse took it, set it down with the rest and swept her off her feet into his arms. He carried her into the house, kissed her, and set her on her feet. "Welcome home. This is your house.

Make any changes you want. Just don't tell me you want to start with a bulldozer."

———◦———

Kevin and Carley Bradley had gotten together with Doc Nalls and Helen to put together a big-time, Texas shindig at the Bradley's baronial estate to celebrate the marriage of Jesse and Holly.

On a sultry summer night under a sequined sky with a quarter moon, a multitude of lanterns lit the revelers on the wide lawn. While a whole pig spiraled on a spit, strolling mariachis strummed wailing love songs in the night. Half the hill country had turned up. Judge Lamar and his wife Leona, ropers, doctors, lawyers, cutters, cowhands and ranchers, accountants and polo players, students, artists, feed merchants and Texas rangers, Digger and Brantley, had come to see the woman from Colorado. She danced with the men and charmed even the most brittle and envious of the women. Jesse was a proud and happy man. A dream he'd never dared to dream had come true.

83

A Pregnancy in Progress

Holly had been riding the mare, San Mamacita, every day for weeks. They'd cut a bunch. Holly could now ride into a herd like a pro. Her innate elegance combined with the soft feel and flowing balance of a ballerina was a thing of beauty. Jesse delighted in it. A bond of deep feeling had formed between her and the mare in foal. Though she rode several other horses learning to turn-back and hold the herd, she'd come to think of Mamacita as her own and looked after her needs with the zeal of a lioness minding her cubs. Jesse was in the arena working the black colt as she finished bathing the sweated mare. Slick and round, she had seven months to go; two before beginning to swell. She was burnished bronze as Holly led her to the sun to dry. She stood at the mare's head and stroked her face in the way that Jesse did and whispered woman things that only she could hear.

84

They spun along the I-10 at eighty. Holly said, "What do you think about the idea of creating a therapeutic riding program for handicapped people?" She went on with great knowledge of its psychological and physical benefits. When he said he thought it was a good idea, she launched into the telling of a clearly thought-out plan. What its objectives should be, what it would take to get it going, the licenses, the affiliations that could be made with the local hospital, the assistance they could get from Walter being on the board, and Kevin with all his friends. "And Helen and Carley, they'd love to be involved in something as wonderful as that, don't you think?"

"Yeah," he said, impressed with how much thought she'd put into it.

"Oh, and we'd probably have to get at least three really quiet old horses." She raised her eyebrows enthusiastically asking for his input.

"Yeah, we can. We could do that." He shook his head as if to recover from a blow and laughed.

"What?"

He laughed. "Nothing...you just amaze me. I think it's a great idea."

"I've been thinking about it ever since we did the benefit for the cystic fibrosis kids. That was so rewarding."

At the stoplight before the entrance to Home Supply, Holly absently turned to look out the window and said, "Cool car."

Jesse leaned forward to look around her at the Pre-owned Cars of Distinction lot and spotted the candy-apple red 1976 Mustang convertible. Cherry and indeed, cool. It was perched on a ramp like a rocket ready for launching. The light turned green, the Mustang stayed still while Jesse drove on.

They picked out the new kitchen floor at Home Supply and then stopped at Alex Goland's to take care of business about the video, which was selling extremely well. Alex showed them an accounting of what was going where, including Bear and Holly's percentage. Jesse said, "Looks like we could afford to take you to lunch, come on."

While they dined on blistering Tex-Mex cuisine that would cause a gorilla to reach for Mylanta, Alex told of his sister's daughter with multiple sclerosis and its devastating effect on the family. Jesse brought up Holly's idea for a therapeutic riding program. Alex responded with enthusiastic encouragement and a willingness to help.

———※———

Holly had been engrossed in the kitchen rehab and was cleaning up when she heard the dually pull in. Jesse came in and admired the work. He put his arm around her, "It looks like a magazine. Come on outside, I want to show you something."

He opened the screen door and let her walk out in front of him. She stopped as the door closed behind them. At the foot of the steps right in front of the house was the gleaming red Mustang convertible, as yet uncoated with ranch dust. She said, "That's the car we saw in the lot."

"Yeah, it is…"

"What's it doing here?" she asked, "Whose is it?"

He slipped his arm around her waist and whispered in her neck. "Yours."

85

The Laundry Room

In the yellow afternoon light, an iridescent glow about her face and naked arms, Holly fed the machine in the laundry room at the back of the house. She wore wide-legged cut-offs, droopy red anklets, and dirty white running shoes.

Suddenly, he was behind her, pressing against her as she arched over the machine. His arm around her waist, she straightened up. He spoke into the back of her neck, "All you need is a bamboo pole and a can of worms." She leaned into him and he smelled the apple-sweet willingness rising in the heat. He freed the brass buttons at the bib-top and the overalls pooled at her feet.

A half-hour later, he was juggling turkey, mustard, bread, and beer as he kicked the fridge shut and set the fixings on the counter. She turned him around and spoke with the huskiness of sex still in her voice, "I like it when we make love like that. Unplanned. Not in bed."

"Yeah, we need to try it in a restaurant. Or a mattress store. You want tomato on yours?"

"Or in Kevin and Carley's bathroom while there's a party going on. Yes, please. Mustard...and mayo."

He took her in his arms and looked in her eyes. Emotion had risen unannounced and moistened his eyes. It seemed he had something to say but not the skill or means.

86

Bombproof Horses and Red Tape

Kevin had about as much chance as a snowball in hell when Holly invited him to lunch at the Mexican place in Kerrville. "It's not just teaching handicapped people to ride horses. I've seen miracles occur in Colorado. It works not only on a physical level, but psychologically as well. They spend most of their lives in wheelchairs looking up at the world. Imagine the sense of self-esteem they experience on the back of a horse. They're suddenly nine feet tall and they're doing something not everyone can do. With each step the horse takes, he creates a changing need for balance. The rider has to constantly adjust. It improves their sense of balance with no conscious effort. And instead of being in a stuffy clinical environment with white coats, they're out in the air with horses and hay. Kevin, this is an opportunity to do something so worthwhile for people who suffer terribly. And I've never heard one of them complain. Ever."

Her speech had arrested the motion of his arm in mid-delivery of a Margarita from the table to his lips. His jaw had gone slack, his brow raised in awe. When she paused, he snapped to and said, "Holly Marie, you need to run for governor…and I'll damn sure back you."

Jesse worked three horses culled from twenty-odd until he was certain they would remain unflinching under a surprise attack by a Mongol horde in a lightning storm. One was a big hammer-headed, kind-faced dun. Another was a small, round, mutton-withered old gray. Jesse's favorite was a seventeen-hand Clydesdale giant, donated by a friend of the Anheuser-Busch family. A magnificent beast, gentle as a lamb, with a foot that could cover a trash can. Dense, long, white hair feathered his fetlocks and a bright white blaze ran between soft brown eyes. His name was Mr. Bud.

Abbie actually leaped when Holly first revealed her thoughts about a therapeutic riding program. Abbie told Holly that she and Mason would be volunteers. They'd learn CPR at the fire station and take whatever classes were necessary to comply with licensing and insurance requirements. They could design T-shirts with logos for the program, and on and on she went with recommendations extending in all directions.

She helped Holly send faxes, fill out forms, and mail stuff. She rode the horses, did all the barn work she'd always done, shared her woman stories with Holly, sought her advice, and with diminishing relish, attended the university.

87

San Mamacita Takes Holly for a Ride

It was a small cutting, but the competition was keen. Holly's face had the sheen of a tallow candle. She sat the polished mare tall and straight staring at the herd as if they were lions. Jesse, beside her on a turnback horse, leaned toward her and said, "Just have fun. You know what to do and so does she. Just get inside of her, cut a cow, and let her go to work." Holly nodded her head stiffly. He rubbed his hand between her shoulder blades. "Shrug your shoulders and wiggle your toes. Go on."

The announcer welcomed her to the sport and declared the good fortune of Jesse Burrell to have won such a prize as Holly for his wife. The pretty face, a frozen mask, managed to rearrange itself with a smile of appreciation as she heard the announcer ask the audience to make her feel at home and the applause that followed. Then she moved from poise into tranquil harmony with the task. Her concentration absolute, and making no mistakes, she put in a run that was near to perfect. Twenty minutes later she was declared the winner of her class. First was the whooping and whistling then the pats on the back and a barrage of congratulations till her cheeks ached with smiling and saying thank you. In Jesse's arms, her eyes filled with tears as she said, "I've never won anything in my life. Thank you, Moolie."

"You're welcome, but you did it."

"Mamacita did it."

"You helped her, you didn't get in her way. That's a lot easier said than done." He kissed her and spoke quietly into her mouth. "I'm proud of you."

88

News

The night was as black as the inside of a rubber boot. The owls were silent. The dogs lay still in the barn, bedded in shavings. A small yellow glow from the barn was dimmed by mist. A pitcher of iced tea sat on the rough table between them. Strains of Bach came faintly from the house. It was the end of a long exciting day, well past bedtime, but neither felt like sleep.

A scratching match flared in her hand. She held it to a candle in a glass on the table. "It's too dark. I want to see your face."

He reached out and touched her hand. "I was so proud of you today."

For a time, silence stood between them. Even the candle flame was still. When she spoke, her voice was soft, almost distant. "Jesse, there was a mommy on a mommy in that arena today."

She heard him draw in a breath and let it out with a soft chuckle. Then as one might react in awe to the stunning sight of a whale exploding from the surface of the sea, he said, "Oh, wow!" He got out of his chair and knelt between her legs, taking her hands in his. "Oh…wow," he said again. Then he placed her hands around his waist and took her in his arms. He saw in her face glowing like a lantern the anticipation of his response. "Man…Holly…God…" His eyes began to fill with tears as realization made its way through shock.

"Are you happy?" She wanted to know, to hear it.

"Yes, I am. I am happy."

"You're sure?"

"I'm sure." He looked in her eyes and laughed. "You're a mommy."

Then in a little girl's playful voice, she said, "And you're a daddy."

He laughed again and put his head against her stomach. "Hello in there. What's going on? Hello…?" Then he looked up at her and asked, "When did you find out?"

"I did a home test this morning. But I've known since it happened."

"When?"

"On our honeymoon, at the Fairmont."

"How could you know?"

"I could feel it."

He stood and brought her to her feet. Pressing against her, holding tight, he told her he loved her, and then led her into the house.

——⬥——

Walter set them up with an obstetrician whose appearance, he warned, belied his personality and skill. Dr. Elliot Adashek had the pallor of a mortician who had himself already joined the choir invisible. His gray skin draped on a spare frame seemingly devoid of flesh and possessing only enough muscle to provide mobility. He was, however, warm and friendly in nature, meticulously scrubbed, and stylishly attired. He wore cologne pleasing to the nose. Holly liked him immediately. Jesse called him "the Count," and went about the house saying, "Good evenink. Velcome to my office."

89

The Horse as Healer

Holly and her troops triumphed over bureaucracy, fatigue, and negativity to emerge with a licensed, modestly funded, excellently staffed, therapeutic riding program. Flags, balloons, music, and lunch launched the festive first day for Miracles Unlimited. Eight eager clients, children from four years to eighteen, were ready to begin. Anxious parents hovered. Newspapers, radio, and TV journalists had arrived. Walter and Helen Nalls, Kevin and Carley Bradley, most of the local medical community, polo people, ranchers and lawyers and local politicians, the mayor, and Judge Lamar were all in attendance. Holly was everywhere at once, smiling, bowing, shaking hands, explaining how the therapy works, and photographing everything.

Kelly Dale had brought her twelve-year-old son. Wiley'd been dealt a rough hand at birth. Afflicted with cerebral palsy, he listed starboard in a wheelchair, his mouth open, head lolling to one side moving in a small circle as if trying to right itself. His eyes were

kind and soft under a brow that seemed to be waiting for an answer
to a question unasked.

The volunteer staff wore white T-shirts bearing the Miracles
Unlimited logo. Abbie and a therapist named Charlie, who could
flip through the air as if the earth were a trampoline, helped eager
Wiley to his unwilling feet. A system of braces in stainless steel and
leather straps encircled his waist and supported his legs with rods
that ran to his ankles, hinged at knees and hips. Wiley's mom
explained that he had never been near a horse. She was real nervous
about it. Wiley was not. As they got him close to the old round
gray, now known as Casper, an energy began to emanate from the
boy. His face glowed with desire reaching out to connect with the
horse. It seemed as if he might speak. Instead a sound of delight
completely his own came from his lips as his arms stretched to
touch the gray. His hand came in contact with the warm shoulder
and moved up to the neck. His mother watched, her lip caught
between her teeth. As Wiley stroked, he became consumed with a
rapture that caused him to tremble. The sounds of joy he made
seemed a safeguard to keep him from exploding. His face contorted
into a smile that would turn winter into spring. His mother drew in
a gasp of air and clamped her hand to her mouth. Tears flooded her
eyes as she looked for someone to lean on. Jesse saw and came
quickly to her side. He put his arm around her shoulder. She sobbed
into her hand and said, "He's twelve years old, and that's the first
time I've ever seen him smile...ever."

———≼⊹≽———

The fan spun above them stirring the warm night. Jesse inhaled
through the strands of her hair across his face. "You did it. You
got her done. When I saw Wiley smile that incredible smile and wrap
himself around old gray...and saw his momma crying, I felt..." He
took an emotional breath in and blew it out. "I felt like I was worth a
little something...like we had done a good thing." He put his lips to

her ear. "You gave me the opportunity to feel that. It meant more to me than I can tell you. Thank you, my beautiful woman."

She put her slender fingertips to his cheek and said, "It never would have happened without you."

90

Portrait of a Baby

Alone in the bathroom, she stood in profile before the mirror measuring the making, stroking her belly, caressing the child within, seeing breasts filling. Jesse had confirmed she was beginning to swell. Her eyes appeared to have seen something wonderfully radiant and borrowed a brilliance that lived in them now.

She had turned off the light before opening the door and stood there with a candle in her hand, a phantom image from another time, a world of coaches and horses, mansions on country estates, rustling gowns, lounging hounds, and string quartets. A tortoise comb held her hair up-swept, wayward wisps curling along her ears and down the length of her neck to the band of her gown. The pale pink creamy fullness of her was showing through. In one smooth move she was cross-legged on the bed with the candle placed on the table. A small, flat tin was in her hand. She wore her mysterious smile as she fondled the tin, then opened it and held it out for him to see. "They're colored crayons. You can dip them in water and paint with them. We can paint our bodies. They're from France."

" All right!" he laughed. "What a cool idea." A thought came instantly. "Can I go first?"

"Okay. There's a glass of water right there." He knelt in front of her and took her face in his hands. He touched his lips to hers and felt her breath. He reached down to the hem of her gown and lifted it slowly as she raised her arms to allow passage over her head. She shook her hair across her shoulders and lay back, pale silk and cream and blood beneath. He wet the green one first and touched it to her skin to the right of her navel and moved it in a curving line. "Don't look till I'm done."

Nearly an hour had passed when he asked if she'd fallen asleep. She hummed a no. He applied some final strokes and paused to appraise his work before declaring it done. Then he took her by the hand, told her to shut her eyes, and led her to the antique mirror on the wall of their bedroom. He stood naked beside her. "Okay. You can open your eyes."

She looked bewildered before the words came to her lips. "Jesse...it's beautiful...I didn't know you could do this..."

"Neither did I," he laughed.

The curving form of a baby enwombed was perfectly drawn on her belly and around it a wreath of green leaves on woven vines with two tendrils emerging at the top and growing up one to each breast where flowers bloomed. A rose on the right, a sunflower on the left, nipples as painted pistils. And just above the delta at the joining of her legs were four pink flowers and little green leaves.

"Your turn." He said.

"Maybe tomorrow." She reached up her arms, a look of rut in her eyes, and wiggled her fingers to draw him to her. He felt her painted skin against his own as her arms pulled him in. He moved down her body till his mouth was at the baby and his hands caressed a rose and a sunflower, then slid to the dampness of the delta where the orchid opened crimson and purple and engulfed him in its mystery.

He was always first awake and felt like a kid getting away with something to watch her sleep. Each breath blowing a wisp of hair, away and back. She had her own way of warring with bedding, twisting sheets and slinging pillows. Almost always on her stomach, one hand in her groin, the other slung, a long bent leg sticking out and half a buttock bare. She gave the impression of a mummy that had been granted a brief return to life and, midway through escaping her wrapping, had grown exhausted and fallen asleep. He kissed the plump mellow melon of her rump as he reached to press the hollow just above. She groaned and, stretching long and yawning, turned.

Water steamed over them. The baby and the painted garden on her flesh washed away in rainbow rivers flowing down her thighs as he knelt in the shower sliding the soap over her skin and pressing his cheek to her belly, her fingers in his hair.

He took her by the hand and led her to the porch. Before they stepped through the door, he told her to close her eyes. "What now?" She said.

It was a rocking chair. A hand-done, intricate weaving of bent willow with thick quilted cushions on the seat and tied with bows to the back. "It's a momma's chair. You can sit and rock-a-bye-baby in your arms." She smiled and closed her eyes as she settled her head against the back. He sat on the rail and watched her. All doubt, all fear, had vanished as if it had never been. There was something private and female in this state that she was in, a harmony between temperament and circumstance, a special warming joy distinctly hers.

293

91

Falling Leaves

He rode out the back gate on a long loose rein, his shadow riding before him lay long and thin upon the patchy ground, the colt completely at ease but ever alert. He could think of little else but how this horse seemed to have been sent to him by some design beyond his understanding. With a talented horse, bred to the task, it would normally take twice as long to get to where Soot was now. He reached out and stroked the sleek black neck.

The sun had fallen and the blue gauze of evening settled over the hills. The dark outline of the cottonwood stood against the hammered sky more like the ghost of a tree than the actual thing. He stood down, hobbled the colt and sat against the tree. He closed his eyes. A hissing rub of branches came to his ears on a soft breeze.

"Did you send me this colt? I like to think of it that way."

He opened his eyes and looked up. A leaf loosed its grip and spiraled down between his feet. He picked it up and brought it to his lips, then put it in the pocket of his shirt.

Holly stood in San Mamacita's stall talking to the mare about the relative sizes of their burdened bellies. She had a towel in her hand stroking the brilliant copper skin, when Jesse rode in. He was still ten feet away when he declared, "You smell good." A soft cotton dress, blue with tiny flowers, flowed about her ankles above deerskin moccasins closed with a silver concho. Her hair hung in a big, loose braid.

When he finished putting the colt away, he turned to find her. She was gone. He called her name. Walking the length of the barn he called again. He walked out back to the great cottonwood where Damien's childhood swing hung and called once more.

A soft voice came eerily out of the tree above his head, saying, "Shhh."

He looked up to see her pale legs dangling from a stout limb near the top of the tree. "What in the hell are you doing? You are a pregnant woman. You trying to kill yourself? Stay right there. I'm coming up."

All the clamber up the tree, he muttered about having married a lunatic, thinks she's a damn chimpanzee. He finally got to her and fixed himself in a notch and began to scold her again. She put her finger to his lips and told him to hush and listen to the night. Moonlight fell upon her through the leafage in strands of silver-blue, imparting to her tranquil face a bloodless look of marble. She turned her eyes to him and smiled. And for a moment he thought he could see inside of her, the shape of her thoughts, the industry of her woman's nature forming bones and brewing blood. He placed the flat of his palm against the fullness under her dress as if to feel the turnings of the wheels.

92

Fort Worth, Look Out

A cold, mizzling rain was falling in the dim just before dawn as the last of the horses clambered into the trailer. Chauncy's neckbell tinkled as he hopped in and found his place near Soot. Jesse made a final tour around the truck and trailer, checking doors and the hitch. He got behind the wheel and buckled in. Abbie in the back seat nestled among a pile of jackets, pillows, and down coats, squirmed with excitement. They were going to Fort Worth to win The Futurity. Holly reached over and touched the back of his hand on the gear shifter and smiled. It penetrated his heart. He brought the back of her hand to his lips and kissed the pale blue highways of blood beneath the see-through skin and asked if she'd pour him a coffee.

———◦◦◦———

On the interstate at seventy miles an hour, he passed a familiar road sign. Seeing it triggered memories of driving home last year a hollow man, as empty as a straw, with little purpose and frail desire. Now his business was blooming, his soul enriched by the miracle of Miracles Unlimited, and most important of all, he had found the love of his life. He put his eyes on her beside him in the full blossoming of motherhood and felt a flush of heat in his loins.

"What?" she said.

"Nothing," he answered, and ran the flat of his palm softly over her face.

A quarter-mile behind them a black muscle car doing at least eighty-five miles per hour weaved recklessly in and out of lanes. A red car of the same type was chasing the black car and doing at least ninety. Each car packed four teenagers. Jesse was checking his mirrors constantly. The black car roared up on his left side and had to brake hard for the vehicle ahead. The young driver attempted the impossible, swerving hard right and cutting right in front of Jesse. Forced to brake again, the car was thrown into a sideways skid. Jesse had no room to maneuver. He hit his brake swerving right onto the shoulder as another car plowed into the rear of Jesse's trailer.

Chaos ensued. Traffic at a halt. Six vehicles wrecked. Jesse's rig banged but functional. Two horses were tied outside the trailer. Jesse led Soot out of the trailer on three legs. The left hind leg would barely touch the ground. Chauncy followed.

Holly and Abbie watched in stunned silence as Jesse examined the black colt.

In the stabling area at the Will Rogers Coliseum, Soot stood in a stall, the hind leg cocked, toe lightly touching the ground. Jesse, Holly, and Abbie stood in mute attendance. Dr. Dale Schmidt, a practitioner of equine chiropractic and veterinary medicine palpated the colt's spine. "He's got a vertebrae wrenched out of place causing a spasm in his loin. I'll try some manipulation, see if we can't move it back. Then I'll place some acupuncture needles to control the inflammation and pain. When I'm done, run cold water over his back for twenty minutes and give him two grams of bute. Then all we can do is see what morning brings and go from there.

298

———◦✦◦———

They came from the corners of the country, and a handful from Europe and Asia. Most though were Texans. It was a glamorous roundup of coifed hair, diamonds, gold and silver, bosoms in silk, and feet in dead reptiles wearing silver spurs under miles of denim and felt.

Cutting had come a distance from its origin on dusty pasturelands in cactus and scrub under blazing suns and drenching rains. But the men and women who really were the lifeblood of the sport were still the cowboys, the dawn-till-dusk, down-in-the-dirt men and women who love horses and working livestock, who would every now and then find themselves with a taste for silver and silk, and a want to gather with friends and see who had the better horse.

Jesse rode the colt through the solemn corridors and under the archway into the loping pen behind the judges' stands. The air was hushed and serious. The dominant sound, hoofbeats muffled in the sand. Holly, Abbie, and Dr. Dale walked beside him. When the colt came up on his toes for a good gander around, Jesse nudged him forward. Holly and Abbie found the portable steps that took them from the arena floor to the box seats. They sat and watched the colt move into a trot and join the traffic circling the pen to the left. Dr. Dale watched from the side.

Thirty-odd horses were walking, trotting, mostly loping, to take the edge off and get them relaxed enough to concentrate on the job. Jesse trotted three circles and then rode over to Dr. Dale. "What do you think?"

"He looks good. How does he feel?"

"Good."

"I know you don't want to hear this, Jesse, but I've got to tell you. If he injures himself again, it could jeopardize his future both as an athlete and as a breeding stallion."

"I hear ya, Doc."

Jesse turned the colt and joined the traffic at a lope. The
colt's neck soon began to soften and his stride evened out. He
finished a circle and rode over to the working area entrance at the
end of the row of judges' stands. He dropped his reins in a loop
across the colt's neck and leaned forward to study the herd and
watch the competition.

The cattle were young, quick and healthy. He spotted two or
three he'd try to avoid. They were high-headed, squirrely looking,
not involved in the solace of the herd. They could be runners, rather
than wanting to get down in front of a horse and try to get by him.

There were three horses to go before him. He felt a touch at his
leg. Holly was looking up at him. He bent down to kiss her. She
whispered against his lips, "Go get 'em, Jesse." She ran her hand
under his chaps and tickled his thigh.

"Thanks," he said.

Thirteen minutes later, he took three deep breaths, blew the last
one out, and moved toward the herd, loosening his shoulders. He
went deep into the herd and cut his first cow. Soot was keen and
sure, even patient as he waited, confident, quivering, to see what the
cow would try next. When it moved, he was right in its face. He
appeared as a lustrous black shadow darting here and there without
effort or sound, a graceful manifestation not of this earth but
ephemeral and spirit-like, capable of vanishing instantly.

The buzzer put an end to his defeat of the third cow. He rode
out of the herd to an eruption of applause. Ten minutes later, it was
announced they had won the first go-round. Out of six hundred
and fifty-three horses, Soot and Jesse were judged to have performed the best. They'd now be among the two hundred and forty
horses going into the second go-round.

He wanted more than anything to simply head off with Holly
and Abbie, have a quiet dinner as if nothing had happened, and
speak not one word about it. Instead, he was set upon like he was
one of the Beatles in the sixties. He smiled and said thank you a
hundred times.

Holly had jumped on the phone to Bear and Ruby who let out a "yeow" and a "way to go" loud enough for Jesse to hear six feet from the phone. He got on and said thank you one more time and grinned as he snaked his arm around Holly standing there.

Back in the stall, Holly and Abbie worked brushes and towels to polish the lustrous colt. Jesse stroked the sleek neck as Dr. Dale pressed fingers along the colt's spine and hip. "There's some instability right here. Let's see what we can do." He began to make an adjustment on the colt.

The second go-round wasn't much different from the first. Jesse Burrell and the black colt destroyed the competition, leaving the owners and riders of two hundred and thirty-nine horses thinking they might just as well have remained abed. Again, Jesse felt that overwhelming desire to be off alone. To not speak of the glowing success as if to deny its reality. When Holly took him in her arms, she knew and spoke not a word. She held him with increasing pressure until she felt him come to her and begin to breathe in synchrony with her. They looked into each other's eyes for a brief moment and then let go. Abbie was waiting for her turn. She looked up at Jesse and said, "What else? I didn't expect anything else."

Bobby Hunt, a rival cutter, walked up. "Jesse, if I'd known what you had, I'd a stayed in bed. Congratulations, pard. Two down."

Almost six hundred horses had been excused from further competition when the sixty remaining began to warm up for the semifinals. The living greats, with several hundreds of years of experience riding with them, were all there with super colts. There was an undercurrent of attention on Jesse's colt as he rode into the warm-up area. They all knew this was the one to beat. But no one got it done. Not that day.

For only the third time in the history of the event, one horse would be going into the finals having won all three preliminary go-rounds. And this time it was Soot— the urchin, the mutt, lacking any known royal lineage, indeed the progeny of dubious parentage, devoid of any documentation of age or legitimacy.

Against the cold December night, Jesse wore a heavy, wool mackinaw that looked like it came out of an old Northwest lumber camp. He had on his good Black Gold hat, brushed clean. He walked down the barn aisle toward the colt's stall. In about two-and-a-half hours, he'd be riding for the gold. Soot raised his nose as if to search him out in the air. Holly and Abbie with brushes and towels fussed around the colt like court attendants at a coronation. Charlie the therapist and Mason had arrived and hovered, trying not to get in the way. Abbie would find no end to the brushing of Soot's mane and tail. He stood alert and calm, a splendid work of God's art, as breathing black marble with a lustrous glow that came from within.

Chauncy stood aloof in the corner, the silent faithful companion, proud of his service. Holly, in spite of her belly, had polished his hooves. Mason and Abbie had put the dull rich sheen to the leather and rubbed the silver conchos to a bright shine. Jesse placed the green and white Navajo blanket on the horse's back then swung the saddle up and wiggled it into its fit. He pulled the cinch up snug but not tight. He ran his hand along the sleek neck and combed his fingers through the thick forelocks that fringed the coal black eyes giving the colt a look of the rascal about him. Holly put the final touch. A dab of Vaseline to the colt's muzzle and around his eyes made him a shining thing.

Twenty horses, the best in the world at three years of age, were about to compete for a big chunk of a quarter of a million dollars. A sober silence kept from being absolute by an undercurrent of guarded murmuring resembling the muted tones of a requiem. The whole of the hill country had come to Fort Worth in support of Jesse and the colt. Mason's mom and dad, Billy Diggs and Kathy Sue had driven down, so had Floyd Cox and a truckload of ropers. Dr. Nalls and Helen with Judge Lamar and his wife Leona had flown in on Kevin and Carley Bradley's private plane. They all sat together in Lamar's box. The judge, with some humor, had gone on nonstop chiding his wife for forcing him to get rid of the soot-colored colt, and bragging about his uncanny eye for horseflesh, at the same time lavishing praise on Jesse for his amazing talent. "He put the spit and rub to him. Nobody else would have even tried." He turned to his wife and shook his head with a tight-lipped grin. "Leona, you cost me a million dollars." She cocked a brow and looking at him out of the corner of her eye, replied, "It's not the first time, cowboy. Besides, I probably saved your life. And darlin', that's worth much more than a million."

The judge laughed big and loud. "You know she's probably right…about me being worth more than a million, that is." Larry Littlefield had come down from Colorado to announce the celebrity fund-raiser and to film a segment for his TV show. And like he said to Jesse, "I come down to see you win this thing, boy."

Though Soot had been the brightest star by far up to this point, all previous scorings were discarded now and this work alone would determine The Futurity champion. Anything could happen, as they all well knew. And no one better than Jesse. Thoughts of last year's tragedy kept trying to poke their way into his brain. He drew in deeply and blew them away on his breath as he watched the behavior of the herd during the last work before his turn to go. The colt was ready, the wildness in him always there. He had his own way of doing things and to ask him to do something he was just fixin' to do on his own was an insult he didn't take kindly. He had a lot of draw to him. He made a cow want to try him. Jesse reminded himself, above all, trust him. Don't panic if he waits a heartbeat longer than you think he should before hurling himself into that explosive turn. He's just having fun letting the cow think she's got a chance.

In the aisle behind the five judges' stands, Jesse nudged him forward at a quick trot and sat him down. One turn-around to the left and one to the right and stop. Drop the reins, stroke his neck, and let him relax. He heard his name called as he headed to the working area. Jesse sat tall and slim in a white shirt, black hat, and cream-colored fringed chaps. He wore a pair of silver-mounted spurs that Holly had ordered handmade especially for the occasion.

The colt was a thing to behold, burnished blackness with the touch of silver sparkling here and there, his front legs from the knees down were wrapped in white. He moved in delicate contact with the earth as if desiring to leave it undisturbed by his passing. His neck long and low as he approached the herd, his ears flicking like antennae, he almost seemed to crouch like a panther stalking.

Jesse knew what he wanted to cut and went after it. The judges like that, a decision to go for a specific cow right from the start. It makes for a higher degree of difficulty and this was no time to play it safe. He was against the best. The scores were high. The only way to win was to let it all hang out. He drove ten head out. The judges could see that he was focused on one cow. If he were to change that focus to another, it would cost him a penalty of five points on his score and certainly the championship. But if he cut it successfully, he would gather points in his favor.

He dropped the colt in front of the one he wanted—a perfect cut, right in the center. Somewhere in the vastness of God's consciousness, in His sense of humor, in the poetry He puts into life, He must have created this particular cow to be the ultimate challenge for this particular horse. It seemed as if the cow and Soot came from the same source that had produced in them a fierce combativeness, the resourcefulness and extreme desire to achieve their end. They seemed inspired by their tasks and the opposition to its accomplishment. The eager heifer seem to say, "If you think you're going to stop me, you got another think coming." The heifer then made a move like a bantamweight.

So sure was the colt of himself, he didn't even hurry; he seemed to take more time than wise, and yet a blur occurred. Just as the cow thought she would make it to the herd, she found in her face the hot blowing breath of Soot. Now savvy to the fact that this was not going to be as easy as she thought, she pulled out every instinct and lightning quick reflex with which she'd been endowed. And at every bone-crunching, muscle-tearing turn the cow found itself staring into a mirror reflecting not herself but the shining black face of the fire-breathing demon glaring her defeat. He began to give her a head start like a boy racing his sister. He'd blow right by her just a little and sink into his melting stop, watching her without turning his head. Then he'd hesitate a millisecond before cracking over his hocks in a hazy arc and cut her off. Jesse could feel the dirt against his foot as a stirrup brushed the ground.

The swelling roar of the crowd reverberated in the rafters of the coliseum. The valiant little heifer had been worn down. Fatigue had taken hold and stopped her dead in her tracks. No cow had ever tried harder. As Jesse lifted his reins placing his right hand at the withers to signal Soot to relax, the audience went to bedlam.

He turned the colt back to the herd and cut his second cow. It wasn't the one he wanted but he was under the pressure of the clock. He had no choice. It was a wild-eyed, high-headed thing that looked like it just might try to leave town rather than get back to the herd or out of sheer frustration, decide to run right through him. One bad move here could cost him the farm. He told himself he had to stay cool, trust this colt. There was something about Soot that made a cow try harder. The cow wanted to run rather than play but Soot cut her off and danced in front of her saying, "Come on Show me what you've got." The cow made a move toward the wall. Soot waited. Way too long. Jesse's heart stopped. He was sure they'd blown it. The crowd quit breathing. When what seemed like an eternity ended with a spine-cracking whirl over his hocks, Jesse thought he heard the sound of bone break. His blood ran cold. He felt himself for a millisecond having to catch up, so quick was the move.

The colt lunged in front of the cow and boxed her in. The cow shuddered and darted toward the herd. Soot waited that agonizing wait, then swept his graceful blur of an arc and blew in her face. He tapped his front feet in the dirt, his nose inches from the ground in front of the cow. The audience roared. Jesse knew he was on the edge. He wanted to quit but it would have meant being back in the herd when the buzzer sounded. He needed to end his run with Soot working a cow, and leave the judges with that image. So he took the risk and stuck it out. At the last second, the cow surrendered and

305

stood trembling in front of the quivering wound spring of a black colt ready to pounce. The buzzer sounded on a perfect portrait. Jesse slowly lifted the reins in his left hand and gently placed the fingertips of his right on the horse's withers, signaling they were done. The colt came out of his crouch to the throbbing roar of tumultuous applause, whistles, and cheers. He bent low and whispered something holy to the colt as he stroked the gleaming neck. He lifted one rein just an inch and Soot turned his face back toward Jesse's knee so he could touch between his eyes. The Will Rogers Coliseum had never heard the sound it heard that night.

Twenty minutes later the announcer voiced the obvious, that Jesse and his colt had won The Futurity.

He talked about the stud colt's lack of pedigree and his awesome ability and said he'd like to be selling tickets to Jesse's front door to folks with mares to be bred. He believed this colt would be the start of a dynasty.

Lamar, in the box with the Nalls and Kevin and Carley, turned to his wife and said, "Hear that? More than a million. Way more than a million." They all laughed and made their way to the arena floor to congratulate Jesse.

Though he felt a rush of emotion, it was a quiet thing. He had always thought that if this moment would ever occur, that he would let loose a yahoo and toss his hat in the air or some such extravagant gesture of joy. But it wasn't that way. He felt humble and quiet and private again. He brought Holly, Abbie, and Mason into the circle while they presented him the trophy and took the photos. He spotted Lamar in the crowd and called him into the circle. Larry Littlefield, microphone in hand, was asking about the horse. Jesse drew Lamar close and introduced him as the man with the golden eye. "He found him…while he was fishing."

Larry said, "Fishing? You didn't pull him out of a lake did you?" He held the microphone to Lamar.

"No, sir. I think he came out of the sky. God made him, I stumbled on him, and Jesse showed him how to become what he is.

It was a match that was meant to be."

Jesse felt a sudden surge of emotion and tipped his head toward the roof and silently said, I love you, Zack. I know you're here.

Larry moved next to Jesse and said, "Any final thoughts, Mr. Jesse?" He held the microphone out.

"Yes, sir. I do have one request. I would like to purchase that first cow we cut and take her home and retire her at my place."

Larry laughed and said, "Just right…just right."

93

The Bounty of Success

He did buy the cow and take her home. Holly called her Moonie. Jesse called her Money. Orders for the video were pouring in faster than they could fill them. Everyone with a promising mare wanted to breed to The Futurity champion. Local TV and radio wanted interviews. He used them to promote their non-profit Miracles Unlimited program by taking Holly with him and having her talk about the benefits of therapeutic riding. The Lazy JB was alive with comings and goings. Abbie had to find them a secretary to help with the increasing volume of work.

She was already in bed when he came still steaming from the shower and squirmed up against her. She'd loosened her hair and let it spread on the pillow. A time of great calm between them had arrived. Their relationship had developed in leaps from one pinnacle to another leaving valleys yet to be explored. He began to talk of his father. How important it was for him to impress ol' Clyde. "I still don't know if I ever did." He chuckled at a thought.

"What?"

"He was a piece a work." He shook his head. "Sometimes he could make John Wayne look like a sissy. He was gonna teach me to swim. So he threw me into a pond. I mean slung me in there. Now I never was one of those kids who took naturally to water. I didn't much care for it. I damn near drowned while he stood there and watched…" He quit breathing. He shook his head and made the sound of air leaving his lungs.

"What happened?"

"I just scrambled and flailed and somehow managed to get to shore."

"What if you hadn't?"

He snorted through a grin. "You want me to tell what I really think?"

"Yes."

"I believe I would've drowned."

"You think your father would've stood there and let you drown?"

"I don't believe he ever considered it as a possibility. He was just teaching his boy to swim."

"Can you swim?"

"Kinda…I'm about halfway handy in the pond up at the creek. Course, I can stand in it." He grinned in the corner of his mouth. "He was a good man, though. A real good man."

"Bear was a great swimmer. He still is. And my brother, wow, he could outrun anything. He won more trophies in high school. My grandmother was crazy about him."

Jesse could see in her eyes the voyage back as she said, "Grandmama," she continued, " always spoke so softly. Always full of love. I miss her so much. I always wanted to be like her. It's so hard having people get dead on you." She laughed at herself and went silent.

There was some need between them to catch up on each other's lives before they met. He moved until her head was cradled in his shoulder and his hand found the splendid fullness of her breast, her nipple swelled between his fingers. He knelt above her and helped her free of the gown. He looked at her with wonder, as a child at a conjurer. "There has never been anything as beautiful as this." He gently placed his hands on her full round belly and stroked the taut apricot skin as tenderly as fingers have the art to do. Then slowly did his hands caress and circle the warm throbbing bloom of her bosom. The moisture flowed and he felt the life within her. "Is it all right?" he asked.

"Yes," she replied as she offered herself. "It's fine."

"I want you so much. You're sure it's okay?"

"He said as long as it feels all right. And it feels just fine." She reached out her arms.

94

Parturition

The morning was damn near as dark as night. Mamacita was due to foal any time. She shifted restlessly as he undid the door to the foaling stall. He began at her head and gently ran his hands over her body. Her shape had reached an extreme of enlargement. The pelvic bones had loosened, her udder had sprung and the yellow waxy colostrum had formed on her teats, all the definitive signs of imminency. Each evening, Ricardo bathed her hindquarters with antiseptic soap, wrapped her tail and made sure the bedding was clean. Most horses deliver at night following a feral heritage. There are fewer predators on the prowl then and by hunting time, a foal can be on its feet ready to flee. Jesse told Ricardo to keep a sharp eye.

After supper that night, he sat with Holly and watched a Batman movie. Then he tucked her into bed and told her he was going to spend the night in Zack's loft. "I think tonight might be her time."

She looked up at him from under the covers and said, "I want to be there. If it's going to happen, you call me, okay?"

"Yep."

"Promise?"

"I will." He kissed her and left.

Jesse laid abed, his senses as near to waking as a junkyard Rottweiler. It was two in the morning when he sensed unrest below. He was out of bed on his way to the door when Ricardo hit the steps. Jesse opened the door.

"The mare, she's coming pronto. Maybe there is some problem."

The barn was lit. The dogs had emerged. Chauncy had assumed a stoic post in the corner of the foaling stall. The mare's hide was darkened with patches of sweat. Jesse placed the flat of his hand on her flank. She turned her head. The big chocolate eyes were rimmed at the top with white, glaring. Wetness gathered in the anxious furrows of her brow.

"Call Holly and fix a bucket of hot water." The words had barely left his lips when she appeared at the doorway sleepy-eyed, bundled in down. "I just told Ricardo to call you."

"How is she doing?"

"She's having a problem." He took her pulse at the jaw and dropped to his knees to check it at her foot. "Her pulse is out of control. Call John on the cell phone and bring it to me."

Holly stood at the mare's head cupping her cheek and wiping her face with a cold cloth. Jesse described the mare as very distressed, shocky, pulse speeding, eyes rolling, gums white. He listened to Dr. John tell him it sounded like she ruptured the artery that feeds the uterus and would bleed to death very quickly. The foal would suffocate. Mamacita shifted her weight, drawing her hind legs under and squatted as if to sit. It was a brief pose before she moved again, dropping her weight weakly to one hind leg and then the other in search of relief. She dropped a shoulder, tentatively, then tightened in spasm as her uterus contracted in a great expulsive effort. Jesse said, "She's fixin' to lie down." Then he listened to the doctor and covered the mouthpiece to tell Holly, "If she wants to lie down, let her."

The mare lowered her shoulder to the ground and flopped on her side with a heavy groan and troubled breathing. Holly went down next to her, murmuring sounds of comfort with a hand against the horse's cheek. Jesse said, "Okay, I got it. Get here quick as you can." He folded the phone.

The mare wasn't down but seconds before she thrashed her legs and struggled in pain to regain her feet. Jesse had added a bottle of glycerin to the bucket of hot water. He put his folded arm to the shoulder in the bucket, dabbed a gob of Vaseline on his fingers and over the back of his hand and watched it disappear under the mare's tail. At shoulder deep, the pressure threatened to paralyze his arm and render fingers useless. Sweat-beads showed on his brow and cheeks. His face twisted shut as he groped to try to discover what was wrong. The mare spasmed again. Jesse bit his lip. "It's wrong. It's all wrong. The head is turned completely back. I can't feel the front legs, they must be folded underneath." He pulled his arm out and plunged it in the bucket working circulation back to his hands. "I'm gonna try to get a hold of the nostrils, see if I can't pull the head around."

He pushed in again while Holly held her head, whispering. The mare tried to contract again but her strength was gone. She sighed in resignation. Jesse found the nostrils. With his thumb and middle finger hooked, he pulled as hard as he could. His shoulder muscles bunched, his neck corded, eyes squeezed shut, he placed his left hand against her rump and pushed as he pulled with his right. His grip slipped free of the foal's nose. The head stayed. "Shit. I can't move it. I might be able to get a wire around the jaw and pull it around and maybe get it out. No matter what, it's the end of the foal. This mare's going fast. We're gonna lose 'em both." His eyes held a long questioning look at Holly. Then as if he found an answer, he turned and ran to the house and back in under a minute.

Holly's eyes were wide, staring as he stepped into the stall. How could eleven months of anticipation come to this? "There's no other

way, Holly. They're both gonna die. I'm gonna try to save the foal."
Holly's eyes would not leave his hand. "Why don't you go outside.
We've got to do this quick." He glanced at the mare. "There's no
more time."

"No. I'll stay. I want to be with her."

"I don't think you should."

"I'm going to stay, Jesse." She moved to the mare's side and
slowly stroked her bulging ribs. She draped her arm across the
mare's back and squeezed her eyes shut as Jesse moved to the head.
Tears ran in streams down her cheeks, her chin trembled as she
spoke softly to Mamacita.

"She's gonna drop, Holly. You've got to step back. Be careful
she doesn't fall on you." Jesse placed the muzzle of the Smith and
Wesson to the hollow above Mamacita's left eye angled toward her
right ear. He glanced once to see that Holly was safe and closed his
finger on the trigger. The explosion echoing in the stirred-up barn,
San Mamacita blew a noisy gust and collapsed into the straw. A
small movement occurred in each leg at once, then she was still. The
other horses pranced, snorting in their stalls. Jesse had his big pocketknife in his hand as he knelt to the swollen belly. He grabbed a
handhold of skin and pushed in the serrated blade, sawing the full
length of the belly exposing the warm still living viscera. Holly covered her mouth and nose and turned her head but only for a
moment. Then with resolve, turned back to watch. She wiped away
her tears and held her shirttail over her nose.

The clack of iron-shod hooves drumming the walls of neighbor
stalls and squeals of annoyance came to their ears. He put the knife
aside and squinching up his face, dug through the hot tangle of
entrails. He clutched and tugged until he freed a shining white sac,
like the soft skin of a monstrous egg. He took up his blade and
punctured the thick membrane, then tore the opening wide with his
hands. Holly had moved to his side. A dark little head with wet
pointed ears appeared. Jesse's hand cleared away the viscous fluid
from its nose and mouth. A gasping breath was heard, followed by

another…and another. Jesse pulled away the sac and held the filly in his arms, covering his chest with blood. He looked up at Holly and said, "It's a girl."

95

Lost in a Thorny Wood

Dr. John was a thoughtful, studious man, big and kind. He explained to Holly that there was nothing else that could have been done. "He did exactly what I would've done. He even collected the first milk. Very important. He knows how much you loved the mare and he wanted to be sure that you understood that there was no other choice. I'm sorry…" He touched the back of her fragile hand. She nodded silently, then smiled a sad smile and said, "Thank you, John."

They named the filly Buenacita, and took to calling her Cita. They started with a handheld nippled bottle until she became adroit and graduated to a hung bucket with a nipple at the bottom. Abbie called her Beebee for Bucket Baby. Holly fussed over her like a child with a favorite doll. But she was not the same Holly who was waiting for the birth. She grew silent and withdrawn.

She continued her commitments to the therapeutic riding program. But underneath her practiced facade, darkness brewed. In the evenings before Jesse got home, she'd have her rocker time alone to read, relax, or meditate. But now, the pictures flowing into her mind uninvited were of death. They came in battalions without mercy, to occupy and leave no room for hope and joy. Her brother's murder, the beloved Grandmama, Jesse's son, her twenty-six-year-old valiant cousin, tortured, killed by cancer, Buckshot…and now the beautiful Mamacita who gave her life so the baby might live.

All death seemed to have but one faceless presence, a gray oppressive force that sucked away her spirit, leaving her defeated, lost in a thorny wood, unable to find the open air.

Jesse's attempts to cheer her went for naught. A wan smile was the best his efforts would yield. Even the relentless fervor of Abbie fell before the wall of Holly's depression. Jesse spoke to the vampire obstetrician who assured him her health was fine but to bring her in. "Will you call her, Doctor? She's got kind of a hair trigger lately and I don't want to set her off. She seems to be about an inch away from crying most of the time."

She was already in the bed, staring at the wall in the almost dark, when he came in and asked her if she'd like a massage. "No. Thank you." He could see that her face held the tight grimace of a child preparing for tears.

He sat on the bed and touched her arm. "What is it Holly? What can I do? Please tell me. I need you to talk to me."

"I don't know. I'm sad."

"Why? Everything is perfect. We should be happy."

"The happier I am, the sadder I become. I miss my brother so much." The chin trembled, she bit her lip. "He should be here to see this." The tears gushed and she cried in earnest. Loud sobbing gulps. He held her in his arms and rocked her, whispering, "I know, I know…"

He felt her stiffen in his arms as she clenched her fists and pounded the bed, an instantaneous flare of red-faced anger. "I want him back."

Jesse was stung with a feeling of impotence. "He's not coming back. But I'm here. I'm here. I love you and I'm trying to fix it. All I do is try to please you and you're making me feel like I don't exist." He felt badly and stupid for getting angry so he attacked her even more. It grew to a fury, until they were on their feet at opposite sides of the bed, Holly screaming at him, till she ran out of fuel and stood exhausted, tears running down her face, arms limp at her sides, a waif. He went to her, wrapped her in his arms and held her close. She whimpered, "I want my mommy," and then laughed a weak, little laugh. He put his hands to her wet cheeks and kissed her tear-drenched lips. He said, "I want my mommy, too. I can get you yours a lot easier than you can get me mine." They laughed.

96

Ruby

Ruby, always the brightest of lights with her ready smile, and eagerness to please, was more than welcome at the Lazy JB.

Cita was a red sorrel like her mother, with a narrow white strip down her face. Jesse had imprinted the foal from her first breath. People were a magnet for her. Ruby said she was the most beautiful thing she'd ever seen and would not leave off wrapping her arms around the filly and petting her from head to tail.

They had a couple of hours before a Miracles Unlimited session was to begin. Jesse had his arm around Ruby as Abbie arrived leading the huge Clydesdale, Mr. Bud, and said, "Your steed, madam."

Ruby bit her lip and turned her head as if to find a way out. "Jesse, are you sure I need to do this?"

"Of course you do. He's a baby-sitter."

Holly was twenty paces away leaning on the top rail of the arena, watching. She whined in mockery, "C'mon, hurry up, let's go. Get on the horse. I wanna see you ride. You're such a fraidy-cat, mommy."

Her face made an abrupt change of expression as she felt a twist in her guts. It was sudden, intense. Shocked, she gripped the rail, fearing she'd go to the ground.

Abbie saw it on her face gone white as an aspirin. "Holly, you all right?" She called. Jesse and Ruby turned to see. Jesse came on the run and put his arm around her. "What is it?"

"I think…it's starting…" She squeezed it out in a clenched whisper as he took her weight in his arm. Ruby was at her other side.

"Can you make it to the house?" Jesse asked.

"If I can't, you can put me in a wheelbarrow." She started to walk, Jesse holding her on one side, Ruby on the other. She turned to her mom and, referring to Mr. Bud, said, "Looks like you lucked out…for the moment."

Abbie gave Mr. Bud to Ricardo and caught up with them. "What can I do?"

"Get the Mustang and pull it up in front of the house." He felt Holly tense in his arm and stop. She bent at the waist, winced, and let loose a sharp, one-note, high-pitched cry.

It was only yesterday, she had told Carley, "I feel like I've got a balloon inside me filled with fifty gallons of water and one big fish. And it's about to burst at any second."

And just then, it did.

Ten feet from the porch, she felt the quick tear and a gush of fluid course down her leg and splash at her feet. She cried, "Ohhhh…" and looked down half expecting to see the fish.

Labor began in earnest as they pulled out of the ranch. Ruby, in the backseat, leaned forward to work her fingers in Holly's shoulders and stroke the back of her neck.

"I sure am glad to have you here, Ruby." Jesse said. She reached and touched his shoulder. He handed her the cell phone and said, "Why don't you call Bear. We've got about a twenty-minute drive." He looked over at Holly and took her hand.

An obstetrics resident, an elegant woman with glossy raven hair, soft black eyes, and the lyrical inflections of India, examined Holly and assured her all was well. She said she would call Doctor Adashek and give him her report. "As you get closer to delivery, he will be here. I think you will be a few hours. Your husband and your mother can be with you."

Holly said, "Oh, yes, that would be good."

Dr. Elliot Adashek walked into the room, an incongruous smile on his cement-colored face, and performed a quick examination. He informed Jesse and Ruby that everything was progressing normally and that they were about to take her to the delivery room. "Jesse, the nurse will fix you up with a gown."

"Thank you."

"Sorry, mom. They limit it to daddy only."

Ruby nodded, gave Jesse a hug, and as soon as he followed the nurse, she went to the phone and called her husband again. He had booked a flight and was getting ready to leave.

97

Harley

Jesse had wrapped her hand in his and matched her squeeze for squeeze as he stroked her head and whispered words of love. She'd been laboring for almost four hours. As he looked at her struggling, red, squinched-up face, he loved her more than ever and thought she was never more beautiful. Something she would not have believed. One thought kept hammering into his mind. Please God let this child be whole. Let these doctors be correct. Don't let anything go wrong, please. There came a point when he could think of nothing else.

The nurses in their familiarity with this everyday event bantered lightly. "So what are you hoping for? A boy, right? Cowboys all want boys."

"I like girls…" he managed to get said.

"You got names picked out?" The voices came anonymously from masked faces.

"Harley, if it's a boy. Alexandra, if it's a girl."

Just then, Holly howled, perspiration popped in beads across her face. A faceless chorus chanted the word "push." Jesse stood by her head, mopping her face as she sucked air in and blew it out on a shattering scream, nearly crushing his hand. He heard the sounds in a blur of movement and turned to see the doctor holding their baby and swabbing it clean. The nurse held a pair of scissors out to Jesse and he cut the cord.

And then she handed him his son. How fragile, his tiny fuzzy head cradled in his palm and how insistent in his effort to rise up and turn to see the world. The sweet, newborn smell of him was that of life itself. The scent of a miracle. All his parts seemed where they belonged. Jesse brought him gently to his chest and felt complete…then he carried him to Holly and presented their son to her outstretched arms. Once in her possession, she scanned him like a laser. Satisfied, she mouthed, "He's a smoogie, Harley." She then took him to her bosom and closed her eyes.

Later, in a private room, Jesse sat on the edge of the bed holding her hand. Doctor Adashek had taken Ruby to see her grandson. He squeezed her hand and said, "Well done, Holly Marie. You did a helluva job. I'm so proud of you. We've got a son. We've got a Harley." He felt his eyes well up and turned to look at her.

Her hand had felt lifeless when he squeezed it. Her eyes were closed. He pressed her hand again and said, "You want to sleep?" A sharp panic surged through him as he sensed something wrong and called her name. "Holly?!"

There was no response. He reached for her shoulders and moved her gently, calling her name. There was nothing. He flew from the bed and ran into the hall calling for help. A nurse came quickly to the room. In minutes, Doctor Adashek, the Indian woman, another doctor and several nurses hovered at her bedside. Jesse had turned to stone, out of their way, letting them work. Ruby came to his side. They put their arms around each other, stunned.

Doctor Adashek, rigid-faced, came to them and very quickly said, "She's in coma. We're taking her to intensive care immediately."

With that, he turned to a flurry of activity that sped her from the room leaving Jesse and Ruby mute, frozen fast to their place.

The emergency team moved with elegant precision at a furious pace. Complex procedures were carried out with astonishing dispatch. Blood pressure, pulse, temperature, heart rhythm, and blood oxygen monitors were attached. Electrocardiogram, electroencephalogram, and a CT scan of the brain were performed. Within minutes, computerized blood tests were completed to evaluate for the possibility of various organ or gland malfunctions or chemical imbalances in the blood—all unlikely in a young woman so healthy, but Doctor Adashek took nothing for granted. He knew he stood in the presence of a grave complication.

He called in an intensivist to manage the myriad details involved in caring for a comatose patient and a neurologist for the specialized evaluation of the possibility of a central nervous system disaster. After his examination and reviewing test results, it was determined that his clinical suspicion was correct. The CT scan had shown an intracerebral hemorrhage, bleeding into the substance of the brain. It was confined to the right frontal lobe. A neurosurgeon arrived promptly, performed a neurological examination, reviewed the test results and confirmed the diagnosis.

Abbie had met Bear at the airport by holding up a sign saying, GRANDFATHER BEAR? She drove him straight to the hospital where their bright expectant faces turned immediately to clay.

Four white-coated doctors came through doors and arced around Jesse, Ruby, Bear, and Abbie. The family faces, drawn and creased had taken on the color of the walls.

Doctor Adashek spoke first, then deferred to the neurosurgeon. He was patient, compassionate. His eyes went to each family member as he spoke. "At this point, the exact cause of this event can only be a matter of speculation. Intracranial hemorrhages occur very rarely, and totally unpredictably in normal, healthy women. Some recover with residual disability of varying degrees, and some make total recovery with no permanent effects at all." Then his calm, educated face took on another hue as his poise crumbled some. He fiddled with a nonexistent itch at the end of his nose as he said, "And you do need to have the full picture, at least to the extent that we do. In some instances, these events…they can prove fatal. I'm sorry to have to say that, but I'd be remiss if I didn't. Now we've got a lot more testing to do and we're going to get right to it. We need to do a cerebral angiogram. She could have an aneurysm that ruptured. We just don't know." He scanned the pained faces before him and smiled as warmly as he could. He stepped close to Ruby and touched her arm saying, "We'll take care of her." He placed his hand on Jesse's shoulder for an instant, then turned and left followed by two doctors.

The cold sparseness of his form belied the warmness of Doctor Adashek's heart. "Doctor Wilson is one of the best neurosurgeons in the country. If I had a problem, he's who I'd want. Have you seen your new grandson, Mr. Bassett?" Bear shook his head. "Come. We'll show him off to you. And for whatever it's worth," he turned back over his shoulder as he led the way, "her hemorrhage had nothing to do with the pregnancy or the delivery." They all fell in behind, Bear with his arm around Ruby. Abbie mustered enthusiasm for what should have been a pure and joyous thing, corrupted now with fear and anxiety.

Doctor Adashek put the baby Harley back in his tiny chamber. "It's going to be some time," he said. "So if you want to leave, get something to eat, whatever…I'll call you the minute we know anything."

"If it's all the same, Doctor," Bear responded, "we'll stay."

98

Vigil

The night arrived without notice. Phone calls were made to Dr.
Walter Nalls, Kevin Bradley, and Billy Diggs. Abbie called
Charlie the therapist who had developed a special bond with Holly
in their work with the kids. He arrived with a stack of deli sand-
wiches, coleslaw, potato salad, pickles and soft drinks. He spread it
out for them to choose their preference. Whether they knew they
were hungry or not, it served as a distraction and supplied nutrition
for bodies stressed.

Doctor Adashek was the first coming down the hall with
Doctor Wilson half a step behind. Everyone tried to read their faces
as they came to a halt. Wilson told them that the angiogram
revealed no demonstrable abnormality of the cerebral circulation
and therefore no indication for surgery. He explained that it was not
possible to surgically remove a blood mass from within the substance of the brain. "So we're going to set up a maintenance program of support and then we're going to monitor her progress.

We'll have her in a room pretty quick and you'll be able to see her…and be with her as…much as you like. Do you have any questions?"

They had many. Doctor Wilson answered them as well as he could. Walter had arrived to lend his personal and professional support, confirming Doctor Adashek's regard for Wilson's skills. An hour later, they gathered around her bed. A feeding tube had been passed through her nose into her stomach through which a liquid formula was fed at a calculated rate. A catheter had been placed in her bladder. She lay there amidst a web of tubes, wires, and patches connected to a network of gauges and graphs like some fragile prey ensnared for future devouring by a monster arachnid. For Jesse, it was the dreadful reenactment of the torturous days sitting next to Zack before they pulled the plug.

There was a difference. With his son, he soon came to know that the form in the bed was no longer inhabited. It breathed mechanically. At the flip of a switch, it would have ceased to move. Holly was not invaded by a ventilator. The shallow rise and fall of her chest were her own.

A quiet strength from an unknown source began to grow inside of Jesse. It seemed as if the more he was assaulted, the stronger grew his resolve. Ruby looked as if a breeze would cause her to disintegrate like a cone of burnt incense. She had already lost a son and now stood held together by will alone.

Sometime in the middle of the night, Bear and Ruby kissed Jesse and allowed Abbie to take them back to the ranch. A nurse's aide had provided Jesse with a folding bed next to hers. But he remained on the edge of her bed, leaning close to her face, trying to feel if heat would rise to his cheeks as he spoke to her—words of love, any words, any sounds, structureless phrases, all with one intention, one definition. In the still dark just before dawn, he moved from her bed and found his way to the glass wall behind which his son lay sleeping. He stayed for a time looking through the glass and then left. As he made his way back to her room, he thought, she might just be awake.

He sat on her bed and wrung a cloth into a steel bowl, then moistened her lips and wiped her brow. He kissed her face, fixed her covers, and moved off her bed to curl up on the cot. He punched up the pillows under his head and pulled his knees to his chest. He closed his eyes. In the darkness behind his lids, a thousand thoughts and pictures ran amok.

Six days and nights fused as one dark torment of time without relief from the sun. It was a heart-stinging, stomach turning, mind-wrenching roller coaster ride through an inferno of emotions. Ruby had become a shadow of her fragile self. Bear, always big and bright, grew dark and drawn. At wide unexpected intervals, a mirthless, nerve-driven laugh would escape. Had they been required to face the onslaught of emotional pain without nature's armor plate of shock, anguish might well have been their executioner.

Jesse almost never left her room. Only at Ruby's insistence would he go home to shower and change, then he'd come right back. What little sleep came upon him happened in the small bed next to hers. He sat there all the days in a bedside chair, his arm on the bed and his hand over hers. His fingers moved on hers to let her know that he was there. He had his headphones and a stack of magazines and books and the TV. But most of the time, he talked to her. He told her about the music he was listening to, the articles he read, the horses that were waiting for her at home, who had called, who had been to see her, and who the flowers were from. And he would describe the flowers in finest detail, holding one inches before his eyes and then offering it under her nose. And he told her about their son. What a perfect treasure he was and how she had to get well to enjoy him. His voice grew ragged from the unfamiliar marathon of chat. But he believed that she could hear him.

Not an hour passed without the coming and going of medical personnel. Her vital signs were monitored on a fixed schedule. She was turned at regular intervals to different positions to prevent mucous collections in her lungs. She was moved and massaged to prevent blood clots in her legs.

Twice in the week, on his way home and on the way back to the hospital, he stopped at Holy Rood Cemetery. He prayed, then stood and waited, but he felt no sense of a presence there. So he left, after having implored God for mercy, to please give him back his wife.

A constant stream of friends flowed through with kindness, hope, and love. Larry Littlefield came down from Colorado and sat with his friend. He was there when the neurosurgeon and Doctor Adashek came in, and just behind them, the woman from India. Instead of hope and aid, they had come to represent to Jesse a cold, damp wind heralding the horror they were in. They checked the charts and graphs. They touched her here and there. Dr. Wilson ran a key along the soles of her feet. Her big toe moved upward. He lifted her eyelids and shined a light in her eyes. His face gave nothing away. Jesse wanted to say something, ask him something, but he couldn't form the thoughts. He also sensed the answers might be better left unsaid. Wilson made some friendly comment, words with no meaning other than to try to show compassion. The doctors left. Jesse had caught his lip between his teeth and held his breath. He felt the tightness in his chest and let the air out.

Ten minutes later, Doctor Adashek returned and asked if Jesse would come with him. The doctor led him to an office, ushered him in and shut the door behind him. Doctor Wilson sat, staring at a sheaf of papers. He stood and asked Jesse to sit. They all took chairs. Wilson took off his glasses and ran his palm from his brow to his chin as he placed the papers on the desk. He looked at Jesse directly. "We need to talk about a couple of things, Jesse. Holly's heart could quit at any moment. In which case there are decisions that fall into the province of the family. In the event that were to occur, do you want us to do CPR?"

"Which is what?" He felt his guts writhe.

"Resuscitation to restore a heartbeat."

"Is that a mechanical thing?" He tried to strangle a newborn agony.

"Well, it involves calling in the resuscitation team. They

surround the patient and start chest compression to mechanically get the heart pumping blood. They would put a tube in the windpipe and hook her up to a ventilator and then they would use various intravenous medications to support the blood pressure…"

"Then she would be on that mechanical support system at that point?"

"Right. The upside is that we can perhaps restore the heartbeat. The downside is that if the circulation has been stopped long enough, and no one knows what long enough is, there can be permanent brain damage." Wilson stopped and waited, looking at Jesse, giving him all the time he needed to absorb the devastating information.

Jesse tipped his head down and shut his eyes. He gripped his temples between his thumb and middle fingers as if to forestall the explosion of his brain. When he looked up, he said, "I want you to do whatever it takes to keep her going."

"We have to tell you, Jesse, things do not look good. There is absolutely no encouragement to us, objectively, that she is going to come out of this. So at some point, you'll have to give some thought to whether you want us to terminate life support and let nature take its course." Again he paused to let it sink. "I am not recommending that at this time, but we do need to prepare you for the possibility."

Jesse walked from the office feeling like Mamacita with her guts on the ground, only he was still alive. Larry was pacing the hallway. He knew, as did Jesse, that when Doctor Adashek led him away, it wasn't good. The proof was there on Jesse's face. He asked Larry to give him a few minutes alone but not to leave.

He went into the room and shut the door. He climbed onto the bed, with a knee on each side of her. He took her hand in his and leaned close to her face. He told her he had a plan. He needed her help. "I know you're there. I know you can hear me. You can come back. I know you can. You have to want to. I'm going, for just a little while. Going for help to talk to God. And when I get back, you're going to come back to me…and our son, Harley. You wanted him so much. You've got him now. You can't leave him, Holly. You can't."

335

He called Larry in and told him what the doctors had said and what his plan was. They got on the phones and made a bunch of calls. They climbed into the pickup and drove to Holy Rood Cemetery. It wasn't long before the assembly convened. Jesse had asked Ruby to conduct. There was Walter and Helen, Billy Diggs, Kathy Sue, Lucas and Mason, Abbie and Charlie, Ricardo and Nellie, Kevin and Carley, the judge and Leona, Kelly Dale and her son, Wiley, in his wheelchair and half a dozen more who had been summoned by the network of friends, and Bear and Ruby, Larry and Jesse.

They circled the grave of Damien Zachary Burrell and linked their hands. Ruby spoke but a few words about why they were there. She asked them to please be aware of the power of communal prayer. "It is a potent force that God recognizes. It cannot go unheard. So if each of you, in your own way, silently or aloud, would ask that Holly be returned to us, I am sure our request will not go unheard." A field of energy grew so intense as to seem as if it would whirl into flame. Without knowledge of passing time, they stood in prayer. No one tired, not one shifted. The concentration on their purpose was absolute.

They parted solemnly, in whispers.

Jesse stood alone, staring at the gravestone. Then he looked to the sky and said, "Please, dear God, don't take her from me. Whatever thy will is, please grant me the strength to accept it."

Larry, Bear, and Ruby drove back with him to the hospital in the truck. Jesse asked that Bear and Ruby visit her first on their own. Then Larry went in for a brief time alone.

When he came out, Jesse entered the room and shut the door. He knelt over her and peered down at her face. He could see that the life force within her had grown dim, distant.

She was leaving on a long, slow journey through a bright expanse of light where time and distance had no consequence.

Before her eyes faint forms began to shape, emerging from within the light as if self-created, as people, faces that she knew. How pleased she was to be in the light as light itself. The cast-iron weight of earthly pain, of grief, of guilt, the doubts and fears of human heritage had vanished as if they'd never been. Then there among the faceless shadows was her Grandmama wearing an apron, holding a trowel, a knuckle-track of earth smeared across her cheek, beside herself with joy at seeing her daughter's daughter. "But oh so young, my darling child…"

Moving along the path of light she was still able to turn her head and see Jesse on the bed, kneeling over her, begging her to stay. She could hear him saying, "I know you can hear me. I know you're still in there. I know. I've seen the difference. I knew when Zack was gone. You're still here, I know you are. Don't leave me, Holly. Turn around, come back. I need you to help me raise this Harley boy."

But on she went into the white gold until there in the glow she saw what she wanted more than anything ever. Her brother Brad stood there before her, his chestnut hair askew, his lopsided grin around the brightest teeth, the Bassett smile. In life, they would have hugged with crushing force, but what existed here was far more intoxicating and complete than pressing flesh. Oh, my, my, my, how very sweet it was to feel her spirit intertwine with his, become a thing unto itself. What ecstasy to feel again the mischief in his soul, to see it dancing in his eyes. He stepped a little to his right.

A shadow shape behind him soon revealed itself to be the golden boy. Damien Zachary came forward and bowed in a way Holly appreciated, almost as if to kiss her hand. They now stood side by side, Damien and Brad. A soothing tide of peace and calm sought for all her life was now upon her. Her brother spoke first, then Damien. They told her she had to go back. That it wasn't yet her time. She had to raise a son, be a wife. She stood, a recalcitrant child prepared to disobey. Her brother said, "We'll be waiting for you.

You can go back now, knowing that we're all right and that we'll be together again. You need to love your son and your husband. They need you. We'll be here to take you in."

Jesse put his thumb to her eye and raised the lid. The light was gone. The eye had begun to dull. A fierce, dark, and desperate rage possessed him as he felt his whole being collapsing in despair. His eyes rolled up as if to examine the underside of his brain. He felt her hips between his knees, then gripped her shoulders, lifting her from the bed and shook her gently. His tears fell upon her cheeks. "Oh,…God, Holly…come back…don't go." He placed her head back on the pillow and took her hand and brought it to his face. He put his lips to the back of her hand.

And then from somewhere outside of what he thought was real, he felt her fingers tighten. His breath stopped in his throat as he squeezed her hand and felt her pressing back.

The sound of his voice rattled the windows as it echoed through the corridors bringing medical personnel, Bear, Ruby, and Larry on the run.

99

In The World of Blood, Tears, and Joy

The following day, her eyelids fluttered and opened briefly, then remained open and slowly began to focus, as she became aware of her surroundings.

Two weeks later, they wheeled her to the curb, Harley in her arms. With Jesse on one side, Bear on the other, she handed the baby to her mother and stood up from the chair. Settled in the car, Ruby put Harley back in her arms. As they drove away, the Count stood, waving, wearing a huge smile.

———◆———

The aroma of livestock, shavings, hay, grass, and grain came to her sweeter than a bed of roses. She carried her three-week-old son through the barn to meet their unique world. She handed him up to his daddy astride Soot and watched as he went for his first ride. Harley was three weeks old.

That afternoon, she was at her computer; photos scattered on the table at her side and covering the floor. She was putting together the newsletter for Miracles Unlimited. Harley lay content in his crib next to the desk.

Jesse hung up the last bridle and headed toward the house. Dozer lumbered at his side. It was the sweetest hour of the twenty-four. Warm for March. The sun had gone and left a somber purple shroud over a flame of light spreading along the hills. In the east, a deep blue began to darken and reveal a solitary star. The moon would not be far behind.

He neared the stone steps to the porch and looked up. She was sitting in the rocker in the fading glow of day, cowled in the poncho, its hood framing her face, its soft folds keeping Harley warm. She turned to smile at him as he stepped to the porch and leaned back against the post. He folded his arms across his chest and tilted his head back and looked at her. This image of living flesh and spirit, he thought, would not, in all the time stretched out before him, exist again, not as it is right now. He felt he had to fix it in his mind, treasure it, and hold it there for use as comfort at a time of need.

He walked up behind her and felt the lovely sloping bones of her shoulders under the wool and looked down at his son nuzzled at her breast. Then he moved his hand until he felt beneath his fingertips the soft fullness of her lips.

A shrill cry, keen to the senses, pierced the air above them. Jesse looked up at the male golden eagle circling low on motionless wings. He watched its spiral descent until he could see clearly the color in its eyes fixed on his. It shrieked again, turned, and flapped its wings as it headed for distant trees. A copper-colored feather floated toward the ground and settled at Jesse's feet. He picked it up and turned it slowly between his fingers, then bent to kiss the top of his wife's head as his hands followed her arms to their son and whispered the word, "Yes."

The End

Epilogue

Though much of this book is made up, it all started with my efforts to recover from the loss of my twenty-six-year-old beloved son Damien Zachary. For more than a year after his departure, I was paralyzed. Unable to think, not knowing what to feel, wanting to quit feeling, to pull the covers over my head and shut out the world. My world, of course, still existed under the covers. There was no escape.

One day, I threw the covers off and sat down to write about Zack. That's what I called him. Zack. I stared at the blank page for a long time with no knowledge of where to start. Eventually, I began to write unconsciously, letting my fingers work without guidance from thought. I did the same thing for three days in a row. On the fourth day, what had started as a catharsis began to evolve into the novel you hold in your hands. I felt I now had a reason to go to work each day, spurred on I believe by the spirit of Zack.

When I wrote the final sentence, the manuscript was six

hundred and twenty-four pages long. A stream of consciousness. Then began the real work of rewriting and cutting mercilessly.

The first page, however, exists today exactly as it was the first day I sat down to write about Zack.

Then I met my wife, Susannah, and what had been a fantasy became reality.

My wish for you is this: know your children, guard them, question them, and know if they are not telling the truth. Demand that they do. You might just save their lives.